THE BURSAR'S WIFE

ALSO BY E.G. RODFORD AND AVAILABLE FROM TITAN BOOKS

The Runaway Maid (March 2017)

THE BURSAR'S WIFE

A GEORGE KOCHARYAN MYSTERY

E.G. RODFORD

TITAN BOOKS

The Bursar's Wife
Print edition ISBN: 9781785650031
E-book edition ISBN: 9781785650048

Published by Titan Books
A division of Titan Publishing Group Ltd
144 Southwark Street, London SE1 0UP

First edition: March 2016
10 9 8 7 6 5 4 3 2 1

Names, places and incidents are either products of the author's imagination or used fictitiously. Any resemblance to actual persons, living or dead (except for satirical purposes), is entirely coincidental.

A CIP catalogue record for this title is available from the British Library.

Printed in the USA.

This one is for my lovely spouse.

1

I HATED THIS BIT OF THE JOB, THE BIT WHERE THEY STARTED crying. I pushed the box of tissues over, and Albert ('call me Al') Greene took one, blew his small red nose with it until it ran out of dry, then took another. I looked wistfully at Sandra's empty chair; she knew how to deal with the criers, it was the ones that just sat there grinning that worried her. But Sandra only came in twice a week to do what little admin there was, and I was struggling to pay her for that, so I had to deal with the tears myself. Greene, an overweight, pasty-faced school teacher, took another tissue and blew hard. I picked up the photographs he was staring at and shuffled them. His wife Trisha Greene featured in all of them, all with the same man, all telling a story starting with sitting in her car outside a popular walking spot. Al Greene struggled to compose his voice.

"And you're sure they were there together?" He was a drowning man grasping at straws.

I nodded, and referred him to my notes. I had spent an hour either sitting in my cold car or muddying my knees taking photographs in the dimming light. Many of the pictures I'd taken showed only the top of Mrs Greene's head in her companion's lap, or her back as she sat astride him, but I restricted the ones I showed to her husband to some heavy snogging, since I judged him a sensitive soul. He threatened tears again.

"Do you know who he is?" he asked, once he had used several more tissues – I made a mental note to up his bill.

"No," I lied. I thought him unlikely to seek physical revenge – he seemed too in touch with his feelings for violence – but I saw no benefit in him knowing who the man was; and you never could tell how people would react to this sort of news. Besides, I'd also omitted to tell him that the man in the photo was not the only one that Mrs Greene had tested the suspension of her cabriolet with; I'd counted three others in the three times I'd tailed her to the car park. It was a known spot for casual sex.

"My mother was right about her." He shook his head in the belated realisation that he should have listened to his mother. "I gave her everything she wanted." His round face crumpled, and I resisted the temptation to tell him that there were obviously things she wanted that he couldn't provide, but instead I looked through the window at the grey Cambridge skyline. If I twisted my neck and looked up Lensfield Road through the dirty glass I could just make out the clock jutting from the corner of Our Lady and the English Martyrs. It was lunchtime, but my stomach had told me that twenty minutes ago. I turned to my client.

"Do you love your wife, Al?"

He nodded hard. "Yes, of course."

"There's no 'of course' about it. I mean do you still love her despite this?" I fanned out the pictures in front of him. Mrs Greene was not unattractive, and I had come to know some of her endearing mannerisms, like how she tilted her head up to look at someone under her fringe, or how she pulled at her bottom lip with her forefinger, or studied herself in the courtesy mirror in her car when speaking on her mobile phone, possibly even to Al here.

He nodded again, this time with feeling.

"Then I suggest you go home and ask her whether she is having an affair. Sometimes people are just waiting to be asked."

"And if she denies it?"

"Then you have two choices. You can ignore it and say no more, or you can tell her you hired someone to spy on her, in which case your marriage is as good as over anyway." He shredded his wet tissue.

"And if she confesses?"

"Then you either leave her or forgive her." He did not look convinced by my pearls, and who could blame him. I opened a drawer in my desk. "Listen, if you do choose to forgive her, you both may have certain issues to work through, in which case you could do worse than talk to someone. If Mrs Greene were game, that is." I flicked through a stack of business cards, given to me by the other occupants of the building: homoeopathist, acupuncturist, herbalist and nutritionist. I chose one with intertwining rings on it that read "Couples Counselling" and gave it to him.

Although the other occupants had often made clear that an investigation agency did not fit in with the spiritual ethos they were trying to engender (their words not mine), they did not turn away my referrals of highly strung clients they could pummel, prod, listen to, or ply with expensive herbal extracts. I still remembered the days when I had occupied two rooms in the building and the others were taken by a book-keeper, a literary agent and a Freudian psychotherapist. But times had changed, and I suspected that these happy therapists hoped I would leave so they could complete their little band with an aromatherapist or crystal healer.

Someone whose job it was to rake through the muck of people's lives looking for evidence to feed the worst suspicions of loved ones or checking that disability claimants weren't skateboarding in their spare time did not sit well with their wholesome vision. And if work continued to decline as it was doing, they would soon have their wish.

With Al Greene gone I scribbled a note for Sandra to invoice him and checked the appointment book. I had a free afternoon, so I put my feet up on the desk and planned what to do with it. I would start with lunch, then an afternoon film at the Arts Cinema. Knocking interrupted my planning. Maybe Al was back to ask me if I was sure it was *his* wife I had photographed. I called the knocker in and the door opened to let in the nutritionist who had a room downstairs. She looked like a walking advertisement for her profession, and leant against the open door, folding her thin brown arms.

"Nina, what a pleasant surprise," I said, and meant it; she was the only person in the building I could have a conversation with. I swung my feet off the desk. She took in the room with amused disdain – the walls cried out for paint, the carpet for more fibre. Only a couple of pot plants on Sandra's desk provided an oasis of life. Nina's dark skin and hair contrasted with the starched whiteness of her coat. A small pin sat in her lapel, which I assumed showed membership of a professional body, but I had never been close enough to examine it. "Have you come to join me for a Big Mac?" I asked. "You can go large for an extra 30p." She smiled with almond eyes and too-perfect teeth; an uninhibited smile that stirred something in me. Sometimes, if I'd had a couple of drinks, I worried about what Nina wore under her white coat. She was at least ten years my junior, but it had been ten months since my wife had found that women were more exciting than men and moved to Greece with one. Consequently I was having difficulty getting close enough to appreciate them, never mind read the badges on their lapels.

"I can see you're busy, George, so I won't keep you. I just came to tell you that there's someone downstairs asking for you."

I checked the diary again and shook my head. "I've nothing more today."

"You sure?" she asked, in mock surprise. "I'd have thought that people were queuing up to find out if their partners were cheating on them." I gave her a crooked smile.

"It's not all I do, you know. Besides, wouldn't you want to know whether you were being cheated on?" She unfolded her arms and looked at the flaking ceiling, taking the question seriously.

"I'm not sure. I think I'd rather not know. Or if I suspected someone I'd rather just ask than get a private eye to spy on them." I got out of my chair, hoping she would notice that I hadn't let myself go completely. It was pathetic, anyone over forty would not register on her radar.

"Maybe we could go for that burger and discuss it?"

She smiled and opened the door.

"I always bring lunch to work, George. And anyway, I don't eat meat." She put her hand on the door. "I just came to tell you about your glamorous client." I followed her out of the office. She started to walk away, and I wanted to ask her whether dinner was an option, but I'd left it too long and was relieved when she disappeared. Like I said, it was pathetic.

Dull November light filtered through the frosted glass window of the shared waiting room. It was empty except for a woman with oversized sunglasses and a silk headscarf who sat thumbing through an ancient copy of *HELLO!* magazine. She might have sprung from the pages of it herself, and I wished that I had spent more money on a suit. She lifted her head as I approached her, showing angled cheekbones and the sort of lips some women pursued through collagen injection. She appraised me through the dark glasses and I hoped she didn't go on first appearances.

"George Kocharyan?" The accent was educated, clipped vowels, but difficult to pin down and a little strained. But then that described many people in Cambridge.

"I'm impressed, most people get Armenian names

wrong," I said. She stood up and smoothed her white, thigh-length raincoat. It cinched her waist with the help of a wide vinyl belt.

"May we talk in your office?"

Indeed we may, I thought, smelling money in her perfume.

2

MY OFFICE SEEMED MORE GRUBBY THAN USUAL WITH MY fashion magazine guest in it. I offered her a seat and she hesitated before sitting down, as if waiting for me to brush it off.

"So, Mrs, Ms...?"

"Mrs. It's Mrs, erm, Booker. Sylvia Booker." She blushed momentarily at this revelation, but soon recovered. It was an effort for people sitting in her chair to reveal basic facts about themselves; they'd come this far and then struggle at the last hurdle.

"Mrs Booker," I said. "How can Cambridge Confidential Services help you?" She looked round the room in case anyone might be lurking before taking off her large glasses. I was rewarded with piercing turquoise ovals. She undid her scarf revealing hair that spent many hours in a professional's hands and small earlobes that sparkled with tiny diamonds. She studied my face as if she were trying to place me.

"It's my daughter, Lucy." She peeled off skin-tight gloves. Her nails must have been seen to while her hair was being done and another diamond on her finger kept a thick gold wedding band company. She put the gloves in a small handbag on her lap and I waited. From afar she'd looked early thirties but this close I put her just the wrong side of forty. Her right hand fussed with the rings on the other, with what I took to be nerves, unless of course she needed a drink, but then she'd have had one before coming here and wouldn't have been the first.

"I've heard it all before, you know, you can't shock me," I told her in my most reassuring voice. She took a breath.

"I'm worried about her. I think that she may be running with the wrong crowd." Her voice was low and smooth, like Grace Kelly in *Rear Window*.

"And what makes you think that?" I was curious as to what colour you would call her eyes. Was turquoise an eye colour?

"Her behaviour of course. She's started at Emma this year."

"Emma?"

"Sorry, Emmanuel College."

I nodded. I knew where she meant, I just didn't like her taking the knowledge for granted. Some people assumed the whole town revolved around the university.

"I don't mean to question your concern, Mrs Booker, but isn't this normal behaviour for a teenager?" She gave me a look telling me she wasn't here for my insights into human behaviour.

"It's more than that, there's something else going on. She's distracted when she's at home, she's deliberately picking fights." From what little I knew of kids this sounded perfectly healthy to me – I must have looked sceptical.

"Do you have children, Mr Kocharyan?"

I shook my head.

"Lucy is a fragile girl, always has been. She's easily influenced, manipulated even." An interesting choice of word, *manipulated*.

"Do you think she's taking drugs?"

She looked genuinely shocked.

"No! Absolutely not, Lucy would never take drugs." Right. And she's probably never had sex either.

"Is Lucy's father of the same mind, Mrs Booker?"

She shifted her gaze fleetingly over my shoulder and brought it back. "How do you mean?"

"I mean, does he know you're here?"

"Does that matter?"

"It would make things easier if I took the case, that's all."

"I can't bother my husband with this. I'd rather that he knew nothing of it."

"Why's that then?"

She was annoyed at my question, annoyed that I was asking questions at all.

"He has enough on his plate. He has a position of responsibility at the university."

Shit, not a university bod. I tried to stay clear of university business; a more inscrutable lot you couldn't find. Like most educated people I'd had dealings with, words came from their mouths that did not match what they were thinking.

"I assume he isn't a porter there?"

Her fine cheeks reddened and I almost felt sorry for her.

"No. No, he isn't." She studied her handbag. It was like pulling teeth.

"So what does he do?" Again with the blushing.

"He's the Bursar at, erm, Morley." My jaw tensed and I felt myself redden. It was bad enough he was a university big cheese, but to be at Morley of all places. I didn't want this job; I wanted to be down the road watching a 1970s Italian crime film. They were showing one every afternoon this week at the Arts Cinema. I wrote MORLEY in capital letters on my pad.

"Have you tried talking to Lucy? Sometimes people just want to be asked whether anything is wrong."

"Yes, yes of course I have, but she clams up. I know there is something going on, something she's keeping from me. A mother knows." Right. If mothers knew, I wouldn't have them in here asking me to find out for them. My stomach grumbled for the sandwich waiting for me round the corner on Hills Road.

"Will you help me, Mr Kocharyan?"

"Perhaps you could call me George. Look, I'm not sure how I can..." Her impossible eyes shimmered and tears leaked onto her cheeks. Little sparkly jewels rolling out of bigger ones. I pushed the tissues towards her. I had a silly notion that I should dab the tears away myself, but I kept it a notion.

"I'm sorry, I'm just so worried." She blew her nose and blotted her cheeks. She was either under a lot of strain or a very good actor.

"I'm still not sure what it is you want me to do," I said. She took a silver compact from the bag on her lap. She opened it and checked her face, speaking as she wiped mascara tracks from her cheeks.

"Just look for unusual acquaintances. Anyone a fresher shouldn't be consorting with."

I wasn't sure what sort of person that was, never having been a fresher myself, but imagined it included the sort of person your parents warned you about in the first place. I felt doubtful regarding the whole thing, it was too vague. She snapped her compact shut and looked at me with renewed confidence.

"I can pay in cash," she said, fixing me with those turquoise eyes. They were like a weapon she could use at will. I was annoyed at this appeal to the mercenary in me but then I thought of paying Sandra this month – Mr Greene's payment might not come through for weeks. I also thought of the Inland Revenue and the looming MOT on my ten-year-old Volkswagen Golf. On the plus side, the job would make a change from watching disability claimants to see if they were faking injury, which I hated. Stacked against it though was the fact it involved the university, which I also hated, and Morley College of all places. It was a question of which I hated more.

"It could get quite expensive," I said, "depending on how long you want me to look." She smiled for the first time, a triumphant lengthening of the lips which faded quickly.

"Money is not an issue, Mr… erm, George. I can even give you a retainer." She opened the little handbag and retrieved a crisp white envelope, holding it by its edges as if tainted. It looked satisfyingly thick. "Would a thousand pounds be enough?" It was my turn to smile and I took the envelope, relishing its heaviness. I considered opening it, but counting money in front of her would have appeared cheap.

Instead I put it down, opened a drawer and pulled out a standard contract with my terms and conditions on it. She shook her head and her hair swayed.

"Must there be paperwork?" she asked. "I'm prepared to trust you."

"I'm flattered, but my assistant likes paperwork, it keeps her in a job." She filled out her details on the form and I gave her a receipt for the money.

"I hope we can resolve this quickly, George." She pushed the form across the table. She'd put her address as the Bursar's Residence, Morley College.

"Shall we shake on it?" I said. She raised carefully shaped eyebrows but let me briefly hold her limp kipper of a hand. "I'll need details of your daughter's lectures, her regular movements, that sort of thing," I said.

"It's all in the envelope. There's her weekly schedule, the names of her tutors and a photograph." That explained the thickness of the envelope.

"I'm impressed. If only all my clients were so efficient."

She favoured me with her first real smile and stood up, putting on her silk scarf and glasses. I could see my reflection in each lens.

"Is there some way I can reach you? Discreetly of course."

She hesitated before removing a card from her bag. In an elaborate cursive font it read 'Sylvia Booker' and a mobile number, no occupation, no address. I passed her one of mine. I suggested we meet in a week unless I had something before. She nodded guardedly, as if reluctant to make any commitment, then looked at a tiny gold watch on her wrist.

I followed her perfume to the door.

"By the way, why did you choose Cambridge Confidential, Mrs Booker?" She stopped and looked back at me through the dark glass.

"I chose you, George, because I recognised the name on the website of your private eye association."

I could have asked her what she meant but she'd stepped into the hall. Besides, I knew what it meant. It meant that she'd known my father at Morley.

3

I COUNTED OUT TWENTY-POUND NOTES FROM SYLVIA Booker's envelope as I ate my sandwich al-desko. I reached a thousand when the phone rang. It was Jason, Sandra's eldest.

"Boss, why aren't you having lunch with the fit Nina?"

"First, you can't call her fit, I'm told it's sexist—"

"But she is fit, boss, she's a nutritionist and she obviously works out." I rolled my eyes pointlessly.

"Second, I'm not a student like you, I can't just ask women out."

"Really? So how does it work when you're an old geezer? Do you have to fill out a form and apply? Like planning permission but for dating." He chuckled at his own joke and I thought of the dating agency website Sandra had emailed me the link to; I couldn't even complete my profile on there. It just seemed a bit desperate, which of course is what I was becoming.

"Why am I discussing this with you, for fuck's sake?"

He laughed down the line. "Relax, boss. She's just a woman, not an alien. She might even be into older men."

Jason was nineteen and doing a part-time music technology course at Anglia Ruskin University. His mother kept two jobs, one of which was with me and the other Jason knew nothing about, one which I had only learnt about a few months ago. I wished that I could offer Sandra more work but I struggled to pay her for the stuff she did and even that I could do myself if I could be bothered. But I'd known them a long time – ever since I'd established a few years ago that Jason's father had skipped the family and country to concentrate on furthering his drug-dealing career.

"What can I do for you, Jason, besides teach you some manners?" I unfolded the sheets of paper that were in the envelope with the money. A head-and-shoulders photograph was paper-clipped to the front: Lucy Booker. Lucy had not inherited her mother's looks. She had a tense face that reflected little joy. She looked familiar, of a type, mousy with a nose too big for her face. I had a nose myself, so I knew what I was talking about. I was curious to see what her father looked like.

"I'm just checking in, boss. See if you had any jobs going." I glanced at the photo and then at the money. I could do worse than throw some of it his way.

"Something has come in which might need a younger face than I can manage." I looked at my reflection in the window. "My windows also need cleaning."

"OK, I can come by in the morning, but I'm not interested in cleaning windows."

"Choosy bugger, I'll need to run it by your mum first."

"For fuck's sake, boss, I'm over eighteen."

"Yeah, well, that's the arrangement she and I have." He muttered down the phone. I sympathised, but Sandra did not compromise when it came to her kids. She was determined they would stay on the straight and narrow, and that Jason would go to college and not straight into a job to support her and his young brother. Nothing was to get in the way of him finishing his course, not even any extra money that I knew they could use.

Sandra and Jason had also been there for me when Olivia had gone over. Others had been sympathetic but also either embarrassed at the circumstances or unaware of the personal blow to the old machismo – I believed that I must have failed somewhere on the manliness front.

"It was nothing you done, boss," Jason had told me, a couple of weeks after Olivia had flown with the other woman – from her book group – to Greece to set up an artists' retreat in an old farmhouse. I was still drowning my self-pity in beer at the time and Sandra would send Jason round to stop me from drinking too much. "She was probably into women all along but didn't realise it," he'd said.

"Right, so I just tipped her over the edge, is that it?" He'd had to put me to bed that night, bless him, just as Olivia had done once or twice when she had started to wind down the heterosexual phase of her life. I don't suppose getting pissed had helped put the case for men, but I hadn't realised I was making a case at the time; just that she was drifting away.

My train of thought was happily derailed by the thousand pounds in front of me. I returned nine hundred of it to the envelope and placed it in the small office safe. With my feet on the desk I read the neatly printed sheets Sylvia Booker had given me on her daughter. It was all there, the life of one

Lucy Booker – daughter of Morley College Bursar – laid out in single-spaced, small-fonted detail, with her photo paper-clipped to the front, including a breakdown of her weekly lecture schedule – she was doing English Literature – and the societies she belonged to. Someone had gone to a lot of trouble putting it together, almost more trouble than I go to myself when tailing someone and writing a report.

There was nothing contentious, political, or even mildly exciting about what Lucy did, at least on paper. In fact her interests outside the course looked quite boring, and I wondered if they had been picked by her mother: Cambridge University Debating Society, Cambridge University Bridge Club, Cambridge Christians, hill walking, rowing team. Jesus, I was surprised she had time to get up to anything that didn't meet with her mother's approval. I also noted that she still lived with her parents on Morley College grounds – I hoped I wouldn't have to go there.

I rang Sandra at home and prayed she wasn't still asleep. She picked up on the third ring, sounding tired. She worked an adult chat line three nights a week and slept late the following mornings.

"I didn't wake you?"

"No, you're OK, I'm just on my way out to pick up Ashley." Ashley was six years old and had a different father to Jason. Another bloke who didn't hang around long. "Did you fill in your details on the dating site I sent you, George?" I decided it was easiest to lie.

"Yes I have. No matches yet though."

She snorted. "You're lying to me, George, I had a look

last night for new entries. You haven't filled anything in. One day I'm going to answer my premium rate line and you'll be on the other end asking me what I'm wearing." I felt my face warm at this image and didn't know what to say. "Maybe you're more of a webcam kind of guy, though. Thankfully I haven't got the body for that sort of work. At least on the telephone I can wear my bathrobe and keep my legs hairy." Now she was deliberately trying to embarrass me but knowing that didn't lessen my discomfort.

"OK, I'll do the bloody questionnaire."

She laughed down the line, sounding like a train coming to a halt. "Sorry, George, but you do need a kick up the bloody arse."

"I actually rang because I've got some work for Jason." She calmed down.

"Is it marital stuff?"

"No, it's a case of an overbearing mother unnecessarily worried about her offspring. You know the type."

She snorted. "Are you taking the piss?"

"As if. Seriously though, it's easy money." She told me that as long as it didn't interfere with his coursework then it was fine. "Tell me it's not dangerous, George."

"No," I said. "It's not dangerous."

Later that afternoon I watched my 1970s Italian *poliziesco* film, one of only seven people in the cinema. I then drove home with a pizza for company. I made it a threesome with a bottle of Pilsner and we all got on just fine. I put on the Goldberg

Variations (one of Olivia's more successful attempts at improving me culturally) and then fired up the old computer to check my online vitals. While it was going through its interminable start-up routine I went round to the other side of the dining table where I had a chess problem set out on a large wooden board, the wooden pieces pleasingly heavy and tactile – a set that had belonged to my father. The board was out permanently now that Olivia was gone, and dinner parties a thing of the past. I'd also moved the computer down from the bedroom, thereby turning the dining room into my study. The chess problem was for white to mate in three, and the solution had eluded me for a couple of days. I made some half-hearted movements and returned to the computer.

Olivia had emailed me with another update of her restoration plans, which I couldn't bring myself to read. Instead I found the email from Sandra with the witty subject header 'Getting back on the horse' and clicked on the link to the dating agency website. Eventually – I still connected to the Internet using a modem and my telephone line – a conventionally attractive couple (him brown, she white) appeared on the screen, grinning stupidly as they ran through a sun-drenched and daisy-covered meadow hand in hand. I sighed and brought up a blank search page and Googled Sylvia Booker. Her name appeared in links to a couple of local charities, and a quick scan of the sites told me she was a trustee of both. One related to homelessness, the other to rehabilitating ex-drug addicts. I also looked up her husband, who turned out to be one Elliot

Booker, although I didn't get as far as finding pictures of him. Then I got distracted and ended up checking out a few other women completely unrelated to the case, none of them as attractive as Sylvia, but all of them in fewer clothes. Like I said before, it was pathetic.

4

I LIVE NORTH OF THE RIVER CAM IN A HOUSE I INHERITED FROM my parents which I could not afford today if I tried to buy it. The area has become gentrified with the type who drive people carriers and go camping in France when they can afford a beach holiday in Tenerife. It took me no longer than ten minutes to drive to the office and park on the small forecourt, because I avoided the nine-to-five traffic. I walked round the corner to Hills Road and bought a black coffee to go from Antonio's, one of the few remaining independent coffee shops in the city. The clock on Our Lady and the English Martyrs told me that it was nearly ten, my usual time of arrival if I'm in the office. When I got back to my building an unmarked police car was parked on the double-yellows outside, hazard lights flashing. I could tell it was a police car because a plain-clothed copper was sitting at the wheel, and you can't mistake a plain-clothes. They'd also removed the hubcaps, so they don't come off in a high-speed chase. The driver was picking his nose, rolling his harvest into a ball before examining it and flicking it out the window.

I was about to enter the building when a skinny woman in

a blue trouser suit came striding out the door. She squinted at me with ice-blue eyes that were a bit too close together.

"George Korkyan?" She had her hair pulled back painfully hard in what Sandra called a Croydon facelift.

"No," I said. She stepped forward, and I could hear a crackle of static in her shiny suit.

"You're not George Korkyan, private investigator?" She had a reedy voice high-octaved with tension.

"No. I'm George Kocharyan, private investigator. And you are?" She whipped out a badge from inside her jacket; it hung on a chain round her sinewy neck.

"I'm Detective Inspector Stubbing. Guv'nor wants to see you." She made her way towards the unmarked car, expecting me to follow without question.

"Well the guv'nor, whoever that is, knows where to find me," I said to her back. I walked into the building and went upstairs. I left the door to my office open and sat at my desk. I'd just taken the lid off my coffee when she strode in, giving me a look that would strip paint. She put her palms flat on either side of the desk and leant over.

"Listen, Kockerhead, or whatever your fucking name is, Detective Chief Inspector Brampton is waiting at a crime scene, and unless you come with me now, I'll haul you over to Parkside to wait for her there, and she could be some time." Her spittle sprayed my coffee and I looked at her to see if she was bluffing, but all I saw were the straining tendons in her neck and a throbbing vein in her temple.

"You didn't come through the fast-track graduate scheme, did you?"

She gave me her paint-stripping stare and her lips quivered dangerously so I got up before she exploded.

"Why didn't you say it was Brampton?" I said. "She's like a mentor to me." I left the coffee on the desk.

I sat in the back of the car alone as nose-picker drove and Stubbing sat silently beside him. Brampton's and my paths had crossed last year, at some management seminar run by a management consultancy firm which was coordinating efforts to license private investigators. Brampton was a speaker, introduced as a Cambridge graduate who was bringing industry management practices to the police force. Her speech was peppered with jargon that I didn't understand and no one had bothered to explain.

We drove south past the small city that is Addenbrooke's Hospital towards the Gogs, the highest point outside Cambridge. I felt a tightening in my gut. It got tighter as we turned right towards Magog Down and were then waved under the yellow tape held up by a uniform into the car park where I had photographed Trisha Greene and her friends, and was fully knotted by the time I saw the police cars and vans surrounding Mrs Greene's little blue cabriolet, an exclusion zone round it defined by more yellow tape. A tent that had been erected to prevent the rain washing evidence away was being dismantled. Stubbing got out and I followed her lead.

"This way," she ordered. We walked up to where DCI Brampton was talking to an elderly woman cradling a small dog in a coat. We stood at a distance, waiting. I gathered from what I strained to hear that the woman had found the car early this morning. I noticed that underneath her open raincoat Brampton was wearing an expensive and well-cut version of what Stubbing had on, and also had her hair tied back, but less severely than Stubbing's eyebrow-lifting effort. She was stocky and looked like she was on a richer diet than Stubbing. We approached when the woman had been led away by the uniform.

"George, thanks for coming up," Brampton said, in that pleasant way of speaking educated middle-class people have even when they are shafting you. She did not offer to shake hands. She reminded me of my headmistress at secondary school – severity wrapped up in charm. Her round nose and pudgy cheeks were red with cold.

"DCI Brampton," I said. "Thanks for dragging me up here. If it wasn't for community-minded policing I'd never get any fresh air." She gave me the sort of smile bad poker players give you when they know they are holding a better hand than yours.

"Step this way, George." Stubbing, grinning at me with gappy teeth, lifted the yellow ribbon surrounding the cabriolet. Brampton stepped under and then Stubbing let go of the tape as I was about to follow. I lifted it myself and caught up with them.

"You're just in time, the SOCOs have finished," Brampton said. We walked up to the car, me wishing that forensics still had several hours' work to do and I could delay seeing what I knew I was about to see. Brampton shooed away a photographer in protective white overalls. The driver's door was open and Trisha Greene, naked from the waist up, was slumped in the seat. I say slumped: her neck was fastened by a wide leather belt to the bars of the seat headrest, her head lolling forward in an unnatural position, her eyes still open, as if surprised at her own topless state. Her dress had been ripped open at the front and pulled down over her arms; it had also been pushed up her parted thighs and was bunched at her waist. Her body was relaxed, which made her neck look longer than I remembered. Brampton turned to me. "I think you come up here more than you make out, George. I think you might know this woman." There seemed little point in lying about it; they obviously knew I had been watching her, although the swollen, purple face I saw now bore little relation to the pretty, animated one I'd photographed last week.

"Know is a strong word. I've seen her from a distance, through a camera."

"Pervert," said Stubbing. Brampton smiled.

"Detective Inspector Stubbing here has a strong moral streak," said Brampton. "She disapproves of people spying on other people who are having sex."

"I think that's the idea, isn't it? They come up here to be seen," I said.

"By other perverts," spat Stubbing. Brampton raised her bushy eyebrows and asked her to go and check something with a scene of crime officer.

"Would you mind identifying the woman in the car, George, just for the record." I did the necessary, then tore my gaze from Trisha Greene and turned to Brampton.

"I'll assume you're holding the husband, since he's not doing the identifying?"

She pulled her raincoat round her and shrugged to keep warm.

"He's made a statement, we're just confirming his story. He says he hired you to watch her and that she was having an affair." I told her the truth about Trisha's activities, omitting the fact that I'd advised her husband to confront her.

"He doesn't seem the type," I said, as we walked back to the cars.

"There isn't a type, George, just motive and opportunity." She signalled for the waiting forensics team to remove the body. "I'm not pleased about this," she said, in a tone suggesting that it might be my doing. "I try to keep a clean patch, and this sort of thing is not good for Cambridge. The press are going to love it, especially if it involves private investigators and public sex." She stared at me and I didn't care for the way she linked the two things.

"The press won't get anything from me, it's your lot you need to worry about. And Mrs Greene didn't die because of something I did," I added, mainly for my own benefit. She said nothing, but studied the forensic team carefully removing Mrs Greene from the cabriolet into a black body bag, removing the belt that had been used to strangle her. I could now see that it had a brass buckle and tried to remember whether Al Greene had been wearing it when he'd been in my office.

"There must have been people up here who saw her."

"You weren't one of them, were you?"

"No. I was not. The case was over, as I'm sure the husband has told you."

"You may have become infatuated with her, George. She was quite pretty, wasn't she?"

"I was at home," I said, alarmed at the direction this was taking.

"Alibi?"

"Do I need one?"

She ignored me and spoke to someone about getting the car picked up.

Stubbing came over and ignored me as well.

"We're ready when you are, ma'am." Brampton nodded at her and turned to me.

"Don't go anywhere, George, we'll need to take a statement and some DNA and see any other details you've collected while you were following her. Stubbing will liaise with you." Stubbing leered at me as if Brampton had promised me to her sexually.

"I can't wait," I said.

"Play nice, George," Brampton said. "By rights we can just seize your computer and files. But I prefer we all be singing from the same hymn sheet."

"Come by the station first thing tomorrow," Stubbing said, as if I worked for her. They walked over towards the unmarked car, one a cheap imitation of the other. Arse-licking Stubbing opened the door for Brampton. I obviously wasn't getting a lift into Cambridge. Stubbing closed the door on Brampton and shouted to me, "You can go back with Mrs Greene, get one last gawp at her."

She got into the driver's seat and I watched her have a good laugh with the driver at my expense. As the car pulled out she stuck her hand out of the window and made a wanking gesture at me below window level where Brampton couldn't see it.

5

I TRAVELLED INTO CAMBRIDGE IN THE BLACK VAN THAT TOOK Mrs Greene to the morgue at Addenbrooke's Hospital, upfront with the driver and his mate. From there I had to catch a bus into town, cursing Stubbing all the while.

Jason was sitting at his mother's desk when I got into my office; he was logged onto her computer and moving the mouse about on its mat. It was one of those mats you could slot your own picture into and Sandra had put a photo of Ashley in it, a little brown kid with curly hair and a mischievous smile. Jason, on the other hand, was a pale long-limbed youth with wavy brown hair that he had to push back to see the screen. He was so engrossed he didn't look up when I crossed to my desk. He wore his usual jeans and a hooded sweatshirt, always with the hood down. I sat at my desk and looked at my cold coffee, contaminated with Stubbing's spit.

"I hope you're not surfing for porn," I said.

"I'm updating your virus software, and your system is riddled with malware. And another thing, when's the last time you did a backup?"

"Ask your mum." This is why I didn't have a computer

myself at work; I just couldn't be bothered with all that stuff.

"I'll do one now." As he worked he wittered on about the importance of backups, and the technicalities involved, but I wasn't listening. When I didn't say anything he said, "You can thank me later."

"Have you been here long?" I put the lid on the cold coffee and placed it in the bin; I wasn't ready to exchange bodily fluids with Stubbing.

"Yes," he said, typing fast and looking at the screen. "Why are you so late?"

"I've been getting some fresh air," I said. "Do you know how long you have to wait for a bus in Cambridge?"

"You should get a bicycle, boss."

I got the Booker file out of my desk, and removed Lucy's photograph. "There's a student at Emmanuel College I want you to get some info on." He scooted over on the wheeled chair and looked at Lucy's picture.

"Let's hope she's got a big personality," he said.

"What does that mean?"

"It means she's not gonna win any beauty contests, is she?" I rolled my eyes. "What? It's the truth, right?" I ignored him and gave him the low-down on Lucy and her mother's worries. He shrugged and flicked his hair.

"I've been out with this girl Rowena from Emma a couple of times, but I think she's a year ahead of this Lucy. There's a group of the posher ones who like to mix it with the real Cambridge, know what I mean?"

"You mean they like a bit of rough?"

He laughed and his smile and big brown eyes made him

look like his mother. I could see why he had no problem attracting girls. "That's right, boss. They want to experience the real thing before they have to get hitched with people who speak like them. This girl even plays bridge and polo. Right la-di-da she is. Get this, her work experience was at that advertising firm that did those cool car adverts, the ones where the cars turn into trainers. Her dad arranged it for her." Jason's work experience had been as a plumber's mate.

"You're not saying Lucy is part of this group?"

He looked at the photo and shook his head. "No chance." Something that Jason had said earlier nagged at me.

"Rewind, Jason, to what this Rowena does." He shook his head. "Plays. You said she plays something."

"Bridge and polo." I skimmed through the details on Lucy Booker provided by her mother. Lucy was a member of the university bridge club that met every Wednesday night.

"Do you still see this Rowena?"

He nodded. "Not regular like. She's a bit loud, if you know what I mean. But she's coming to a gig this weekend." He started to tell me about how the band playing were mates of his but I wasn't really listening. My plan was for Jason to follow Lucy around for a bit, in his free time, since he would be less conspicuous than me in a student setting, while I would check out her extra-curricular activities. But his connection with the college might provide a quicker way in. I asked Jason to see if Rowena knew Lucy through the bridge club, find out a bit about her, which crowd she mixed with etc.

"Without arousing too much suspicion, that is," I added.

"I don't want Rowena running to Lucy telling her someone is asking questions."

He picked up the photo, studied it and said, "Don't worry, boss. I'll tell Rowena I know someone who fancies Lucy, she'll get a kick out of that." I gave him fifty quid cash and sent him on his way. I wondered whether I should have a chat with Jason about the birds and the bees, and how condoms were cool. But I wasn't his father, and knowing Sandra she'd probably terrified him into putting one on every time he phoned a girl, never mind touched one.

I put my feet on the desk and thought about Trisha Greene held up by the neck against her own headrest. I could not believe that I'd been so wrong about Al Greene, who only yesterday had been sitting opposite, exceeding his quota of office tissues. The whole thing bugged me. Did he drive up there with her to understand what it was she was looking for, maybe try it for himself, and then flip? Or did he follow her up there and catch her at it with someone else and *then* flip? Brampton seemed to have the whole thing sewn up already, although she was keeping her cards close to her chest. I knew I shouldn't worry about something I couldn't influence, especially since I hadn't had my morning coffee. I got up to get my coat when the phone rang. It was Sandra. I filled her in on the Greene murder.

"What's the world coming to when you can't meet a stranger in a car park for sex without being murdered?" she said. I pointed out that most people are murdered by someone they know.

"Maybe so, but I met the husband, and I don't think he was up to it. Too much of a lamb, bless him. If he was a brooder, then maybe, but he wore his heart on his sleeve." I agreed with her and switched to the Booker case, such as it was.

"Who do we know at Emmanuel?" I heard little Ashley in the background, demanding something in an annoying voice. Sandra's voice went faint and I heard her tell him she wasn't at home to Mr Grumpy.

"Sorry about that. What about Jack, he knew your dad, doesn't he work the kitchens there?" I told her Jack had retired. "There's the girl next door but one to us, she makes beds there occasionally." Sandra lived in an ex-council terraced house in King's Hedges, an area of Cambridge that doesn't feature in postcards of the city. Her ex-husband had seen fit to spend some of his drug-earned money on buying it outright from the council, then cladding it in what looked like crazy paving and putting it in Sandra's name. Sandra didn't care; it had no mortgage, three bedrooms and a strip of garden she had made bloom, in contrast to some of her neighbours who saw their gardens as somewhere to store old furniture and appliances they no longer needed.

"It's unlikely she knows Lucy," I said. "She doesn't board at Emma; she still lives with her parents at Morley."

"You'd think they'd have kicked her out, they could easily have wangled her a room right in the college. I'd have kicked Jason out long ago if he could afford anything in this overpriced city." I told her I thought the same and she reminded me to water her plants. I wondered whether it was Lucy's choice or her mother's that she continued to stay on

Morley premises. Initial impressions suggested the mother, but experience told me that despite their strong lure, initial impressions were usually wrong.

I watered Sandra's plants, put on my raincoat and locked the office. I met Nina coming up the stairs.

"Everything OK?" she asked. "A very rude policewoman was here this morning demanding to know where you were. It upset some of the customers. It's not what they expect when they come for a massage."

"Yeah, sorry about that, she's lacking in basic social skills." We stood there awkwardly, me one step higher. "Listen, I'm going to get a coffee across the road. Do you want to join me?"

She pointed over my shoulder up the stairs. "I have a client waiting. Besides," she said, "I've had my caffeine quota for the day."

"Maybe some other time then, when you haven't had your quota."

She smirked and shrugged. "Maybe," then passed me. I wasn't sure I liked the way she said 'maybe'; it left me feeling that she knew I was desperate and was playing me. I was too old for such playground shenanigans.

Later, at home, after I'd heated something covered in plastic and sat with it over my chess puzzle, I was rung by Kamal, a friend who worked as a porter at Addenbrooke's while he tried to make it as a writer. He wondered whether I wanted to go for a drink. I watched the steaming, spreading mess of dinner and said yes, even though I knew he just wanted to tap me for stories.

6

PARKSIDE POLICE STATION IS A BRUTE OF A BUILDING STANDING in good company next to the fire station. They both look over the large square of green in the middle of Cambridge that is Parker's Piece, drooled over by developers and protected by Our Lady and the English Martyrs, who watch over it from one corner. The lamp post in the middle used to be called Reality Checkpoint by some of the more toffee-nosed students to mark for them the end of the university bit of the town and the beginning of the 'real' bit. Nowadays of course a lot of students venture beyond the lamp post and into the real town, for cheap accommodation if nothing else.

I arrived at the police station having walked from my office through a mean drizzle, carrying my photos of Mrs Greene on a memory stick, along with a file containing her movements. When I wasn't following her I'd captured her car journeys on a tracker placed under the bumper of her cabriolet. I had removed it a few days before giving her husband the low-down on his wife's activities.

Stubbing, bless her, kept me waiting in reception after I'd announced myself and I spent the time watching unfortunates come and go – it was not a place people came to happily, unless they'd come to recover something they'd lost that incredibly someone had handed in. The ones who arrived under the insistence of the police usually did so round the back entrance, out of the way of the tourists who had strayed across the road from Parker's Piece.

Stubbing's face, pinched and pale, appeared at a glass window in a door. She caught my eye and snapped her head at me to follow. We walked without talking and Stubbing held open the door of a small interview room where a bored-looking young plain-clothes sat at the metal table reading a *Daily Mail*, which he quickly folded up when we came in. I could smell Stubbing's cheap deodorant as I passed her. There was a small table in the windowless room with a tape recorder on it, much like you see on TV, but without the dramatic lighting, which in this case was overhead, harsh and fluorescent. We sat on hard chairs facing each other across the table. I felt like a suspect even though I was just giving a statement, a feeling reinforced by the fact that my chair would not sit on all four legs at once. The other detective pulled his chair up to the table and flipped open a pad. I half expected him to lick the end of a pencil but instead he took a fancy-looking ballpoint from inside his jacket.

Stubbing got straight down to business.

"This is Detective Sergeant Turner," she said, tilting her head towards her colleague. "Mr Kocharyan, please tell us when you first met Albert Greene." Stubbing's hair was still pulled back in headache-inducing tightness and she was wearing the same nylon suit. A thin gold chain with nothing on it sat at her bloodless throat.

"I'd just like to say how pleased I am to be able to help the Cambridgeshire police in any way possible," I said, trying to get my chair level. Turner coughed a word into his hand. I ignored him. So did Stubbing. "Albert Greene came to me three weeks ago suspecting that his wife Trisha Greene was having an affair. I agreed to investigate. I followed her on four occasions over two weeks and also tracked the movements of her car over the same period." Turner scribbled onto the pad.

"Tracked her movements how?" Stubbing asked.

"Using a standard £200 GPS tracker you can buy in any electronics shop." I gave her a breakdown of the exact times I'd followed Mrs Greene myself and then I took the USB stick from my pocket and pushed it across the table. "On here is a spreadsheet detailing all her car journeys over the two weeks the tracker was fitted." Stubbing told Turner to make a note. "You'll see that most of them are to her workplace or the gym but there are also regular trips to the car park, where you found her. That is where I took most of the photos I have of her; they're on the memory stick as well. Mr Greene confirmed most of the addresses; there were a couple he didn't recognise but I assumed they were friends or people she preferred to, ah, visit indoors."

"You didn't check those out?"

"I'd already confirmed the client's suspicions at that stage. He wasn't paying me to follow everyone she was sleeping with. I'd like the memory stick back, it's expensive."

She picked it up. "You can have it when the case is closed."

Turner grinned and Stubbing handed him the memory stick, asking him to take it over to the high tech unit and to get a receipt. He left the interview room and she pulled the pad round and read the statement. She sat back in her chair, clasped her hands behind her head and glared at me. "It's a grubby job you've got, Kocky," she said.

"It pays the bills. Besides, yours isn't exactly wholesome."

She looked at me with disgust.

"Is Greene being held here without charge?" I asked. I checked my watch. "Surely he's been here twenty-four hours already." It was as if I hadn't spoken; she was giving nothing away. I forced myself to maintain eye contact with her icy stare. She cracked first.

"He's a detained suspect. Do you know what that is?"

"It means Brampton likes him for the murder."

"DCI Brampton to you, Kocky."

"It's Kocharyan."

"Yeah, whatever. What sort of name is that anyway?"

"Armenian." She looked no wiser. "Is the belt his then?" I asked.

"You ask a lot of questions about things that don't concern you."

"I don't think he did it," I said.

She sat up in her chair and crossed her arms. "It's a good thing that your opinion doesn't matter then, isn't it?" She turned the pad round and asked me to read the statement. I was reading through it carefully when DS Turner came back in and went over to Stubbing. He leant down and whispered something in her ear. She frowned and gave him a questioning look. He shrugged. "You'll have to wait for that receipt," she told me.

She leant forward, looked me in the eye, a hint of a sneer on her face. I thought she was going to say something but she very quickly stood up, scraping her chair legs on the floor. "We'll have a look at your material and get back to you if we have further questions. Sign the statement. DS Turner here will show you out." With that she picked up my report and left the room.

"Not even a 'thank you for coming in'," I said to Turner as I signed the statement, reassured that words hadn't been put into my mouth.

"Not from DI Stubbing, sir. She's—" He stopped, perhaps realising he was being inappropriate. "This way, sir," he said, opening the door.

"She's what then?" I insisted, following him into the corridor.

"She's a good detective, sir."

I got back to the office after stopping off for lunch to find Sandra at her desk and on the phone. She raised her eyes to the ceiling to tell me she was suffering a fool on the other end. Sandra's telephone manner was brisk and businesslike. She used a slightly harsher one to chase up payments and I imagined it was the same one she used when talking to her premium-rate callers. She was big, or what women, when being kind, liked to call 'curvy'. She called herself fat. Her killer smile could clear your worries like morphine and she had a penetrating brown-eyed gaze that worked like truth serum. She put down the receiver as I put my feet up on my desk.

"That was Work and Pensions. They have another benefits sponger they want you to check out."

"I hate that work, Sandra, you know that."

"It pays bills."

I tried not to look smug as I said, "There's nearly a grand in the safe. A retainer from Sylvia Booker."

She opened her mouth to say something that would no doubt burst my bubble when thankfully the phone rang and she had to answer it.

"Cambridge Confidential Services, how can we help?" she asked. Sandra always said 'we' when she answered the phone, insisting it sounded like there were lots of us, not one man and his part-time PA and her odd-job son. She listened and frowned. "Where are you? Why aren't you in class?" I smiled as I imagined Jason doing some fast talking. Sandra gave a sceptical grunt and transferred the call. I put the handset to my ear. Hubbub formed background noise.

"Boss, why don't you get a mobile, or use the office one? I wouldn't have to go through Mum to speak to you."

"Because you don't own a mobile phone, Jason, it owns you." Sandra made a derisory snorting sound. Loud uninhibited female laughter drowned out Jason's reply. "Where are you?" I asked.

"The Flying Duck. Hang on, let me move somewhere quieter." The laughter dimmed and Jason's voice grew clearer. "Guess who I've just had lunch with?"

"I don't know, Britney Spears and Paris Hilton, by the sound of it."

He laughed. "No, the complete opposite I'd say, now that I've met her." He paused gratuitously for dramatic effect.

"Spit it out, boy."

"Lucy Booker."

7

JASON HAD EXAGGERATED THE NATURE OF HIS LUNCHTIME tryst with Lucy Booker, as I discovered when we met later that afternoon at Antonio's. Jason didn't want to come in to the office since his mother was there and would no doubt question him about something or other he should or shouldn't be doing. Antonio took his time making an espresso and a cappuccino while I quizzed Jason, who smelled of beer and crisps.

"So you didn't actually speak to Lucy then?" I'd already established that he'd met with Rowena at the Flying Duck for a lunchtime drink, which explained why he was there in the first place – it was an undergraduate hangout only frequented by the likes of Jason to pick up girls or pick fights with male freshers philosophising in that annoyingly loud way freshers do when drinking.

"She came in with her rowing crew. It's a favourite pub of theirs after practice. She drank half a shandy. The others had pints of bitter. She spent most of the time looking down into her beer and blushing at the jokes. You should hear some of the jokes these girls tell, boss – some of them make me blush. There's this one about three men and an old lady with no teeth, right—"

"I've heard it, Jason, it's disgusting." Antonio came over with our coffees. He was fifty-something with a large paunch and impossibly thick and wavy hair lined with grey. It gave him the appearance of gravitas he did not possess.

"You want some almond cake, Georgio?"

"No thanks, Antonio, I need to watch myself." I patted my stomach.

"Forget about it. The ladies don't want sticks like young Jason here. They see your stomach as a sign of your appetite for life."

"More like a sign of your appetite for cake," said Jason. He started hooting loudly until Antonio walked away, shaking his head. I looked at Jason to show him I wasn't laughing; I was, after all, paying him for his time.

He registered my face and settled down.

"Did you learn anything useful while boozing at my expense?"

"Yes I did, as a matter of fact." He sucked noisily at his hot cappuccino without lifting the cup from the saucer and then smiled at me with a frothy moustache. "They belong to the same bridge club." He wiped his upper lip with a napkin. He'd missed a bit but I didn't say anything; sometimes I felt the need to punish his youthful cockiness.

"Excellent work, Jason."

"Well yeah, boss, but this is the thing. I asked Rowena whether I could play bridge, you know, to like raise the subject, and that got the biggest laugh of all, like I'd asked if I could meet her parents, right? Anyway, she goes to Lucy like," – and here he put on a passable version of Penelope Keith in *To The Manor Born* – "'Do you think Jason could master the subtleties of bridge, Lucy?' and Lucy looks at me under her fringe and shrugs. 'I don't see why not, he doesn't look stupid,' she says. And then she asks me, as brazen as you like, 'You're not stupid are you?' and all the while her eyes are flicking between me and Rowena, like the question was about me and her, not about bridge. Anyway, it got to Rowena 'cause I could feel her arse tighten on my hand."

At this point Jason took in more of his coffee and I was left with the image of a tensing Rowena with Jason's hand under her buttock. I waited for him to carry on, looking around the four-tabled place wondering how Antonio survived the saturation spread of coffee-shop multinationals. Only one other customer kept us company; an old man who was studying the inside of a Cambridge *Argus*. I could see the headline and my own buttocks tensed: DEAD WOMAN FOUND IN POPULAR DOG-WALKING SPOT. Jason was shaking his head, ready to resume.

"Quiet as a mouse she'd been up till then," he said. "Then Rowena asks Lucy why she never goes to bridge club any more, and whether it was because she'd finally found a boyfriend, and Lucy goes the colour of a baboon's arse and makes her excuses." He shook his head and looked down at the table. "When she'd gone they all had a good laugh at her expense," he said, in a low voice. There was hope for the boy yet.

* * *

I bought a Cambridge *Argus* on the way back to the office, where Sandra was typing on the computer. I sat at my desk and put my feet up.

"Any messages?" I asked. Sandra just snorted without breaking her flow and I started to read the inside page article on Trisha's murder. It gave little detail, no mention of the belt. I'd just got to the bit about a man helping with enquiries when the soothing clickety-clack stopped.

"I rang Work and Pensions, told them you'd take the benefits case."

I sighed and put the paper down. "I've told you I hate that work, Sandra. It's bad karma, ask any of the women who work in the building."

"Yeah, well, they have a long line of people ready to part with cash in return for some hocus-pocus. You, on the other hand, have a long line of bills waiting to be paid." I sighed again, wondering whether it wouldn't be better to sack Sandra and replace her with someone younger who minded their own business and let me be. I heard the buzz-buzz of the inkjet printer spraying words onto paper. I went back to the murder story. Thankfully there was no mention of me or Al Greene, only DCI Brampton. It was early days though, and although the *Argus* was not celebrated for its investigative journalism, it was only a matter of time before the sexual nature of the crime came out and the potential quadrupling of sales made someone curious. My worry was being linked with the case; the last thing I needed was a reputation as some sort of sleaze-ball private eye whose clients ended up in jail. The printer stopped and Sandra placed a page on my desk.

"The details of the benefits case; he's claiming he can't walk. He lives out in Cottenham, so you could kill two birds with one stone."

"He probably *can't* walk."

She switched off the computer and picked up her bag. She stood there fixing me with her big brown eyes and that disarming smile.

"You live in the clouds, George, you need to get a business head screwed on, like the girls in the building." She leaned on my desk and it creaked dangerously. She'd lost the smile. "Jason tells me you've been sniffing round that skinny Asian bird."

Jesus Christ.

"Skinny Asian bird, Sandra?"

"She's not what you need right now." Really? It seemed to me Nina was just what I needed: uncomplicated, attractive, sexy.

Sandra looked me up and down. "I know that you probably need to get laid, but believe me, Nina is not the answer. You need to get onto that dating website." I took my feet down and tucked my bottom half under the desk in case of some embarrassing physical manifestation of my needing to get laid. She was going to say something else, then regained the smile and said she'd pop in the next day for a couple of hours. When she was gone I tried to fold up the newspaper but it got tangled up so I ended up screwing it into a giant ball and stuffing it into the waste basket.

I snatched the piece of paper from the desk and examined it. The address was indeed in Cottenham; if I left now I could get there half an hour before the end of visiting hours and then sneak a peek at my alleged benefits fraudster. I got my camera bag from the desk and went to the door. Then something about bridge club nagged me so I went back to the desk and took out the Booker file. On the list of Lucy's activities Cambridge University Bridge Club was listed for eight o'clock Wednesday nights at Selwyn College, which was in town. Today was Wednesday. In fact it was the only club that took place in the evening; all the others were lunchtime or weekend meets. But according to Rowena, Lucy had stopped going to bridge. Sylvia Booker's business card was in the file. It had grown dark outside so I flicked the desk lamp on, picked up the phone, dialled.

It rang seven times then she answered with a hushed, "Hello?" I imagined Sylvia Booker to be the sort of woman who removed her earring before answering the phone.

"Hello, Mrs Booker? This is George Kocharyan." I could hear a man's voice in the background, the sort of droning you hear at meetings or lectures. Perhaps she was at one of her charity board meetings. I heard rustling and the male voice faded.

"George?" Now her voice was breathless, like she'd been running, and I shook an image from my head of her parted lips next to my ear.

"Just a quick question, Mrs Booker. I was wondering how Lucy gets to bridge on Wednesdays since you live out at Morley College. Does she cycle in this weather?"

"No, I drive her there and pick her up. In fact I'm taking her tonight. Why do you ask?"

"Just trying to get a full picture, that's all. Sorry to disturb you."

"Not at all. Anything else I can help with?" Yes, you could talk softly in my ear like Grace Kelly.

"No. You've been very helpful. Goodbye."

I hung up and went to kill two birds with one stone.

8

HALF AN HOUR WAS ABOUT AS MUCH TIME AS I COULD STAND to visit my father in those days. When he first went into care two years ago I would sit for hours and he would have moments when he knew who I was and occasionally spoke, albeit laboriously. Those moments had grown shorter and more intermittent. I was glad my mother hadn't lived to see his final deterioration (although she'd had to put up with worsening and uncharacteristic outbursts of verbal coarseness and the knocking on neighbours' doors with no trousers on which in time morphed into silence and apathy) and relieved that at least now he had reached a stage where he wasn't aware of his own mental state. Initially we'd assumed it was early-onset Alzheimer's but one doctor had diagnosed Pick's disease, which is rarer but was a better fit of his symptoms.

Inside the home a young care assistant I'd seen a couple of times before led me into the conservatory where the rain pelted down on the corrugated plastic roofing. It was very loud and the care assistant had to speak up.

"We like it when you visit, Mr Kevorkian, you always bring flowers. It's not many men would bring flowers for their father." She smiled at me and I forgave her for mistaking me for the doctor who helped 130 people kill themselves; she was young and since she worked here was probably still idealistic. She took my petrol-station flowers from me and walked off, leaving me with my father who was sitting and looking up at the plastic roofing as it held off the rain. The noise of it was probably what held his attention.

I sat down next to him and patted his hand and he looked briefly at me and smiled, but it was a smile empty of recognition. He turned his gaze back to the roofing and while he was occupied with the rain I surreptitiously checked what I could see of his translucent skin for bruises. I was paranoid about him being abused or manhandled in here, despite everyone that I'd met (and I'd made sure that I'd met everyone) being perfectly nice. Unfortunately, being perfectly nice, in my experience, was no indication of a person's true nature – after all, I'm sure Dr Kevorkian was perfectly nice.

Ten minutes after leaving my father I was getting cold in my Golf watching the curtained house of number twenty-two, home to the supposed benefit fraudster. It was dark and still raining. At least I wasn't conspicuous sitting in my car when it was raining. I was parked three houses down in the narrow terraced street of small drab houses. Satellite dishes were fixed to many of them, and old model Nissans and Fords, some as old as mine, lined the road. Nothing moved, and the flicker of TV screens came through the nets of houses that hadn't yet had their curtains closed. I hadn't come prepared for a proper stakeout: no flask of coffee, nothing to piss into, no snacks. I just wanted to check the place out, get the lay of the land. It was half-past seven. I started the car and headed for Selwyn College.

It was ten to eight when I turned onto Cranmer Road, drove to the end then U-turned and parked where I could see the entrance to the college. The rain had been downgraded to a faint drizzle, the sort that feels like being sprayed with a mister. I could see the building from inside the car, about ten car lengths away. I'd been near here before with Olivia, who'd tried to introduce me to classical music but had chosen the most booming and bombastic of symphonies which put me off going to another concert.

The streets in this part of Cambridge are wide and tree-lined, with buildings set back from the road behind walls and hedges. Surveillance work was a lot easier here than the pack-'em-in streets of ordinary folks, where front doors opened onto the pavement and loitering was difficult. I was soon rewarded with a young couple going in, exactly the sort of nerdy types I thought would be playing bridge rather than getting hammered and having sex. Mind you, Rowena seemed to combine both pursuits quite happily.

I sat there for ten minutes and saw two taxis draw up and several people arrive on bicycles, wondering which of them was Rowena. At ten past a new model Mini Cooper turned onto the road and stopped outside the entrance, the exhaust smoke flattened by the rain. Sylvia Booker was at the wheel, Lucy at her side. I couldn't see them clearly because of the rain on my windscreen. Sylvia seemed to be having a one-sided conversation with her daughter, who was looking straight ahead. Then the passenger door opened and Lucy Booker got out, a knee-length skirt showing under her raincoat. I couldn't make out her features except to see that she had shoulder-length flat hair, which I knew from her photo to be blonde. A slight person, she walked with arms crossed against the cold into the college grounds, a large bag swinging from her shoulder. She was not someone I would associate with a rowing team. The Mini waited, Sylvia watching her daughter until she had gone into the building before driving off. I sank down in my seat as the Mini passed me, turned round at the end of the road and passed me again. I thought about getting out of the car and watching some bridge when the building door opened and Lucy's head appeared. She looked up and down the road, saw that the Mini had gone and came out. I cleared the windscreen with a single flick of the wiper. She had a cardigan and blouse done up to the neck under the raincoat and now put a scarf over her head against the drizzle, or perhaps as a form of disguise. She looked younger than her photo. She walked to the end of the road and I started to get out and follow when she just stopped at the corner of Cranmer Road, her back to me. She checked her watch. I did the same – it was twenty past eight.

On watching Lucy Booker waiting at a street corner, it crossed my febrile mind that she was on the game, and wondered how I would break it to her mother. It is not unknown for undergraduate women to turn to prostitution, but not well-bred middle-class girls like Lucy who didn't need the money, despite the buzz the idea might give sad men like myself. Sandra was right, I needed to get laid – cold showers didn't help. This was not, after all, Histon Road, where the residents had campaigned hard to get rid of the women working the street. I wasn't sure where they worked now; it had been a while since I'd followed an errant husband to pick one up.

I'd calmed myself down when a big fuck-off silver Mercedes pulled up in front of Lucy and my imagination set off again. But she just stood there and a capped driver in a suit got out and opened the rear door, which had a tinted window. He was gym fit under his tight suit, sleeves too short. He took his cap off briefly as she got in and revealed a crop-haired and square-faced head. He did not speak to Lucy as she got in, just gave her a small nod. I had the feeling that I'd seen him before, but he could just have been of a type. I fumbled for a notebook as he closed the door on her, to write down the licence number, which I couldn't see as the car was side-on. The Merc set off and I followed. The rear window was also tinted so I could not see who else, if anyone, was inside with Lucy. I opened the notebook in my lap and wrote the licence number without looking away from the road. It's a skill I've had to learn, like urinating into a cut-off plastic Coke bottle while seated.

I let a couple of cars get between us as we drove down The Backs, then towards Chesterton, near where I live. The Merc was easy to keep in view, even in the rain, and we turned as if to go into town across Elizabeth Way but before the bridge he turned left at a petrol station, went down the road and turned right into a gated residential block. The gates opened slowly, to let the Mercedes in, and I managed to quickly turn into a small open-air car park opposite. The gates closed behind the Mercedes. I yanked the camera with the telephoto from the bag in the passenger foot-well. Through the lens I could see the driver of the Merc unfold a large umbrella before opening the rear door.

The Lucy Booker that stepped out of the car was not the one that had got in. First, her legs appeared, the skirt now unbuttoned to show some thigh. Then her head appeared. She had lost the scarf and her hair was fixed up in a bun. I zoomed in. She had applied red lipstick and black mascara. Her cheeks were rouged. Something sparkled in her earlobes. The most surprising thing though, as I zoomed out slightly when she fully emerged, was that she had taken off her raincoat and undone several buttons of her cardigan and blouse to create some cleavage.

9

BACK IN THE OFFICE I TOOK OFF MY DRIPPING COAT, POWERED up the computer on Sandra's desk and wished I had a coffee machine. I waited for the computer to come to life – starting Windows was like waking someone with a bad hangover early in the morning. I connected the camera to it and waited for the photos I'd taken to upload. I had an interesting evening to mull over.

After watching Lucy go into the building and the driver walk over to a pub opposite, I'd wondered whether I should try to befriend the driver and pump him for info, or stick with Lucy. I decided to stick with Lucy. I went over to the pub and checked through the window; my friend was settled with a pint and a *Daily Express*. Once again he jogged a memory that I couldn't place. I didn't try too hard though; it would come to me at some point if it was there.

I went back over to the apartments. It was a new five-storey block, called River Views, and a plaque on the gate advertised it as being fully serviced and security monitored. The cars in the car park were all executive late models (no people carriers here), and there was no legit way in except with a key or by ringing someone's bell in the panel of about twenty-five that was lit up beside the pedestrian entrance, also gated. Above the gate a camera swivelled slowly. It headed my way. Beyond the gate, in the wall beside the path leading to the lifts, was a mirrored window next to a door marked 'Caretaker'. I studied the names next to the bells but they meant nothing to me. I was about to press them all in the hope that someone would buzz me in with the old pizza delivery trick, when the caretaker door opened and an elderly man came out. I knew him, or rather my father had known him. I'd even done a job for his daughter once. He shuffled over to the gate carrying a big set of keys and a torch.

"Can I help you, son?" he asked, trying to sound officious. He had a cheap uniform on with 'Caretaker' sewn onto the breast pocket.

"It's Eric, isn't it? Eric Partridge?" I asked. He studied me with watery eyes. My father had said he was a drunk and his face seemed to confirm that; the drink had made his capillaries burst and his skin sag. But he did recognise me.

"You're George Junior, aren't you? How are you, son? What're you doing here?" Before waiting for an answer he opened the gate and I was in. I pointed to the door he'd come out of.

"You got a kettle in there?"

Once we were squeezed into his tiny cubby hole he filled the kettle from a tap over a sink so small he had to fill a mug to pour into the kettle. He sat at a small metal desk, gesturing to a small two-person sofa that was designed, size-wise if not quality-wise, for hip-less supermodels. A phone was mounted on the wall to save space and the small electric kettle sat on a two-drawer filing cabinet. Notices on the wall proclaimed various fire and security warnings around a shallow metal cabinet. A small black and white screen on the desk showed a swivelling picture of the car park, then alternated with a view of the outside of the gates. The room smelled of booze and stale farts and I couldn't wait to get out.

"How's your old man, son?" I gave him the low-down on George Senior's state. He became subdued, perhaps brooding on his own mortality. He checked the door was locked and opened the bottom filing cabinet, fishing out a flat half-pint bottle of Johnnie Walker from behind some files. "Let's drink to him." I had a sip from my mug and let him have another on his own. He'd forgotten to care about what I was doing here in the first place; he was just glad of the company. I gestured at the little screen when it switched back to the car park.

"Nice Merc. Is it the S-Class?" He looked out of the one-way window and I realised we could see the car through the glass.

"Yeah, the 320. Sixty grand new. More than what I earn in four years." He looked at me. "You still doing that snooping stuff, son? I never thanked you for exposing that shit of a son-in-law. You saved my daughter from wasting her life on a worthless prick." He shook his head and sipped from his mug. "I mean stealing from his own wife's business. It's like stealing from yourself, isn't it? She's done alright now, she has. Runs a restaurant with her new fella. He cooks, she does the books. You should go and eat there, George." I waited while he wrote the name down and elicited a promise that I would go there and tell them I was a friend of his so I could eat for nothing. I bet his daughter loved the fact that he was so free with her business.

I remarked that it was a bit ostentatious for Cambridge, the car – you might see its sort parked outside a new detached executive home in one of the villages. The kettle noisily filled the small room with steam and then it clicked off. Eric had forgotten all about making tea though and offered me more whisky. I let him put some in my mug so he didn't feel so bad putting some in his own.

"Yeah, you're right there, son. That's Mr Boyd's Merc. Comes up every week from London for a few nights." I pretended to sip my whisky.

"A hit with the ladies, I bet." I noticed a shallow cabinet on the wall, slightly ajar, the sort that held keys. Eric sipped and nodded.

"Right you are. He brings a girl every Friday or Saturday night. But always the same girl on Wednesday nights, always driven here by Mark and always driven home. She never stays more than an hour. She's not a looker, not like the ones he has over on Friday and Saturday nights. They're usually different – sometimes there are two of them; sometimes there's a bloke as well, a thin guy. And sometimes," he leant forward and I got a blast of JW, "Mark and this guy go upstairs with them." He settled back and closed his eyes and I thought he'd gone to sleep. Then he opened them and leant forward again. "Mr Boyd likes 'em young, let me tell you."

"Like how young?" I asked. He sat back and unfocused his gaze. He was making me dizzy with his constant shifting.

"In my day you could tell when a girl was, well, ready, you know?"

I nodded encouragingly.

"Nowadays they look ready when they're not."

Since he couldn't tell an eighteen-year-old from a thirteen-year-old I moved on to safer ground. "And do they stay the night?"

He shrugged. "Sometimes, but not always. Sometimes they leave on their own and Mark drives them home, sometimes he leaves with them. Mark and this skinny guy had to carry one of them out last week, she was pissed as a newt."

"Quite the gentleman, this Boyd. Do you know what he does?"

Again with the head shaking. "I just do nights, son, don't get to speak to the residents much. I just see them come and go, that's all. There's a big turnover here; it's not the sort of place people settle down in, you know? In my day you bought a place and that was it..."

I jumped in before he could continue. "So where's he from, this Boyd?"

"Boyd? He's American," Eric said, nodding, as if this explained everything. He went to the filing cabinet and pulled out a file.

"Quintin, his name is Quintin Boyd. He's got the whole top floor to himself."

* * *

I'd tried to get more out of him but too many reminiscences got in the way and I wanted to be in my car when Lucy came out; according to Eric she didn't stay for long. But Eric hadn't even met this Boyd, just his driver, Mark, a pleasant enough fella apparently, but not someone who liked to chat. Outside River Views I crossed the road and looked up at the fifth and top floor. There were vertical blinds across the tall windows, the sort you see in offices, a soft glow coming through them. I went back to the Golf, watched Mark the driver go to River Views at nine forty-five, took some more photos of Lucy getting in the Merc and then followed them back to Selwyn College.

When she got out near Selwyn, Lucy's makeover was gone; she'd reverted to her plain self – lipstick-free, buttoned up to the chin and down to the knee. I'd waited until her mother had picked her up and now here I was uploading her photos onto the computer.

I left for home, but not before leaving a note for Sandra to do a vehicle check on the Merc's number plate.

At home I let a couple of cold Pilsners nurse me while I switched the computer on. I Googled Quintin Boyd and the top hit led me to the home page of the corporate law firm 'Quintin Boyd'. It could have been a coincidence, a firm with the same name, but on the 'about us' page he was listed as the senior partner who had formed the company twelve years earlier. According to their own publicity they were earmarked as 'fastest growing corporate law firm' by some corporate law body. The page also listed the many mergers and acquisitions the firm had been involved in. There were sixty partners listed, in three different departments spread over London and New York. I could see no mention of a Cambridge office. I clicked back to the partner listings and brought up Boyd's profile. A head and shoulders photo of him stared out, taken at some meeting, looking off at a slight angle. He was smiling, with the sort of teeth you see in Hollywood mouths, and dimples that, if you had them, would make you want to keep on smiling. He was handsome, no doubt, with slightly too much black hair (greyed at the temples), a little long but erring on the side of acceptable for a corporate lawyer. He had the usual dark suit, pink shirt and Windsor knot at his throat you expect to see on those types. He had no extra fat in the face, nothing hanging beneath the chin like *I* saw in the mirror each morning.

I clicked away from him and checked my email. Nothing there but invitations to spend money on enhancing what was between my legs. In my case this would be like souping up a rusty 1982 Ford Cortina, parking it in a garage and throwing away the keys. It did serve to remind me to look at the dating website where I half-heartedly filled in some details against my profile but could not think of a message to write that would make anyone want to contact me. "Middle-aged man who turned wife lesbian and makes living destroying marriages and photographing benefit cheats seeks cuddles and maybe more," was not going to attract the ladies, and I was in no mood for bullshitting. The Pilsner had run out of nurse so I considered opting for the intensive, watch-you-while-you-sleep care only a large whisky can provide. Instead I stood over my chess problem for fifteen minutes until I'd cracked it. I slept like a baby.

10

LEAVING MY HOUSE TOO EARLY THURSDAY MORNING I WAS hailed in a fake friendly manner by the besuited man who lived next door. He drove a new Volvo estate that he washed and waxed every Sunday (and replaced every year) while his harassed-looking wife tried to cope with a couple of shrieking toddlers. I deduced, given his regular garb, that he was some managerial type. He had once complained when one of his precious offspring had scratched her face on a large bramble that had reached through the rotting fence onto his patch, although I don't know why he couldn't have clipped the offending plant himself. I don't intentionally cultivate brambles – my mother was the gardener of the family, and after her death my father just let it go wild. And when Olivia and I had moved into the house after my father went into care, I hadn't the skills or heart to tackle it.

By my neighbour's hearty tone I presumed that he wanted to make some new neighbourly complaint, since it was the only time he talked to me. Sure enough he was asking me about the shabby fence between our gardens and wondered when, if ever, I was going to replace it; it wasn't keeping the ivy and brambles from his clipped and snipped garden. He was trying to make light of it but things like this bother these suburban types. He probably tossed and turned over it at night. I made a promise to get someone to look into it.

"Would you split the cost?" I asked. He made a face and got in his car, my chances at being invited for Christmas drinks blown. I drove off myself, keen to get up to Cottenham before people started leaving for work.

Two butt-numbing hours later I was back in the office. No benefits cheat had left number twenty-two to go to work, and I wanted to type up my report and get together with Sylvia Booker. The case had gone quicker than I'd liked from a financial point of view, but sometimes things were just that simple. Besides, I could possibly get follow-up work with the unanswered questions: despite confirming Sylvia's suspicions about her daughter, which is what I was being paid to do, I'd not really established the nature of her relationship with Quintin Boyd beyond the obvious. Who was this Quintin Boyd and why did he come up to Cambridge several nights a week? On the face of it he came to seduce consenting young women; as far as I knew, hardly a crime.

I was typing up my report at Sandra's desk when Sandra came in, bearing fresh coffee and biscotti from Antonio's.

"We should get married," I said, as she placed the steaming cardboard cup on my desk.

"What, so I can bring you coffee? Sod that." She looked over my shoulder at the screen. "Whatya doing?" I told her about the breakthrough with Lucy Booker. She wanted to see the photos so I relinquished her chair and she brought them up on the screen, studying Lucy's transformation.

"She's obviously tarted up for something or someone," she said.

"There's only one thing she would get tarted up for, isn't there?"

She stared at me as if to check that I wasn't retarded. "Don't be an arsehole, George. A woman can get dressed up for a variety of reasons, not just 'cause she wants sex. She may do it to feel better about herself, or to fit in, or just to be glam for the sake of it. You think women go around dressing up just for your benefit?"

I kept quiet; I knew better than to argue with her, especially when she got that furrow between the eyes. I sat at my desk and Sandra insisted on finishing my report since she used ten fingers to type as opposed to my two. It left me free to ring Sylvia Booker to arrange a time to meet and update her. This time she sounded crisp and professional.

"Let's meet up this lunchtime, George. Do you know Stanmore Barns in Shelford?"

I bumped into Nina on the way out of the office. She was looking harassed and attractively flushed. The cloth of her white coat sounded satisfyingly crisp and freshly starched.

"I've been thinking," I said, before I had time to think about whether it was a good idea. "We should do something, maybe catch a film. What do you think?" She shrugged. I saw some wriggle room in the shrug and tried a different tack.

"I know a place that knows how to undercook a steak," I pursued. She glanced over my shoulder and crossed her arms.

"I'm a vegetarian," she said.

Shit. I was fucking it up and losing confidence like water from a colander. I took heart from the fact that she was still standing there, albeit with crossed arms.

"Then pizza. We can do pizza; I know a place where they make proper pizza." She considered me as if deciding. "You can choose your own toppings," I said, and she smiled. "Would tomorrow night be OK?" I asked. She squinted to consult a mental diary.

"Tomorrow is good."

11

STANMORE BARNS IS A COLLECTION OF UPMARKET SHOPS: AN organic butcher, an overpriced grocer, a couple of nostalgia stores that sell knick-knacks such as 1950s teapots, wooden clothes horses, tin bread bins and laundry mangles. I could make a fortune as I had inherited many of these things when I took over my parents' house – but I still use them. The car park had a good crop of shiny top-of-the-range SUVs with top-of-the-range baby seats in the back. It was a favoured venue for diet-thin leather-trousered mums who left their children with the au pair while they went out for a bite. The au pair would eat a sandwich at home and maybe rifle through her employer's bedroom drawers and then have a cry because she was homesick. I'd had occasion to come into contact with some of these nannies (parents wanting them checked out to protect their precious ones), and they were not a happy bunch.

There is a café at Stanmore Barns that sells you homemade soup and a hunk of bread the price of which would buy you a passable steak and chips in a pub, as well as a pint to wash it down with. I didn't have the place pegged as Sylvia Booker territory (too artificial, too ladies-who-lunch) but perhaps that was why she'd chosen it, so she wouldn't bump into her own kind. The cars towered over my rusting, diminutive Golf and also Sylvia's red Mini, which was parked three cars down from my own. I walked towards the café checking my suit for stains and wondering whether I should do up my tie. The driver window on the Mini slid down with electric ease – some detective I was; I hadn't seen Sylvia sitting inside.

"George, would you mind terribly?" She leaned over and opened the passenger door. I got in and closed it; the seat was too far forward and I had to squeeze in. It was not how I liked to brief my clients, but it wasn't the first time I'd done it in a car park.

Sylvia had tailored trousers on, flared over pointy boots, and a white mac with faint yellow spots on it. A short silk scarf was tied side-on at her neck and she looked the business. I detected a subtle trace of the perfume I'd smelled when she'd first come into my office.

"Thanks for coming out here, George. I hope you don't mind?" She tilted her head sideways and looked at me with her jewelled eyes and I didn't mind, though my knees were pressed against the dash, and I felt it would be too awkward to fiddle about and try and move the seat back – I didn't know the inside of a Mini and I'd have to ask how to do it. She was turned in her seat and looking at me. Did Elliot Booker ever tire of looking into those dazzling eyes? In time, one could take anything or anyone for granted. "You said you had some news." I twisted in my seat – difficult when you can't move your knees.

"Yes I do." I looked away because it was too much to look directly at her. "I've reason to believe Lucy is seeing someone, and has been for a while." Sylvia put her fingers lightly on the steering wheel in front of her and looked towards the butcher's, where an advert for wild boar sausages hung in the window. "It seems she's been visiting someone, a man, when you believed her to be playing bridge." I paused, to see what effect this might be having, but she showed no reaction apart from a slight stiffening of her manicured fingers.

"Go on."

"Before I do, Mrs Booker, please remember that Lucy is an adult, at least in the eyes of the law."

She turned to me. "Are you telling me this man is her boyfriend?" Her voice was soft and controlled.

"I'm not sure if he's a boyfriend, as such. He's an, erm, older man."

Her face hardened. "Who is he?"

"I must stress that at this stage I do not have first-hand proof of the nature of their relationship, just that she has been visiting his apartment." She gripped her hands on the wheel, as if trying to keep the car on the road, but she was still looking at me.

"His apartment? Who is he?"

"He's a corporate lawyer called Quintin Boyd. An American." She turned her face towards the front and her knuckles whitened on the steering wheel. She was breathing quickly through parted lips and she closed her eyes for a few seconds.

"Do you know this man?" I asked. She shook her head

and removed her hands from the wheel, leaving sweaty imprints on the leather. Then she stared at her hands, resting on her thighs.

"It's... well, it's just come as a shock. I mean Lucy isn't ready for this, she..." I wanted to put a reassuring hand on her shoulder but felt it would have been out of order. I did need something explaining.

"Can I ask? Is there any reason that she shouldn't be seeing someone, someone older, distasteful as it might seem?"

"How much older do you think this man is, George?" She didn't wait for an answer. "Is it normal for a girl with Lucy's..." She glanced outside and reconsidered. "Of Lucy's age to be sneaking around visiting a man of this sort in his apartment?" She couldn't know what sort of man he was. I wanted to tell her that I'd seen some odd couplings in my time, and that Lucy being introduced to womanhood by an older man might in fact be preferable to the quick fumblings of a horny fresher. But I wasn't sure how you said that to the mother of the girl in question.

I watched a group of women come out of the café. They stood chatting in the leisurely manner of people who had nothing to do next except spend more money. I knew this because I'd followed enough of them, their overweight workaholic husbands panicking at the thought of their gym-fit, expensively dressed, coiffured, manicured, waxed and pedicured wives with time on their hands while they made six-figure salaries in the City or venture capital or whatever they did. On the whole they had been guilty of nothing more than squandering their lives and their husbands' money, spending their time planning dinner parties after dropping the kids off at one of the many private schools in Cambridge. One or two had found solace in the muscled arms of a tennis coach or even, à la Olivia, the lithe arms of a Pilates teacher. Sylvia was looking at the women too, but I'm not sure she was seeing them, certainly not the same way I was seeing them.

"I'd like you to confirm whether there is anything, uh, you know…" and she had to force the next word out, "…physical going on between Lucy and this… this Quintin Boyd."

"I'd sort of assumed there was, to be honest."

She put her hand to her face as if I'd slapped her.

"I need to know for sure. That is what you do, isn't it, confirm that people are having sex?" Ouch. "I want to know how they met. How did he… this man, get hold of Lucy?" Her voice was rising and then, perhaps realising that she was becoming shrill, she smiled thinly and took a breath. Then she put a hand on my trapped knee. "George." She had taken her voice down an octave. "Lucy is a sensitive girl, and I just need to make sure she is not being taken advantage of by some lothario." The hand was still there. "You'll help me won't you, George? You'll help Lucy." Her eyes brimmed and all I needed was for her to tell me that I was a big strong man.

"OK, I'll try and get some more information on Quintin Boyd, and confirm the nature of their relationship," I said. She took her hand off my knee. I was so easy. "But what happens then? The fact remains that she is probably seeing him of her own free will."

"We all do things of our own free will that we later regret, George," she said, blushing strongly and looking away. You can fake tears, but not blushing. "Anyway, you should know that in your line of business."

I nodded. "Best not to talk to Lucy until I've got back to you," I said.

"Do you need more money?"

I told her no and got out of the Mini.

After I watched her drive off I rubbed my knees to bring them back to life.

12

AT SEVEN-THIRTY THE NEXT MORNING, AS IT WAS GETTING light, Jason and I were sitting in my Golf in the small car park opposite River Views, Jason wearing a woollen hat with ear flaps on his head texting furiously into a mobile phone. He'd put it away but every now and then the damned thing would make a sort of whooshing noise and he would whip it out and check the incoming message, chuckling to himself before thumbing a reply. It was starting to annoy me; I thought students were all asleep until ten. We'd been here since six-thirty, having established that Quintin was in his penthouse by the glow of lights that had come on behind the vertical blinds soon after our arrival.

I was about to pour us some more coffee from the flask Sandra had provided when the silver Merc purred up to the gates and stopped, exhaust discharging into the grey sky. We hunched down so we were less visible. I could see Mark, the driver, talking as if to the dashboard. He didn't have his cap on and from this angle he looked vaguely familiar again, with his square head and number one haircut. A roll of fat had been squeezed from the top of his collar at the back of his neck.

"I wonder who he's talking to," I said. Jason looked up briefly from his phone and whistled.

"Nice car. He's probably talking to someone on a hands free set." I opened the glove compartment and took out the GPS tracker that I was planning to attach to the Mercedes. I wanted to know where Quintin Boyd was going when he was in Cambridge. The tracker was the one I'd used to log Trisha Greene's car movements. It had to be retrieved and connected to a computer to download the log of where it had travelled.

The driver stopped talking, powered down a window and lit a cigarette. He turned towards us to blow out some smoke and I could see he had one of those silly wireless things stuck in his ear.

"Told you, boss. He's a bluetool. So what's the plan?" The plan, and this is why I had Jason with me, was for him to distract the driver while I attached the tracker to the car. It had a strong magnet and, being the size of a mobile phone, would only be visible if someone were looking for it. I opened the glove compartment again and took out an old packet of cigarettes I kept in there. I don't smoke but you never know when the false camaraderie of another smoker will come in useful – I'd learnt many things by striking up conversation with a smoker. I gave the packet to Jason.

"We're going to walk past the car together. You're going to realise you haven't got a light and go back and ask him for one. I'm going to slip this under the car."

"Cool."

We got out and walked out of the car park, just two mates on their way to work nearby. The driver gave us a half-curious glance, Jason getting a fag out of the box. We crossed the road heading to the back of the Merc and Jason was furiously patting his pockets, perhaps overplaying the search for a light.

"Shit," he said loudly, and changed direction to head for the driver's door as I continued to the back of the car. "Excuse me, mate, got a light?" The driver said something I couldn't hear. I glanced up the road and then bent down to untie my shoelace, slipping the tracker under the large rear bumper until I found metal. Jason was making small talk. I tied my lace and stood up, moving to the pavement. I coughed. Jason joined me, throwing the unwanted cigarette to the ground.

"Not very responsive, and not the sharpest tool in the box," he said.

"It is bloody early in the morning."

We crossed the road again and went towards the petrol station on the corner. I sent Jason inside and looked back down the road. The gate to River Views opened and a young woman in a long coat and heels came out. She had cropped black hair cut shorter at the back than the sides. Mark the chauffeur was out of the car and opening the back door before the gate had even closed behind her. Jason came out of the petrol station with yesterday's Cambridge *Argus* as the Merc came up to the corner and turned onto Elizabeth Way, heading out of town. We walked back to the Golf: the blinds were still closed on the top floor of River Views.

The main *Argus* headline was something about a gypsy encampment outside Cambridge but a smaller headline at the bottom of the page read MURDERED WOMAN

IDENTIFIED – HUSBAND HELD and named Albert and Trisha Greene, reporting the fact that he was a primary school teacher. A colleague of his was said to be "shocked" and there was the inevitable quote from a neighbour about how "ordinary and friendly" the couple were.

We sat in my car and finished the coffee and watched several people leaving River Views for work; mainly young professionals in smart hatchbacks. But we'd yet to set eyes on Quintin Boyd. Jason was not used to sitting quietly for long periods and started to explain the differences between Ambient and Techno music, each apparently with its own sub-genres. I tried to make my disinterest obvious; I much prefer stakeouts on my own; they give me time to brood over everything that is wrong in my life.

"I'm thinking about giving up college," Jason said. A taxi drew up outside the gates opposite and the driver looked out to check the address. I half turned to Jason, keeping an eye on the taxi.

"What the hell are you talking about?"

"I'm thinking if I got a full-time job maybe Mum could give up the chat line." The taxi driver was getting out of the cab. I risked a glance at Jason.

"You know about that, huh?"

"Of course I do. Our walls are like, made of cardboard. Sometimes when she thinks I'm out I'm really in my room." I looked at him and he clocked my confusion. "Sometimes I pretend I'm going out just to get some peace and quiet." The taxi driver, a black guy in a cloth cap, was at the doorbell panel next to the gate, looking at the glow of names.

"She's got that job so you can be at college. She'd kill you if you left, you know that." When I checked the driver was talking into the grille next to the buzzers.

"It's horrible though." His voice went wobbly and he turned his face to his window. "I hate listening to it. I mean your own mother saying that..." Shit, this wasn't the time for a heart-to-heart. The taxi driver got back into his car and waited. I glanced up at the top floor and saw the windows go dark. I turned to Jason.

"Listen, Jason. You've got to suck it up, as you like to say. You could quit college, no one can force you to stay, but it would break your mum's heart and the most likely outcome is that she would kick you out and refuse your money anyway." He wiped his eyes with the back of his hand. His phone went whoosh but he ignored it. The gate opened and someone who could only be Quintin Boyd came out; even at this distance I recognised him from his photo online. He paused to close the gate behind him. He looked good in a black knee-length mac. He had no luggage or briefcase and carried himself with straight-backed confidence. I was too far away to see his face properly. He ran his fingers through his hair and got into the back of the waiting taxi. I started the Golf's engine and watched the taxi driver do a three-point turn. I turned to Jason.

"That stuff your mum says, on the phone, it's just acting, she doesn't mean any of it. You know that, right?" I was just repeating what little Sandra had told me about it. Apparently some of her regulars didn't even want to talk about sex, they just needed someone to lament about what a shitty week they'd had. In fact the sex calls were the shortest calls and on a call by call basis made the least money. She'd laughingly told me that she was sometimes too good (not really a positive given the idea is to keep them on the line for as long as possible), and that it was amazing what some sound effects using a tub of yoghurt could achieve.

"You know what else would break your mum's heart?" I asked. He nodded.

"Yeah. If she knew that I knew." The boy wasn't stupid, bless him.

"Why don't you invest in some noise-cancelling headphones," I said, only half joking. He grunted noncommittally as I pulled out of the car park.

"They're expensive, boss."

"Well, you might be able to afford them when we've finished with this job," I said. We eased into the last of the rush-hour traffic behind Quintin Boyd.

13

IN THE OFFICE SANDRA WAS GETTING READY TO LEAVE, watering her plants and putting the computer to sleep.

"I thought you weren't in today?" I asked.

"Just thought I'd put in a couple of hours." She picked up some letters from her desk and went through them. "You need to renew your membership of UKAI or they're going to take your entry off their website. There's your share of the building maintenance that needs paying. The other tenants want a meeting next week and a John rang, something about your garden fence. Oh, and I've done the HPI check on the Mercedes, as well as getting an address from the DVLA." UKAI are the UK Association of Investigators. They are supposed to raise the standards of the profession but for me membership means being in the online directory that potential clients look at – it was how Sylvia Booker had found me after all. They kept sending stuff through the post on the proposed arrangements for licensing private investigators. I never replied to these missives; licensing would probably mean the death knell for Cambridge Confidential. Sandra handed me the letters.

"The DVLA really ought to tighten up their procedure for giving out details."

"You're forgetting that I'm very convincing on the phone," she said, winking at me. I smiled and looked down at the post she had given me. I considered telling her about Jason knowing how good she was on the phone but thought better of it. "Besides, men can't resist helping a woman in distress, can they?" she said, giving me a look full of meaning which I ignored. I took it as a sign of her disapproval of my continuing with the Sylvia Booker case. I'd filled her in after meeting Sylvia yesterday and she'd said the whole thing smelled rotten, and she'd obviously looked Sylvia up on the web.

"I bet if she wasn't posh or attractive or if it had been a bloke you would have asked more questions."

I told her she was wrong even though she may have been partly right. On the other hand she seemed to be leery about any women I came into contact with. I'd also told her the whole thing reeked of money.

"Maybe, but money doesn't cover a rotten smell. I should know," she'd said. "I married a rotten smell with money."

She put on her coat and went to the door. "Has Jason gone home?" she asked.

"He's running an errand for me in London," I said. As I spoke he was actually on the train to London with Quintin Boyd, whom we'd followed to the station after a few hours watching him in town. I would have gone myself but I was worried about missing my date with Nina, even though Jason had pointed out that he also had a date with Rowena.

I figured my need was greater than his. I hadn't said that to Jason when I'd passed him a few twenties and all but kicked him out of the car. I didn't tell Sandra this either, of course, who stopped at the door and looked at me with a warning brewing on her face.

"If he's involved in anything even remotely dodgy, George, I'll have your balls."

With Sandra gone I put my feet up on the desk and looked at the HPI report, which gives buyers an idea of whether the used car they are about to hand over cash for is stolen or has outstanding finance on it. No adverse data was recorded against the Mercedes, which was only a year old. The address that Sandra had blagged from the DVLA was in Royston, just south of Cambridge, and the car was registered to a firm called Chauffeured Comfort Cars.

I put aside the UKAI reminder and the buildings maintenance bill and picked up the number Sandra had written down for John's mobile. I got his voicemail and told him to call by my house tomorrow. I went to the window and tried to rub some grime off but it was all on the outside. Our Lady of the Saints said it was nearing four and I was nearing the possibility of male-female contact. A bath seemed in order but first I needed to transcribe my scribbled notes from the day's surveillance. I sat down again and went through my notebook.

* * *

After we'd left River Views we'd followed the taxi into town and I'd dropped Jason off with Quintin while I went to park and catch up with him on foot. When I finally met up with Jason after calling from the office mobile he was standing outside a camera shop on Regent Street and looking in the window. But he wasn't looking at the display, he was looking inside.

"There you are, boss."

"I had a problem parking."

"He's been in there for ten minutes, talking to the sales guy."

"Camcorders?" I peered in through the window past the cameras and saw Quintin being attended to by an enthusiastic pimply-faced teenager who could sense a sale.

"He doesn't look like he's buying anything," Jason said, and before I could respond he disappeared from my side and I could see him inside the shop, the cheeky monkey. He gave me a wink and stood with his back to Quintin. A few minutes later Quintin emerged with a small plastic bag. Jason told me, as we sauntered after him, that he'd bought some memory cards for a handheld camcorder.

"A camcorder?"

"Yes, the little SD cards, you know, like you have in the digital camera in the office."

"Yes, I know what they are."

We followed Quintin around town for a bit, watched him have lunch, until a taxi took him back to River Views with his shopping bags, where he spent an hour doing whatever he was doing before Mark came back in the Merc and took

Quintin (minus shopping bags but with briefcase) to the railway station where he dropped Quintin off.

That's when I'd sent Jason after him. That's when he'd protested, not just about his date, but saying quite reasonably that he wouldn't learn anything sitting on the train and that tailing him across London was not an option. He was right, except that occasionally you thought you'd got all you were going to get and were about to call it a day or night when something happened that made you glad you'd gone that extra mile or sat in your car for that extra five minutes. Or in this case sent someone else to go that extra mile. If I'd had the time (Quintin was walking into the station) I would have told some poignant story to make my point but instead I just added another twenty-pound note to the ones I'd forked out, urging him to get some lunch and reminding him of the need for receipts. With Jason on Quintin I'd followed the Merc as far as the A10 south out of Cambridge, but mindful of the time I'd headed back into town, disregarding my own advice about going that extra mile. Like I said, it was only occasionally worth it.

I was out of the bath and in the bedroom and worrying about what the hell to wear – the choice was between an old corduroy jacket and a twice-worn Hugo Boss jacket that Olivia had bought me – when the phone rang. Perhaps Nina was calling to cancel, and I was surprised at how much the idea filled me with relief. But it wasn't Nina.

"Boss?"

"Jason, where are you?" It was noisy wherever it was.

"On the train back to Cambridge, hoping I can still make the gig with Rowena." I ignored the resentment in his voice.

"I'm assuming you have something to report since you're ringing?"

"Well, I don't know how important it is. Boyd spent a lot of time on the phone, and I've made some notes." I heard the rustle of paper at his end. I checked my watch; I needed to be out of the house in fifteen.

"Jason?"

"Yeah, I've got them here—"

"Rather than go through it on the phone why don't we get together tomorrow morning?" I looked at the double bed. "Let's make it lunchtime. I'll buy you lunch."

"You're the boss, boss." We agreed that I would pick him up from his mother's and we hung up.

I quickly changed the sheets on the bed before settling on the corduroy.

14

WE WERE IN A LARGE PUB ON REGENT STREET, NINA'S CHOICE of where we should go after dinner. It occurred to me, as I sat opposite her – she looked good in a suede jacket over torso-hugging T-shirt and designer jeans – that the older I got the more difficult it was to go through the initial mating ritual of revealing myself: my likes and dislikes (more of the latter than the former), my view on the latest Julia Roberts film (not seen, not intending to see), whether I'd read the latest book that everyone was raving about (I made a point of never reading books that people raved about), and so on. I was beginning to see, after a long dinner of small talk at The Neapolitan, the sense of using a dating website like Sandra had suggested, thus skipping this initial phase of information exchange. Except that what was the fun in just meeting people who liked what you liked and thought like you did? Not that I was finding much in common with Nina, not that it bothered her, since she spent most of dinner telling me about her plans for setting up her own nutritional supplement line – apparently you could buy generically produced vitamins and the rest was packaging and marketing. Packaging and marketing being the way you got on in this day and age.

The pub was as big as a warehouse, and similarly themed. What's more it was packed with young people decked out in their Friday-night pulling gear and drinking alcopops and lager straight from the bottle. It was the sort of place that needed large bouncers outside the doors weekend nights. I felt like the headmaster at the school disco and now wished I'd worn the Hugo Boss. It was even too young a crowd for Nina, but to be fair she could get away with it in this light.

I was unable to make out whether the evening had gone well or not, or whether it would continue beyond the pub.

"So what sort of films do you like then, if not ones with Julia Roberts in?" Nina was asking.

"Erm… Well, I like crime films, particularly 1970s Italian crime films. There's just been a week of them at the Arts Cinema."

"The Arts Cinema?"

"Yeah, just down the road."

"Oh yes, I've seen it, but never seen a film advertised there I'd want to see. I go to the multiplex at the Grafton Centre." The Grafton Centre is a monstrous temple to money spending that I never set foot in except to follow income support cheats buying sports gear they had no intention of doing sports in. I sometimes wondered where real sports people bought their gear.

We sipped our drinks and I looked around, hoping for some sort of punch-up to distract us, but it was still a little early for that. Then the doors opened and Lucy Booker came in with a group of six; one other girl, the rest blokes.

They were dressed in some finery, gowns and tuxedos, and drew some comments and looks from the people in the pub; although this was not an exclusively townie pub, having gownies in here advertising the fact that they were gownies was unusual for a Saturday night, if not a little foolish. Nina followed my gaze.

"Looks like they're on their way to a ball."

"It's not the season," I said.

The group found a table ten feet away and at three o'clock to ours and a couple of the lads went to the bar and ordered drinks, ignoring the looks and largely good-hearted comments. From the way Lucy was slouched in her chair she had obviously been drinking. She was ignoring a grinning doughy boy who was talking into her ear and smirking. Her hair was done up at the back again. Nina was saying something to me.

"Sorry?" I said. She leant forward and her black hair fell in front of her face.

"I was just wondering whether you want to come back to mine for a drink; it's a bit noisy in here." She was flashing me a smile I hadn't seen before. Blimey, did this mean that I'd pulled? I watched the bow-tied boys take small glasses of colourless drinks to their table. I watched Lucy grimace when trying hers, then drink it down in one to cheers from the boys. The other girl leant over and said something to Lucy but she ignored her.

"Well?" Nina was asking, a little exasperation creeping into her voice. She was probably used to men jumping up when she asked them home – understandably given how attractive she was – and she couldn't quite understand why I wasn't. *I* couldn't understand why I wasn't, except I was intrigued by what Lucy Booker was up to. I watched her down someone else's drink. The boys applauded; the other girl was pleading with Lucy and pulling at her arm but she wasn't listening. One of the boys pushed the other girl away from Lucy, and said something harsh. She said something harsh back and stood up.

"Shall we have one more here first?" I said to Nina, who up till now had been leaning forward over the table, looking at me from under her thickly mascaraed eyelashes, her long fingers encircling her lager bottle. Now, she sat back in her chair and crossed her arms and her legs. She was wearing pointy boots under her jeans.

"I'm sorry. Am I moving too fast for you?" Great, now she thought I thought she was easy. I looked towards the freshers' table and saw that the other girl that had been with Lucy wasn't there. I glanced to the pub doors and saw her disappearing between the bouncers. I turned back to Nina.

"No, no, that's not it. I'd like nothing better than to go to your place, really. I guess I'm just not used to women taking the initiative." This was bollocks of course; it was Olivia that had introduced herself to me at a party. It was she that had taken me home, taken me into her bedroom. Nina uncrossed her arms.

"OK, I tell you what. Let's have another drink then you can ask me home." I saw Lucy's group pass behind Nina, heading for the door. Lucy was being helped by a couple of the boys. They winked at each other behind Lucy's back.

"Let's go for a walk instead," I said, grabbing my jacket. Lucy was being escorted through the doors. Nina followed my gaze.

"You've been watching her since they came in. Is she more your type then, George?" She said it in a jokey way but with a little edge to convey her distaste at being ignored. She stood up. So did I.

"No, it's not like that," I said.

"I don't want to know, George. I'm going to get another drink." She walked off to the bar and I hesitated only for a second before heading for the doors. When I looked back she was laughing with a young guy who had a tattoo on the back of his neck, as if I'd already left. I'd always regarded tattoos as a substitute for character.

Outside I saw Lucy and the tuxedoed lads turning a corner onto Park Terrace off Regent Street, behind the hotel where I'd watched Quintin Boyd lunching with his BlackBerry. My Golf was parked down Park Terrace anyway. When I got to the corner though, I saw no sign of them. I walked quickly down the road and then heard giggling on my left. An office car park behind a closed barrier. It was almost empty. I caught a movement in the dark behind one of the cars. A girl's voice started to say something and was muffled. I walked quickly towards the car, making my footsteps loud on the tarmac.

"Bloody hell, someone's coming," a well-spoken voice said. I could see four tuxedoed lads round Lucy, who was half leaning, half sagging on the boot of the car, the straps of her gown pulled down from her shoulders, her face a mess of mascara and tears. One of the fuckers had her in an awkward embrace and was trying to kiss her on the mouth. Another, when he saw me come into view, started tugging at the back of the guy's jacket. A third was holding up his mobile phone, filming the whole thing. The fourth, a tall Aryan type with a cigarette and a sneer, just looked at me in annoyance.

"OK, that's enough of that," I said, in my clearest and loudest voice. The necker pulled away from Lucy who sank down against the car. He staggered to the rear wheel and threw up onto his shiny shoes.

The confident-looking Aryan said, "Who do you think you are? She wants this, you proletariat fuck." The boy with the phone sniggered, turning it onto me.

When I heard that supercilious, you've-stepped-out-of-place tone I decided to leap. There I was, baring my teeth, flaring my nostrils, clenching my fists and widening my eyes. I snarled and spat. They scarpered pronto, but not before I'd swiped the phone. They left their heaving friend to fend for himself. I left the little shit to it, grinding the mobile phone into the tarmac with my heel.

"Lucy, are you alright?" I took her arm and helped her to her feet. She was bony and lightweight, hardly rowing material.

She said something incomprehensible and I was blasted with the smell of gin – an odd drink for a teenager, I thought.

"Lucy, I know your mother, I'm going to take you home."

"Lots of men know my mother." She giggled and put a hand to her mouth. Vomit boy, obviously confused, came back for a look but a well-aimed kick to the shin sent him yelping. I turned back to Lucy.

"My car is nearby. I'll drive you to Morley College."

"Morley," she parroted, but the mention of it made her straighten up a bit.

"Here, take my arm."

Luckily, or perhaps not (I really didn't know), Lucy seemed oblivious about what had been about to happen to her in that car park. She sat in the passenger seat and was relaxed enough, but that was most likely the alcohol. I drove towards the Backs and Lucy stirred. I glanced at her to see she was looking round the car. She seemed to be peering at my jacket.

"None of Mummy's friends wear corduroy. Do you work for one of her pet charities?"

"Yes, that's right," I said.

"That explains the scary you in the car park. Mummy's friends couldn't do that. They're more into mental bullying, not terribly useful when stopping a gang-bang." She released a high-pitched giggle. So she was aware of what was about to be done to her.

"What happened back there?" I asked.

She looked out of the window as we turned west out of the city. "What happened was I got plastered and decided it would be a good idea to lose my virginity to Toby. That was the plan, anyway. I didn't mean to lose it to all of them at once." She gave another giggle and turned towards me, pulling at her seat belt so she could get closer and putting a hand on my arm. I got a fresh blast of gin. "You're a nice man, friendly. You can have my virginity. I'll give it to you as a gift for saving me, Mr nice strong man." Then she flopped back in her seat and mumbled, "I'm sorry, how terribly rude of me. What's your name?"

I smiled. "George. George Kocharyan." She didn't respond and when I checked, her head was lolling against the door window and she was completely out of it.

15

I'D NOT BEEN TO MORLEY COLLEGE FOR NEARLY TWENTY years, not since George Senior retired early and I drove him and my mother to receive his brass carriage clock from senior management. He'd not been back after that last day, avoiding going into Cambridge during term for fear of running into some of the students. He hated the students, or at least a group of them he called "the tossers". I never really got to the bottom of why he hated this particular group or why he retired early but whenever he wanted to admonish me for some perceived pretentiousness he would warn me against becoming a Cambridge tosser. "Don't ever think you're better than anyone else, Kevork. That's how it all starts." I was never sure what 'it' referred to but he always expressed himself in such extremes. Kevork – the Armenian for George – was what he always called me, even though 'George' is on my birth certificate. Olivia used to call me Kevork during her rare moments of peaking passion, which always left me feeling she would prefer to be making love to someone else. Ultimately, of course, I'd been right.

Lucy stirred as I turned off the Huntingdon Road and the

headlights sought out the entrance to Morley College on the tree-lined road. She muttered something and tried to curl up on the seat. The Golf crunched over the gravel and I cruised into the college car park and tried to orientate myself. Some modern halls of residence had been built overlooking the car park, student accommodation designed by an architect with no sense of humour and a love of concrete. Lights were on in some of the rooms. The fellows and senior staff had accommodation in the original 1800s buildings, which were secluded by carefully managed trees and football-field sized lawns. Although my father had hated it here, this place had kept us fed and under a roof and also, to give the college its due, paid some of my father's care costs thanks to a generous pension scheme.

I found the lane that led to the bursar's residence, driving through a gate and up the drive before stopping behind Sylvia's Mini, which itself was parked behind an older Saab. Lights were on downstairs in the large, ivy-covered house. It was nearly eleven-thirty.

Lucy still being asleep I got out and put my hand on the bonnets of the cars. The Mini's was warm, the Saab's cold. I walked up the stone steps to the covered porch. My presence triggered a carriage light to come on. I stood in front of the big glossy door, readying my finger over the polished brass bell, thinking of something to say if Elliot Booker opened up. I heard voices inside, a man's sonorous voice raised in anger, the unhappy sound of a pleading woman. I checked the surroundings. It was pitch black outside my circle of light and Lucy's face was flat against the car window, drool from the corner of her mouth trickling onto the glass. I pressed my ear against the front door.

It was a solid oak door made two hundred years ago so I couldn't hear clearly. The deep male voice was saying something which included the words, "How long?" He repeated this several times and all I could hear was the plaintive voice of a woman responding. He screamed at her reply. Then I heard him say, "Does she know?" Then the woman: "No, no, no. Lucy can't know." Then something else – it could have been, "Did it happen after a film?" or it could have been, "Did it happen on a whim?" It didn't make sense. I pressed my ear harder but couldn't make it out. Her plaintive voice again, contrite and whiny. Then he was saying, "Why now?" and, "I don't bloody believe it. That fucking man." Her tone was apologetic and beseeching. It was too much to listen to. I checked the car and Lucy moved her head on the glass, smearing saliva onto her cheek. I pressed the doorbell.

It went quiet inside as the two-tone chime faded. I waited and heard a door close. There were steps and a cough and I stood back from the door as it opened. A tall dark-suited man, very thin, with a trimmed salt-and-pepper beard, frameless glasses and sunken cheeks stood in an enormous hall lit by a chandelier too big to get through my front door. One hand was on the door knob; the other clutched a folded letter he'd obviously just been reading. He stuffed it into his jacket pocket when he saw me, but not before I'd caught a glimpse of a logo on it: a spiral staircase.

"Mr Booker?" I thought I could see something of Lucy in him, maybe the disproportionately big nose, the mousy hair.

"Elliot Booker, yes. Can I help you?" he asked, in a tone suggesting quite the opposite. He peered at me as if he'd seen me before in unpleasant circumstances. I gestured to my car.

"I've brought your daughter home, she's been enjoying herself a little too much." He peered at the car and Sylvia Booker came into view behind him, frowning at me with a worried look. She'd cleaned up her face but she'd obviously been crying; you can't get rid of red puffy eyes that easily.

"What is it, Elliot?" she asked, fidgeting with a set of pearls round her neck – worry beads for the rich.

"It's Lucy, the taxi driver says she's drunk."

Sylvia, not bothering to correct him as to my occupation, pushed past me on the doorstep barely giving me a glance. She was in a pink and grey suit that even I could tell she hadn't bought at Marks & Spencer. I followed her down to the car where she rapped hard on the window. Lucy jerked awake, looking confused. Sylvia opened the door and Lucy all but fell out onto the drive. Sylvia helped her up and Lucy leant over the open car door, facing me. She was a sight – pale and sick with mascara-streaked cheeks and blonde fringe plastered to her forehead.

"You silly girl," Sylvia hissed into her ear. "I came to pick you up from the party, what happened?" Lucy looked at me imploringly with bloodshot eyes.

"She went a bit heavy on the gin. I happened to be in the same pub," I said. Sylvia had questions in her eyes, questions I wasn't about to answer. I was struck by the similarity of expression in the two – not just a genetic likeness but a shared anxiety. We helped Lucy up the steps. Elliot had disappeared from the open door. At the threshold Sylvia said, as if I was somehow connected with Lucy's condition, "Thanks, I'll take things from here." I watched them go into the house, Sylvia in her designer suit and Lucy in her gown. Elliot came back to the door. He held out his hand. It had money in it.

"I hope this covers the fare and there's something for your trouble." I stood there, dork-like, and noticed a sweaty imprint of my ear on the glossy black door. Sylvia and Lucy were walking up a wide staircase. "Is it not enough?" Elliot was asking. I took the money; I wasn't sure what else to do. Tell him that as a matter of fact I was spying on his daughter on behalf of his wife, who didn't want him to know about it? It sounded like they had enough troubles as it was.

"It's very generous," I said, because that was what he was expecting me to say. When he closed the door I wiped my ear print off the glossy door with the sleeve of my corduroy jacket.

On the way home I parked on Chesterton Road and walked onto the pedestrian bridge that leads to Jesus Green. I liked to look at the weir and the rushing water at night; it appeared a lot more dramatic than during daylight. When it got too cold I walked back to the car and passed two homeless guys shuffling along wrapped in layers of smelly blankets. I stopped them and gave them Elliot Booker's twenty quid.

16

I WOKE SATURDAY TO THE SOUND OF KNOCKING. I CHECKED the old analogue alarm clock by the bed (Olivia had taken her snazzy digital one with her) to see that it was the tail end of the morning. A pile of books sat on Olivia's side, books left by her for me to read. They were all from her book group days, either prize winners or best sellers. I'd tried them – not very enthusiastically given their association with her book club – getting to page twenty or thirty before putting them down unfinished. I'd mentioned this difficulty at finishing books to my writer and porter friend Kamal. I wished I hadn't. He'd asked me for the titles and shaken his head when I listed them. He said they were too self-consciously clever and stylish, the very thing that seemed to enthral people who gave out prizes. Kamal says that they are written from the head, not from the heart, and are generally produced by English language graduates for other English graduates to read. He urged me to read people I'd never heard of and never remembered. I took his withering generalisations to be a sign of his bitterness at being unacknowledged as a writer. He himself churned out short stories about ordinary people struggling in difficult situations, most of them based on his experiences as a hospital porter.

The knocking wouldn't go away so I went downstairs to put a stop to it. It was John, his Cambridge University Estates van parked on the verge outside the house. That would have the neighbours tutting; they hated people parking on the verges. And on a Saturday.

"George, mate. You wanted me to look at your fence."

"Come in, it's brass monkeys out there." He stepped into the hall, all two hundred pounds of him, and I shut the cold out behind him.

"You want to get dressed, matey," he said.

"You've seen me in my underwear, for fuck's sake, you can handle pyjamas." We played in the same five-a-side football team.

"It's about context. Besides you're wasting the best part of the day."

I shook my head and made for the stairs. "Help yourself to the garden, I'll make myself decent."

Fifteen minutes later I was in the kitchen pouring coffee and John came in with an open notepad and pencil, which he stuck behind his ear.

"Milk and three sugars, matey." I had to root around for the sugar.

"So what do you think?" I asked.

"Well, you've got a long garden there, and it's difficult to get to some of the fence what with the brambles, but you're talking nearly three grand. And that's me doing a price."

"Fuck off," I said.

He laughed. "I'm sorry, mate, but that's almost at cost." He sipped his coffee, frowning at the heat. He was a softie in a big body who you didn't want steaming towards you Sunday afternoon on AstroTurf in his shorts. "I tell you what, mate, since you helped me out with my… problem, I'll do you a favour." He blushed furiously. I went to the sink to spare him. A year ago he'd come up to me after five-a-side and asked me to look for his eighteen-year-old son, missing for five days. I'd found him easily enough – he'd taken himself to London to find a gay community he could feel normal in. If I'd been worried about John's reaction to the news I needn't have, he'd just been pleased that the boy was alright. "The main thing is, is he happy?" he'd asked. I'd told him I thought so. "Then please tell him it's OK with me." John's wife was less understanding of her son's homosexuality, threatening to "kill the little shirt-lifter" if he showed his face in Cambridge again.

"Tell him that his mother needs more time," John had told me at the door, since his wife wouldn't let me in the house. I'd also charged him 'at cost' when I discovered he was working weekends just to pay me.

John put his mug down on the Formica table; blushes receded. "I tell you what, I can do you a favour. We're doing a re-fencing job at one of the colleges. Most of the stuff we're taking off is sound, just not high enough to keep the wildlife out. It may be that I could see some of the panels coming your way, double them up to make it high enough. Call it recycling. Then you'd just be paying labour."

"Great, so that leaves two grand to find," I said. He

laughed and this time his stomach heaved up and down in sympathy.

"So which college is it that needs protection from wildlife?" The idea of the university providing my fence held a certain satisfaction.

He named a college on the outskirts of Cambridge. "We're replacing most of the perimeter; they've got foxes and muntjacs scavenging the rubbish there, even the plastic and paper they leave out for recycling. It's all over the lawns in the morning."

"Muntjacs?"

"Yes. They're small deer. You see them around Cambridge, even in the centre…"

But I was thinking about recycling. Paper. I thought of the letter in Elliot Booker's hand, perhaps the cause of his argument with Sylvia.

"Do you know what days they collect recycling at the colleges then?"

"Don't know, mate, it depends on the college." He frowned and then his face lit up. "Is it for a case you're working on?"

I shrugged noncommittally.

"I could find out for you. Which college is it?"

I parked outside Sandra's house in King's Hedges and tapped the horn, looking to the windows just a few metres from the road. Jason appeared at an upstairs window and Sandra came out the front door with Ashley in tow. She was in a big fluffy bathrobe and matching slippers. She walked down the short path to the car with him. I wound the window down and let out the heat. Sandra had a smirk on her face.

"Good night last night?" she asked. I hoped she hadn't somehow found out about my 'date' with Nina and come to gloat.

"Educational," I said. Ashley whined about being cold. She told him to go inside. Jason called him from the front door. Sandra watched him run to Jason and then turned back to me. She looked warm and inviting, like a downy duvet you want to curl up in.

"Not as educational as mine, I bet." It sounded like maybe I wasn't going to get a ribbing.

"Why don't you get in." She went round to the passenger side and I held five fingers up to Jason at the front door. Sandra filled the car with a freshly bathed smell. She looked round the car.

"You ought to clean this out, George. It's filthy." I took notice of the rubbish-covered dash, empty cans on the floor.

"It's cheaper than installing an alarm. You had something to tell me?"

"I've got one of those telephone headsets, right, so sometimes when I'm working I can do the ironing, or shop online, or it just frees my hands for sound effects." I raised my eyebrows as a warning of too much information about to be imparted. She saw it and smiled.

"Anyway, I was on the Internet last night and I did a search on Quintin Boyd, you know, just out of interest."

"Yeah, I already did that," I said impatiently. "He's a big-wig corporate lawyer." She turned to me and shook her head, patting my knee in mock concern.

"Poor thing. Did you not get your oats last night?" Bloody hell, how did she find out this stuff? I declined the invitation to confess. She dropped the act. "You won't need me to tell you what he's doing next Sunday then?" she asked. I sighed.

"OK, spit it out." She looked past me and waved. I turned to see Jason holding Ashley up at the front window, who was grinning and waving. I waved too and turned back to Sandra expectantly. She was determined to milk it, and was checking her moisturiser-covered face in the sun visor mirror.

"This better be worth it," I said. She flicked up the visor.

"He's the keynote speaker at the alumni lunch, whatever that is?" she said.

"It's where graduates who've made something of themselves get together and pat each other on the back. What alumni lunch?"

She smiled at me before delivering her payload. "The one Morley College is having next Sunday of course. He graduated eighteen years ago, got a first class honours, whatever that is, in Economics and Law."

"It means he's a clever bastard. Let me tell you what I learned."

I told her about my adventures last night, omitting the part about my date with Nina.

"What were you doing in that pub? It's a young person's pick-up joint on a Friday night."

"Wasn't my choice," I said, giving her a don't-ask-me-more stare. I threw her a distraction. "What about the fact that Lucy told me she's a virgin?" She took the bait.

"If I meet her I could tell you either way. If she was pissed she could have been lying, but usually the lie is the other way round. If she isn't actually fucking Quintin then perhaps they have a Lewinsky-Clinton type of relationship. Or, he could be grooming her for something down the line."

"Sounds a bit cynical, even for you. And hang on a minute, when I assumed they were having sex you called me an arsehole. When you do it, despite evidence that they're not, it's suddenly perfectly logical. How does that work?" She flashed me her smile.

"Privilege of being female, George. There aren't many of them."

I didn't tell her that I thought the idea of Quintin spending time grooming Lucy when he had an endless stream of attractive young women silly; I'd learnt to choose my battles with Sandra very carefully.

17

I TOOK JASON TO THE PIG AND WHISTLE IN NEWNHAM: LOG fire, club sandwich lunch, no children. I updated him on last night's shenanigans, omitting the part about Nina going off with a tattooed man. He shook his head either in disbelief or respect, I couldn't tell.

"Lucy Booker ripped to the tits, who'd have thought it."

"Tell me what you got yesterday then," I asked. He took out a notebook and flipped it open. The smell of other people's lunch was making my mouth water.

"OK. Got the three-forty-five to Kings Cross, travelling first class—"

"You travelled first class?"

"Yeah, boss. I bought a first class ticket when I went in. I figured a guy like Quintin Boyd doesn't travel with the proles, right, and if he did I could still travel second class. Either way I was covered, right?" I gave him a nod to acknowledge his reasoning and he went back to his notes.

"He spent a long time on his BlackBerry, emailing and stuff. I couldn't see what he was doing though 'cause I was sat the other side of the aisle. Then he took out some papers, but I couldn't see them. He picked up one of the papers, I'd say a letter from the way it was folded in three, and he made two phone calls." Jason sipped from his beer.

"Have you ever thought of becoming a detective?" I said jokingly.

"Yes I have," he said, dead serious, which took me aback. He took another drink and looked down at his notebook.

"Didn't catch who the first call was to 'cause the woman opposite decided it would be a good time to phone her husband and have a loud conversation about who would pick up the dry cleaning. Anyway, he gave them a reference number from the letter and was asking them about margins of error."

"Margins of error?" A waitress walked towards us with two steaming plates but passed us for another table.

"Yep. He kept asking them how accurate the result was but he was very cagey on the phone, so I didn't get to know the result of what. Anyway, he seemed happy enough at what they said. Maybe it was the STD clinic." He ripped out a sheet from his notebook. "Here's the reference number."

"You said he made a second call," I said, tucking the piece of paper into my own notebook and looking longingly at the door to the kitchen.

"Yeah, boss. To someone called Judith."

"Judith?"

"Yeah, Judith. He told her – she wasn't a girlfriend, the way he was talking to her – he told her that he'd got the result and it confirmed what he'd always suspected from day one. Then he asked her if she'd sorted the other thing." Jason looked at his notes. "Then he listened for a bit and said," – and here he put on a drawling American accent – "'You're asking me what I'm going to do, Judith? Why, I've already done it.' Then he laughed and hung up."

I spent Saturday night alone, reading Olivia's email about how their restoration plans were going, and slightly envious of her and the weather in Greece. I did feel pleased for her, and that she'd found someone who was suited to her. Perhaps I was maturing as a person? After finishing with my emails I looked up some other women online. Claims of maturity were too soon as I longed for a faster Internet connection.

Sunday morning I inspected the fence in the garden, just to make sure I wasn't being over-charged. I wasn't sure how I was going to pay for it, unless I could get more money out of Sylvia. There was also my father's decrepit shed at the bottom of the garden that needed replacing or removing; I'd never been in it and couldn't think what I would use it for. That afternoon I fell asleep in front of Formula One racing – the only thing it's good for as far as I'm concerned. This led to a dream where I was struggling to change gears on the Golf (it has a sticky third) so I could keep up with Sylvia Booker in her Mini. She had a passenger with her, a man, and I was trying to pull alongside to see who it was, but she looked at me and laughed then pulled away. Then something was ringing in the car and I woke up. It was dark and I had a dry mouth. The black and white TV showed people singing in a church. The ringing was still there; it was the phone in the hall. I reluctantly got up to answer it.

"George, it's Sandra."

"Sandra, hi. What's happening?"

"You OK? You sound weird."

"I was napping, you woke me up." She didn't bother to apologise.

"The police have charged Al Greene with the murder of his dogging wife. It was on the local news."

"Well, they needed to charge him or let him go."

"Suppose so. I still don't think he did it."

"Neither do I, but there's fuck all we can do about it." It went quiet and the sound of people singing a hymn started coming from the TV.

"Jason tells me you're doing a rubbish collection tonight."

"Jason needs to learn to keep his mouth shut."

"What has the Bookers' rubbish got to do with Quintin Boyd?"

"I don't know, Sandra, that's why I'm going up there. Listen, do me a favour tomorrow, I know you're not in the office but could you find out what years Sylvia was at Morley?"

"Will do. You think she was there with Quintin?"

"That's what I want to find out; they're about the same age."

"Sure, it makes sense to check it. Erm… listen, George. If you ever fancy a family meal of an evening then you're always welcome here, you know that, right? Ashley's just about house trained and Jason could do with having another bloke about the house." I looked through to the dark kitchen.

"Thanks for the invite." And I meant it.

John the maintenance man had told me, after making a couple of phone calls, that Morley recycling was collected on a Monday morning. Which is why I left home at ten-thirty Sunday night dressed in dark clothes – torch, gloves, and extra strong bin bags in the boot of the car. On the way I stopped at a McDonald's and had a scalding coffee, which I sipped with care. I watched the night-shift truck and taxi drivers sit on their own and wolf down what had been lying in the keep-warm tray – the staff had long stopped cooking.

I brooded over the futility of what I was about to spend a cold evening doing and what a miserable profession I had drifted into when a young woman in a McDonald's uniform and row of gold stars on a badge that read 'Cathy' came up to me. She was holding a large bunch of keys.

"We're closing," she said. "Would you mind drinking up, please?" I looked round to see that I was the only person in the place and half the lights were switched off. I emptied my cup.

"I was savouring the coffee." She gave me a polite grin. She was probably a few years older than Lucy, but with a face toughened by too much responsibility too early. She picked up my empty cardboard cup.

"Sorry, but I have to close up and write something original about hybrid polymers." I stood up.

"Really? Where are you studying?" I asked as we walked to the doors.

"Wolfson College."

"You sound like a Cambridge girl. Am I right?"

"Yeah, one that is actually going to Cambridge University, would you believe?" We stood at the doors and she searched for a key amongst the many on her key ring.

"Tough, is it?" I asked.

"It is when I'm in my final year and have to put in three nights a week here and the customers won't leave." She opened the door and smiled at me. For a moment I forgot that I was about to riffle through other people's rubbish.

18

IT WAS AFTER ELEVEN WHEN I CONTINUED THE DRIVE UP TO Morley in a light drizzle, this time parking in the public car park rather than driving up to the Bookers' house. I sat in the car for a bit watching to see whether my gravel-crunching arrival had made anyone curious. About a third of the lights were on behind drawn curtains in the student block. None of them twitched and nobody was wandering around this late on a cold and wet Sunday.

Once I was halfway confident that I wasn't going to be seen I got out and removed the gear from the back of the car. I stepped onto grass as soon as I could and then headed towards the bursar's house, keeping to the bush-lined edge of the large lawn separating the house from the student residences. When I got to the wall that surrounds the house I looked through the open gate I had driven through last night. I could see a light on in one downstairs room and the Saab was parked in the drive, but no Mini. Staying on the outside I followed the wall round to the back of the house, where compost bins and gardeners' sheds huddled in the gloom. Just outside a wooden door set in the wall surrounding the house there were two plastic recycling containers, one full of glass, plastic and tin, one full of paper. I emptied the paper into one of my bin bags and tried the door in the wall. It was locked.

Instead of heading back to the car as any sensible private investigator would have done, I searched for something to climb on. I pushed a wheelbarrow full of leaves over to the door. With my feet in wet leaves I could just see over the wall into the garden. It was about a hundred and fifty feet to the house. Light leaked from between long blackout curtains at the French windows on the ground floor. The top floor of the house was dark. Curiosity and that little buzz of voyeurism I get from spying on people got the better of me. I pulled myself up until I could get a leg on the wall and then scrambled over the top, dropping heavily onto thankfully soft earth the other side. I had to lie there and catch my breath for a minute; I was getting too old for this shit.

I walked up to the house and the French doors where the light was coming through the drapes. The gap in the curtains was wider at the bottom so I bent down to have a look. I wish I hadn't bothered, because I saw Elliot Booker hanging from the ceiling. Hanging by his neck.

Too early the next morning I opened my front door in pyjamas to stop the urgent knocking that was aggravating my alcohol-induced headache. I was faced with a rain-sodden Stubbing. Behind her a female uniform was noting down my Golf's licence number. Brampton was standing at her car, which they had squeezed onto the drive so it was bumper to bumper with mine. She was under an umbrella and squinting upwards into the rain, looking as if she was appraising the state of my roof – possibly noting that it was the only one on the street that hadn't had a loft conversion done. There was no way they could have traced my anonymous call reporting Elliot's death, and I'd carefully removed any trace of myself from the back garden, raking over my footprints and replacing the wheelbarrow.

"Ah, the witch and her flying monkey," I said, taking advantage of the fact that Brampton was out of earshot. Stubbing's white face reddened and she angrily worked those thin lips as Brampton walked up the drive. The uniform showed Brampton the licence number she had written down. Brampton glanced at it and came to the door. The uniform got in the driver's seat of the unmarked police car to escape the rain.

"George, how are you?" Brampton asked. Up close she was pale and tense, her eyes puffy. "I hope you don't mind us waking you up so early?" It wasn't a question I was meant to answer.

"He probably went to bed late, ma'am," said Stubbing, leering at my pyjamas. Brampton ignored her.

"May we come in, George? It's raining outside," Brampton said. I really didn't want them to come in.

"Is this a social call?"

"Not at six-thirty in the morning, it isn't," Stubbing said. She sounded very tired. No doubt they'd been up all night. I opened the door wide, shepherding them into the sitting room.

They sat on the sagging couch and I remained standing, thinking it gave me some sort of psychological advantage, although what advantage it might have given me was more than offset by the fact I was in my jimjams. "I won't offer you tea, I'm sure you won't be here long enough," I said, even though I was gasping for some myself.

"OK, George. We'll get to the point," said Brampton. "What were you doing in the grounds of Morley College last night?" Stubbing, dripping on the worn rug, was piercing me with those icy blue eyes, intent on my answer. Perhaps I was better off sitting down after all; it would give me time to think about whether they were trying it on or whether I had been seen. Perhaps an OCD-afflicted student sat at his window and made a note of every car that parked in the Morley car park. I couldn't think of a reason to lie; I didn't need to tell them why I was there. After all, I could have been dropping someone off, or making a nostalgic late night pilgrimage to where my father used to work. Lame, I know, but they were ideas to work with. I took a seat in an old armchair, my father's favourite.

"I was there for about half an hour." Stubbing beamed triumphantly at Brampton, who simply looked as tired as the carpet she was staring at. She raised her eyes to me without moving her head.

"What time did you get there, George?" she asked. I didn't say anything, remembering something my occasional lawyer had said about the police trying to place clients at the scene of a crime before they even knew there was a crime, but I'd kind of blown it already.

"Last night sometime. Why, is there a problem?"

"Do you want to tell us what you were doing there?" Brampton asked. Stubbing was piercing into me with a laser-like intensity that was uncomfortable.

"Not really," I said, beginning to feel hot. "Not until you tell me what is going on." They exchanged a glance and Brampton stood up and examined the Bakelite clock on the mantelpiece above the gas fire. A gas fire with asbestos-backed plates that glowed nicely when hot – Olivia had wanted to replace it with an imitation 'real' gas fire with pretend coal but I couldn't see the point in anything imitation. Brampton turned to study me.

"Elliot Booker was found dead at Morley College last night. Someone called it in."

"How did he die?" I asked, my thinking being that it was the first thing I would ask if I didn't know. The vision of him hanging from the light fixture in what looked like his study with a step ladder lying on its side beneath him was still fresh in my mind. I was struck at the time at how high the ceiling was in the house.

"What were you doing there, George?" Brampton asked.

"I was on a case."

"Wherever you go people end up dead," said Stubbing. "Funny that, isn't it?"

"Not really," I said.

"Who are you working for?" Brampton asked. "The Bookers are old friends of mine, you see," she said. Stubbing shot Brampton a glance; perhaps as surprised as I was. Brampton's professional face rearranged itself for a second and I understood that she was upset at Elliot's death. She was friends with the Bookers, but Sylvia hadn't confided in her, or at least Brampton wasn't letting on. It was going to be difficult to keep it from the police now that Sylvia's husband was dead. I decided to play it straight, but without telling them anything.

"I'm working for Sylvia Booker," I said. I stood up, to indicate that it was the end of the conversation. Stubbing stood up as well, watching me as if I might bolt for the door. Brampton turned professional again.

"In what capacity?" she asked.

"That's between me and her."

"Then perhaps we should continue this conversation at Parkside."

"Are you arresting me?"

Brampton slowly got up.

"Well, you were at a crime scene with no reasonable explanation, so in theory you would qualify as a general suspect, if not a specific one. But I would like to think of you as a witness at this stage, George, so you'll be helping us with our enquiries. Unless of course you don't want to?"

19

I WAS PUT IN THE SAME INTERVIEW ROOM WHERE I'D GIVEN MY statement to Stubbing on Wednesday. I was left to stew for a couple of hours, visited occasionally by DS Turner, the same guy who'd claimed on my previous visit that Stubbing was a good detective. I tried to pump him for information but he wasn't having any of it. I counted holes in the foam tiles on the ceiling until Brampton and Stubbing came back carrying a cup of coffee each. It smelled good.

"Don't I get any?" I asked. They ignored me. Brampton flicked through a file and Stubbing wrote at the top of a yellow pad. Brampton examined me and folded her hands on the table, as if in prayer.

"What time did you get to Morley College last night, George?"

"Sometime after eleven and before half past."

"Can anyone verify that?"

"The night manager at the McDonald's on Huntingdon Road," I said. "We had a conversation just before I left. It was just before closing. Cathy, her name was."

Stubbing and Brampton exchanged a look. Stubbing said,

"Blimey, reduced to chatting up McDonald's employees, are we?" Brampton ignored her. So did I.

"Who did you meet at Morley?" Brampton asked.

"No one," I said.

"So what were you doing there?"

"That's between me and my client," I said, even though Sylvia was not aware that I was going to collect her rubbish, nor, I imagined, would she be terribly pleased about it.

"Your so-called client has yet to confirm that she even *is* your client," Brampton said.

Stubbing piped up again. "Even you can understand that the last thing on her mind at the moment will be lowlife like you."

I continued to ignore her and concentrated on Brampton.

"How did Elliot Booker die?" I asked.

"Did you meet with Elliot?" she countered.

"No, I just told you I didn't meet anyone." Stubbing took a long drink of her coffee.

"Did you go near the bursar's residence?" Brampton asked.

"Look, am I a suspect or what?"

"What time did you leave Morley?"

"I wasn't there long, about half an hour."

"Did you go in the house?"

"No."

"What about the back garden?" Stubbing spat.

I shook my head, knowing I had to give them something. "Look, I went there to meet with Mrs Booker but she didn't turn up, so I left."

"You went to her house at eleven-thirty to meet her?" Sylvia asked disbelievingly.

"Yes, well, no. I was to meet her in the car park, not at her house."

"And she can verify this can she?"

I shrugged noncommittally. It was a weak point in my story, but I was hoping Sylvia would see that I was trying to protect her privacy, although she could be forgiven for throwing me to the police at this stage. "So am I a suspect?"

Brampton consulted her file. "When you left Morley you would have driven past the McDonald's you were at earlier, outside of which is a phone box from which a 999 phone call was made at 12.03. Did you make the call?"

"No."

She pursed her lips.

"Bit of a coincidence. You being there and it being the same place someone makes a call from, telling us to go to Morley?"

"Yes it is," I said. "Can I go now, if I'm not a suspect?"

"Perhaps you'd prefer to be one?" Stubbing said.

I made a show of thinking about it: finger on the chin, eyes scrunched in concentration at the ceiling.

"Let's see..." I said.

Stubbing snorted. "Let's book him on suspicion, ma'am, we can place him at the scene of the crime." But Brampton seemed oblivious to Stubbing's eagerness and I knew they weren't going to because Stubbing wouldn't have asked Brampton in front of me.

"Just what are you doing for Sylvia? Does it involve Elliot, or perhaps her daughter Lucy?" Brampton asked. Stubbing shot her a glance, like Brampton had veered from the script. Also, something was wrong about the question but before I could answer Brampton stood up and said, "I'm curtailing this interview for the moment." Stubbing looked confused at this turn of events, but quickly rallied and stood up too.

"Am I free to go?" I asked.

"I'd rather you didn't. I'd like to check your McDonald's story and confirm that you are working for Sylvia Booker and had arranged to meet her." She checked her watch. "If you left I might get the wrong idea and make you stay. That would take a lot longer than it would if I went and made a couple of phone calls; there's so much paperwork involved with charging someone you see, Stubbing here is very meticulous." Stubbing showed me her gappy teeth.

"Can I have some coffee at least? While I'm waiting." Brampton nodded and left the room.

Stubbing stayed long enough to pour the remainder of Brampton's coffee into hers and pass it to me. "There you go, Kocky."

Three boring hours later I left Parkside police station and emerged into a dark but dry Cambridge. According to Brampton, Elliot Booker hung himself at least a couple of hours before I'd picked up his rubbish. She'd come back to the interview room and given me the news in brutal fashion. She also told me that Lucy and her mother had been in London on the Sunday, with Sylvia staying on for a Monday morning meeting and Lucy heading straight for Morley

College. Sylvia couldn't remember whether we'd arranged to meet and I said she must have forgotten. I was just relieved that neither she nor Lucy had been the ones to find Elliot. Brampton had been thinking the same.

"I'm pleased that someone," and here she gave me a meaningful stare, "made that call from a public phone box outside that McDonald's on Huntingdon Road, otherwise Lucy would have been the one to find him."

"Did he leave a note?" I asked. She thought about whether to tell me then said, "No, but they just as often don't as do."

I stood looking over Parkside towards town, wondering whether to walk home or to the office. I pulled my raincoat lapel up against a bitter breeze.

"George?" A familiar voice at my ear. I turned to see Sylvia behind me, having come out of the police station. She was pale, red-eyed and makeup free. She still looked beautiful, but in a tragic and vulnerable way, like she should be in a black and white film with Humphrey Bogart. I wanted to give her a hug but where we were standing was not the place for it.

"Sylvia, I'm really sorry about your husband."

"Thank you. I put Judith right about you."

"Judith?" The name that Jason had overheard Quintin using on the train.

"Sorry, Judith Brampton. You know her as Detective Chief Inspector Brampton."

So Quintin had been talking to Brampton. "Yes, she said

you were friends." Something flitted across Sylvia's face. A concealed emotion involuntarily leaked.

"We were…" She shook her head, then: "I've known her a long time." She looked round at the police station; many of the blinded windows still had lights on behind them. Perhaps, like me, she was wondering whether Brampton was looking down on us.

"Did you tell her why I hired you?" she asked.

"Of course not. Did you?"

"I told her I'd asked you to watch Elliot. She said something about us meeting last night. I told her I couldn't remember, I hope that was the right thing to do?"

"Perfect." That explained why Brampton had accepted my lie about meeting Sylvia. Sylvia looked at me and I waited for her to ask me what I'd been doing at the house. But she had other things on her mind.

"Did you find… Elliot?"

"Yes," I said.

She tipped her head to indicate the building behind her. "I need to get away from this place," she said. "Do you need a lift?" I hesitated, reluctant to impose at this time. "I could do with the company," she said. Surely she didn't lack people to have around her. She read my mind. "There are lots of people I could go to right now, but I need to be with someone outside my immediate circle, someone who didn't know Elliot. Do you understand?"

I sort of understood. Like Sandra, Jason and Kamal had helped me when Olivia had gone, rather than our common circle of friends, who turned out not to be friends at all.

20

SYLVIA SAT ON THE COUCH THAT BRAMPTON AND STUBBING had occupied that morning. She nursed an out-of-date peppermint tea (something Olivia had left) and stared at the glowing asbestos plates in the gas fire. She'd told me in the car that Lucy was staying at her grandmother's while she'd come down to Parkside to talk to Brampton. "I couldn't bear them coming back to the house. They'd been there all morning," she'd said. She shifted around on the sofa, dressed in designer jeans and a soft-looking jumper I yearned to stroke.

"I wanted to thank you for bringing Lucy home the other night. It was awfully decent of you." I shrugged and said nothing because it *was* nothing. "I'm sorry that I didn't acknowledge you, but I hadn't told Elliot about you, and..." Her face crumpled and I had to get up and take the cup from her so she could cry. Despite what romantic fiction writers might claim, no one looks good crying, even a beautiful woman such as Sylvia. One does not, as depicted in films, remain expressionless and simply ooze tears. The face screws up in an ugly grimace, the mouth twists in pain. I wanted to comfort her and pondered sitting next to her and putting an arm round her but instead I went to get tissues; she was technically still a client after all.

"Thanks." She sniffed, taking sheets of tissue from the box I held out and blowing hard. "It's better to get it out now; I can't really do this when I get back to Morley, it would make people uncomfortable." I marvelled at the kind of people she knew that couldn't bear to see her cry when faced with the suicide of her husband. She dabbed at her eyes.

"He made some bad investments on behalf of the college," she said, looking at me.

"You don't have to explain it," I said, although I was dying to know.

"He'd been struggling with it for some time."

"How did you find out?"

She looked away. "I've known for a while…" She was about to continue but started crying again and blew her nose hard. I wondered whether it was a good time to bring up my employment.

"This is probably not the right time to ask, but do you want me to carry on looking into Lucy and Quintin Boyd?"

She sat up straight. "Please, you must carry on. Please don't stop. Please. With Elliot gone there is no one to protect Lucy." Protect her? She reached out and grabbed my hands. "You've got to help Lucy."

"OK," I said, taken aback. "In which case can I ask you something?" She was still holding my hands. Her hands were softer and warmer than I remembered when I had shaken one in my office.

"Of course." It was cruel to ask her at such a time but she

was vulnerable and perhaps more likely to answer. Cynical, I know, but sometimes getting to the truth requires an underhand touch.

"The night I brought Lucy home, what were you and Elliot arguing about?" Sylvia reddened and looked like a frightened deer, ready to bolt. She took her hands away.

"I… I can't remember. What did you hear? Does it matter? Probably about money. He was always telling me I spent too much on clothes." She smiled weakly.

"So it wasn't about Lucy?" She shook her head but seemed to be struggling with something. I got the clear impression that she wanted to tell me, or someone, to unload something she was carrying around. She looked up.

"No, it wasn't about Lucy." OK, so I learnt she was lying; not terribly useful except in confirming my view of human nature. She examined her tiny watch. "I have to go," she said. "There are people waiting for me." She asked me if she could use the bathroom and I directed her to the downstairs toilet, hoping it was clean. The phone rang as she went to find it.

"George. It's Sandra, where the hell have you been?"

"Waiting for coffee at Parkside police station. The service is atrocious."

"I read about Elliot Booker, it was in the *Argus*. Reading between the lines it looks like he topped himself?"

"It looked like that to me," I said. I heard the toilet flush and water running in the sink. I tried to remember if the towel was fresh – Sylvia was used to better things.

"Jesus, George, don't tell me you found him? Is that why you were at Parkside?"

"For my sins." The loo door opened and Sylvia came out. She'd done something to her face – added a little colour perhaps.

"I have to go, Sandra."

"Wait, I've got some news on Sylvia Booker. Remember you asked me to check whether she'd been at Morley the same time as Quintin Boyd?" Sylvia came down the hall and stood there, smiling abstractedly. I held up a finger to her and mouthed "one minute". She nodded and went to the hall mirror.

"What did you find?" I said.

"Well, they were there at the same time, and she was doing Law as well, although not corporate like him, civil. They graduated the same year and get this, they were in the same house. Apparently the colleges have these things called houses—"

"I know what they are."

"OK. You don't sound very impressed."

"It's not a good time." Sylvia was adjusting her hair in the mirror. She'd lied to me about knowing Quintin. Two lies uncovered in one evening.

"Why didn't you say? I have more," Sandra said. Sylvia turned to me and pointed to her watch and then the door. I held up my finger.

"Make it quick," I said into the phone.

"Elliot was also a student there at the same time, same house, did Economics."

"Thanks, that's very interesting. I'll catch you tomorrow," I said into the receiver.

"Wait," Sandra shouted.

"What is it?"

"They all graduated the same year," she said.

"And?"

"It was the year your father left." Jesus Christ. Of course it could just be a coincidence.

"George?" I looked at Sylvia who was finding her coat. "Did you hear me?"

I put the receiver down on Sandra and said to Sylvia, "Sorry about that." I helped her on with her coat.

"Thank you, George, for the tea, for taking me in. I appreciate it."

"Thank you for the lift," I said.

She took a deep breath and released it. "I'd better go and sort things out."

"If you need anything…" I said.

She put her fingers on my forearm. "Find out what Quintin wants with Lucy."

I watched her walk to her Mini and get in.

As she pulled away from the kerb I grabbed my jacket and keys, got into my car and followed.

Sylvia didn't head back to Morley; instead she drove straight to the railway station. It was approaching five, and too many cars were parked outside the station entrance, waiting to pick people up as they emerged. Sylvia pulled into a small space on the wide part of the pavement right outside the entrance. I drove past her and double-parked in the car park where

I could watch her if I craned my neck. She was looking towards the station entrance where a stream of people started to emerge. A car blocked my view and the driver beeped at me. He couldn't go round me as I was blocking his route. I drove round the parking lot, hoping to get back into position. Stupid of course, since everyone was doing the same thing. Cars were following me round, circling as they waited for the people they were picking up to come out of the station. I glimpsed Sylvia approaching someone in the crowd. Some wanker blew his horn at me. I gave him two fingers then discovered it was a woman. She returned the gesture, despite the toddler in the back. I kept driving.

Sylvia was talking to, no, shouting and gesticulating at, Quintin Boyd. I had to drive out of the car park and go past the Mini hoping that Sylvia wouldn't see me. She was too engrossed. I was back into the car park where I pulled into a disabled parking space. When I got out Sylvia seemed to be begging Quintin to get into her car. He, however, was having none of it, and just then his silver Mercedes pulled up and he opened the back door.

Before Quintin got in he said something to Sylvia which made her cringe like a child at a raised fist. The car, with square-headed Mark at the wheel, took off. Sylvia stared after it. She was hugging herself, probably against the cold, but it could equally have been at what Quintin had said to her.

21

THE NEXT MORNING, BEFORE EVEN MY EARLY-BIRD NEIGHBOUR left for work, I was in Cottenham and parked in sight of number twenty-two where the alleged benefits cheat lived. No one came out. If the guy was working he wasn't doing a nine-to-five. Bored, I left, stopping by the nursing home to see my father. They didn't encourage you to stop by at any old time but they didn't forbid it and I liked to surprise them. Megan, the young care assistant, was clearing away my father's breakfast tray.

"You're here early. No flowers today?"

No, I had not brought flowers. I sat with my father as he stared out of the window into the garden. It wasn't a bad view; they'd placed bird tables and feeders on the semi-circular lawn and a cold sun was out. I tried to recall his last year at work, the year Sylvia, Elliot and Quintin had graduated from Morley. There didn't seem to be much significance to attach to this, except that he had retired early on full pension due to, as my mother put it, "Problems at work." I never learnt what these were, but my father made no secret of his loathing of some of the students, who he said treated him like shit.

Hence his endless asides to me along the lines of, "Never let anyone think they are better than you are, Kevork." I hadn't heard him speak for nearly a year, perhaps somehow realising he wasn't making sense anymore.

Megan brought me a cup of tea.

"I think it's lovely that you come and visit, you should see the number of people here that don't have visitors." She put the cup down on a side table. "It was nice of your cousin to visit your father."

"Cousin?"

"Yes, a distant cousin I think it was, not a cousin."

My heart skipped a beat – as far as I knew I didn't have a cousin, distant or otherwise. "When was this?"

"A couple of weeks ago on a Sunday."

"I wonder which cousin it was?" I asked, trying to sound casual. "Did he or she give a name?"

She shook her head. "I wasn't on duty but we talked about it on the Monday because it was unusual for anyone else to visit. Sorry I didn't mention it before. I didn't think it was important."

I shrugged. "I'm just curious, I hadn't realised someone from the family had visited, that's all, and it would be remiss of me not to thank them. Of course I don't want to embarrass myself by thanking the wrong cousin."

"I could find out for you."

"I wouldn't want you to go to any trouble; like I say, I'm just curious."

She smiled. "It's no trouble at all. I'll ask Angela when she's in tomorrow, she was on duty that Sunday."

* * *

Back in Cambridge I got a coffee from Antonio's and took it to the office. Nina was coming down the stairs as I started to ascend, dressed in her crisp white coat and the little pin on the lapel. I had to wait at the bottom to let her come down. Our aborted date seemed a distant memory now.

"Hello," I said. I was half expecting the cold shoulder but she grinned at me and I swear she tossed her hair as she reached the bottom of the stairs.

"I heard about your act of chivalry Friday night. You should have said something." She brushed something from the shoulder of my coat, caressed it even. "Shall we try again? Perhaps you could come to mine. I'll cook something healthy." Now her voice was caressing *me*. I mumbled something, which she took as a yes. She said something about Friday night. I said something about how great that would be. She smiled and walked on. I checked my chin for drool.

I was pondering the ups and downs of dating as I went through the open door of my office. Sandra was sitting at her desk, typing fast.

"Hello, stranger," she said, looking up at me without any discernible reduction in her words per minute. I sat at my desk, put my feet up and looked at my shoes – there was a little dried mud on the sides from when I'd found Elliot.

"Did you tell Nina about my brush with Lucy Booker?" The typing stopped.

"Trust me, George, I was doing you a favour. She was telling anyone who'd listen that you ran off with a young girl."

"She said what?"

"She was telling everyone in the building about your date before it happened and afterwards, you arse. We're women, we talk. Anyway, yesterday she was saying that you'd dumped her for a young girl in the pub. So I took her aside and explained that as it happens you were on a case and to stop badmouthing you. I may have used stronger language." I could imagine Sandra taking Nina aside; that would have been worth paying to see. Sandra started typing again and her words per minute increased, a sure sign she was annoyed.

"OK, Sandra, I was wrong, you were doing me a favour."

"Can I do you another favour?" I grunted at this rhetorical question. "It's not my business, but she's not right for you. Trust me. There, I've said it."

"You're right," I said. "It's not your business." Secretly I was worried that Sandra would find out that I'd just made another date with Nina. I was regretting it myself now having learnt that Nina liked to blab.

To break the awkwardness I gave Sandra a précis of yesterday's session with the police and my heart-to-heart with Sylvia afterwards, ending with her confrontation of Quintin at the station.

"She's really worried about this Quintin Boyd eh? Enough to pretend she doesn't know him."

I turned to her. "Show me where you found the details of Sylvia and Elliot going to Morley." I scooted my wheeled chair over to her desk. She made room for me to see the screen as she brought up a bookmarked website.

"It's a website of Morley alumni. You just type in a name,

if you have one. At first I couldn't find Sylvia Booker but then I realised she'd be under her maiden name." She typed in 'Sylvia'. Three of them came up. She clicked on Sylvia Jessica Patten. "And there she is. Quite a stunner she was, and so young looking." Indeed. I didn't say that she'd also aged very well. She'd been photographed in her graduation garb and it listed her course (Civil Law) and the societies she'd been in. The list looked like a straight copy of her daughter's interests except for something called the Cambridge Blue Club. A small paragraph described her postgraduate achievements. In her case marrying Elliot Booker seemed to have happened immediately after graduation and Lucy was born the same year; they hadn't wasted any time. There was a list of the charities she was currently a trustee of, a couple I already knew about. It looked like she'd never practised law in anger.

Sandra clicked on Elliot's name. He had a first in Economics and was apprenticed at the usual management consultancy firms before becoming bursar back at his old college five years ago. The only society he'd belonged to, apart from the debating team, was the Cambridge Blue Club.

"What do you reckon the Cambridge Blue Club is?" I said.

"No idea," Sandra said. "Something Cambridge related."

"Very good, detective. 'Cambridge blue' refers to the colour worn by university sports teams. Maybe it was a sports club."

"You can also list people alphabetically," she said, clicking on a button. "Boyd is just down from Booker, obviously." She clicked on Quintin Boyd and a picture of a tousle-haired young man with the same strong jawline I'd seen on his company website and in the flesh from afar was at the top. "There's something of George Clooney about him," she said. My eye, however, was drawn to his society memberships. He seemed to belong to most of them, including something called Republicans Abroad and, guess what, the Cambridge Blue Club. But I wanted to check something else. Something that Sylvia had said yesterday when I'd met her outside the police station.

"Go back to the list of names." She clicked back in the browser. There it was, four down from Boyd. Judith Brampton. I jabbed excitedly at the name. Sandra clicked. Brampton, Judith, graduated eighteen years ago. Read Criminal Law, joined the police fast-track graduate programme the year of graduation. A picture of a younger Brampton smiled out at us; it was the first smile I'd seen on her. I scanned for her club memberships.

Member of the Cambridge Blue Club.

"Bloody hell," I said.

"What does it mean?" she said. I scooted back to my desk.

"It means they were all in the same club." Sandra got back to work and I Googled the Cambridge Blue Club with no result. I chewed over things for a while, but the typing was having a soporific effect. I'd got up far too early. The typing stopped.

"Why don't you go, I'll lock up," Sandra said. I picked my feet up off the desk.

"OK, I need to do some food shopping anyway." She

watched me put my raincoat on.

"Buy something healthy, won't you, George?"

"Yes, Mum." She looked suitably pissed off as I left.

It was only when I was downstairs that I remembered that I hadn't told Sandra about the strange visitor to the nursing home, but I saw no point in worrying her.

22

ON THE WAY HOME I STOPPED AT THE SUPERMARKET TO BUY ready meals, some steaks, frozen chips and peas. I also selected milk and fruit and eggs and coffee, enough for a week. I then wheeled by the drinks section and looked for bargains: 3 for 2 offers, bin ends, a litre for the price of 750ml. I had to move the food in the trolley to prevent it from being crushed by bottles and cans. I stood in the queue at the checkout replaying Friday night in my head, when I'd taken Lucy home and listened at the door to Sylvia and Elliot arguing. The woman behind the till was distracting me with excessive chat, asking me how I was and what did I think of the weather. She scanned my stuff coming down the conveyor belt with beady eyes as well as the barcode reader.

"Night in with the lads is it?"

"No. Just stocking up."

"Not very healthy, is it?"

"What are you, a dietician?" She looked taken aback. I was a little harsh I admit, but sometimes a guy just wants to be left alone and not be told what to do by well-meaning women. She went quiet and avoided eye contact.

As I was leaving I heard her say to the next customer, "Some people! You try to be friendly…"

In the car park I opened the hatch of the Golf to put the shopping away and saw the black rubbish bag full of the Bookers' recycled paper. After seeing Elliot dangling from his ceiling I'd put it in the car when I'd quickly left – not wanting to leave it for the police to find – and forgotten all about it.

As soon as I got home I spread out the Bookers' recycling over the dining room table. Olivia had been keen on dinner parties and we'd been to several (all her friends) and hosted a few, despite her being embarrassed at the decorative state of the house, saying it was dark and stuck in the 1950s. She had wanted to knock downstairs through to create one enormous room, an idea I'd put the kibosh on, using the excuse that technically the house still belonged to my father and it didn't feel right turning it into something else while he was still alive, even if he wasn't capable of knowing the difference anymore. Secretly though, I liked the cosy claustrophobia of the rooms and the ability to shut out the knowing chatter of her book group while I watched TV or read. Sometimes I would open the front door to Olivia's bookish chums holding the latest Stephen King or Dan Brown just to annoy her, until one day they stopped coming round, about the same time we stopped having dinner parties, and probably the same time she found intellectual and physical comfort with her new friend.

I poured three fingers of an amber liquid into a glass and

sorted the pile of rubbish into envelopes, newspapers and flyers. The Bookers, or at least one of them, took *The Times* and the *Sunday Telegraph*. There were also some newsletters from various charities with Sylvia's name on the address label. They'd obviously had a clear out: there were several issues each of the *Economist* and *Harper's Bazaar* magazine, which seemed to be full of Sylvia Booker lookalikes. I ignored the flyers and turned to the letters and envelopes. I could find no personal correspondence; they were obviously very careful about what they put in the recycling. The only letters were generic marketing appeals addressed to the householder.

The Bookers were conscientious recyclers though; even the little plastic windows had been torn out of envelopes. Most of them had contained bills or statements that betrayed their origins either with a logo or a return PO box printed on the back – I'd done this enough times I knew the return PO boxes and towns of most credit card companies, banks and utilities. I found an envelope with a five-day-old Cambridge postmark and Special Delivery sticker on it, which meant it had been received on the Friday. Most interesting was the spiral staircase logo I'd seen on the letter Elliot Booker had been holding when he'd opened the door to me. 'Private and Confidential' was printed in the bottom right-hand corner and it had Elliot Booker's name and address printed on a label. I looked on the back for a return address but there was just a PO box with a Cambridge postcode. I turned up nothing else of interest in the pile so I pocketed the envelope and went to the hall to answer the ringing phone – Jason.

"Boss, are we still on the Booker case?"

"Yes we are, my son. I'd like to pick up the tracker from the Merc; it's served its purpose and the battery's probably dead."

The next morning Jason and I drove south out of Cambridge towards Royston, where Sandra had traced the registered address of the Merc to the firm that ran the luxury car rental company – Chauffeured Comfort Cars.

"I'll settle up with you for the work you've done so far when we get back to the office," I told Jason.

"Maybe I can get those headphones you mentioned." Stuck behind a coach on a straight stretch of the A10 I contemplated pushing the Golf round it as I had a wake of cars behind me and could see clear road ahead.

"How's that going?"

"Well, I thought about what you said, boss, about it being an acting job, and that sort of helped... Are you going to overtake that coach or what?" I strained the old Golf painfully past the dirty coach and we pulled in front of it with some relief.

"But I think the real solution is for me to get my own place," Jason said, when the revs had settled down. "It kind of cramps your style, being at home, never mind listening to your mum doing telephone porn."

"Can you afford it though?" I asked. "We might as well be living in London as far as rent's concerned." In my wing mirror I saw a car pull out, overtaking the car that was behind the coach. I thought it was going to pull in behind the coach but it kept on coming. I glanced ahead: the driver would have to get a move on; a lorry was heading towards us. Back in the mirror I could see the car was a Subaru that had one of those vents in the bonnet and a rear spoiler indicating extra horsepower. The driver made it with a car's length to spare. We heard the extended blare of the lorry's horn as it thundered past us, rocking the Golf with turbulence. I checked the rear-view mirror: I couldn't make out the driver because the windscreen of the Subaru was tinted, something I thought was now illegal. I realised that Jason was talking; he'd missed the whole overtaking drama behind us.

"...depending on whether I could get some work to pay the rent. There're plenty of people who work their way through college," he said.

"You're right," I said. "I met one of them the other day doing nights at McDonald's. She looked like shit." I checked the mirror: the Subaru had dropped back and was now letting someone overtake it – odd since it had taken such a risk overtaking the coach in the first place.

"Besides," Jason was saying, "if I could find somewhere reasonable..." We came up to a roundabout and I drove straight on into the outskirts of Royston. The Subaru was still there (now two cars back) but that meant nothing since we were on the main road that went through Royston towards London. "Surely you could do with some extra cash?" Jason was saying.

"What?" Had I missed something?

"You've got three bedrooms, boss. Surely you could spare one." I was looking at street names and it took me a moment to realise what he was saying.

"You want to rent a room from me?"

"I just wondered—"

"Forget it, Jason. I'm no fucking landlord." I passed him the sheet with the directions to Chauffeured Comfort Cars on it. "Get us to this bloody place, will you?" He took the sheet and looked at it.

"Next left. Then third right," he said. The kid was disappointed, I could tell by his deflated tone. But I was not going to have a nineteen-year-old living in the house with everything that entailed – I'd been a teenager myself, and a pain in the neck to my parents. He was a good kid, but I didn't want him as a lodger. Besides, I was getting used to bumbling around the place on my own. Perhaps I'd been a little harsh in the way I'd dealt with it though. I turned left into an industrial area.

"Listen, if you need somewhere to crash for the odd night then that's fine, I'm always happy to lend an ear and a bed. I even know how to order pizza." Jason snorted or chuckled, I couldn't tell. I checked my mirror as I turned right into a cul-de-sac of five or six industrial units and just caught the Subaru turning off the A10.

"It's just here on the right," Jason pointed to a fenced-off area with about a dozen fancy cars parked behind it, one of which was the silver S-Class Mercedes. A sign confirmed that we had found Chauffeured Comfort Cars. I drove past and pulled into a space on the left, in front of a white van. "Why are we parking here?"

"Don't get out, I just want to check something."

In my wing mirror I watched the Subaru slow down at

the junction we had just come off. Although the side windows were also tinted I imagined the driver looking down towards us. Then the car sped up and disappeared.

"What is it?" Jason asked.

"Nothing. Let's get this bloody tracker." But after I locked the Golf and we checked to cross the road I saw the Subaru turn onto the road and stop in the customer parking bay of a trade plumbing outlet. No one got out of the car.

23

A PORTAKABIN SAT JUST INSIDE THE GATE IN THE HIGH-FENCED area that was Chauffeured Comfort Cars. Jason was surprised that they hadn't called it Cambridge Comfort Cars, or Cambridge Chauffeured Cars. I know what he meant; it seemed that every company within a fifty-mile radius of the city prefixed their company name with 'Cambridge' as if it automatically imparted some aura of respectability and learning. The top of the fence was spiked and high enough to put off climbers and there were CCTV cameras mounted everywhere. I peered through the window of the Portakabin where a thin-haired man was hunched over a desk studying a magazine. I managed to make out that it had more photos than words before he noticed me. He quickly got up and came to the door. When he opened it we got a blast of cheap aftershave, which he must have showered in.

"Morning," he said. He was of beefy peasant stock and looked ill at ease in a suit that was cut for someone slimmer and shorter – the trousers didn't cover his ankles, nor the sleeves his wrists. I couldn't tell whether he was the owner or manager of the place. He kept a rictus smile while he appraised our potential worth as customers. "Can I help?"

"Hello," I said, sticking out a hand. "I'm here with my nephew and we're looking for something to take him to his twenty-first birthday party in style." He reluctantly put a clammy hand in mine, rested it there for a second then withdrew it to his pocket where he proceeded to adjust himself.

"Do you have anything in mind?" I looked at Jason who was scouring the cars.

"Nothing too tacky. Just be me and a few girls," he said. I rolled my eyes at him, which he ignored. He pointed. "What about that S-Class Merc, can I look at that?" He walked off without waiting for an answer.

"The boy has no taste," I said. "That looks like a corporate rental to me, am I right?"

"Yeah, that one is booked every week by the same guy," the man said, as we traipsed behind Jason, me feigning a limp to slow us up.

"You OK?"

"Five-a-side. Sliding tackle," I said. "So the same guy rents the same car. You'd think buying one would be cheaper." Up ahead Jason was running his hands over the bonnet of the Merc, like he was smearing suntan lotion onto a woman's shoulders.

"He likes being driven about, that's his thing. He always wants the same driver." Jason moved to the back of the Merc and I stopped next to a stretch limo with tinted glass.

"I think he'd be better off with something like this, no?"

The man nodded, turning to the car and patting the polished roof with his free hand, his other still being used to play pocket billiards. Over his shoulder I caught Jason ducking behind the Merc.

"This is your traditional party rental, the girls love riding in them."

"I agree it would be more suited to the occasion," I said, beginning to sound like a salesman myself. He was giving me some stats about the car when Jason wandered over, grinning, waving the tracker at me behind the guy's back. Then his phone started making that weird noise that passed for a ring. The guy turned and Jason stuffed the tracker in a pocket, pulling his phone from the other. He checked the screen and put it to his ear, turning his back to us. I engaged the guy in talk about rental costs.

"Uncle George," Jason said, a moment later, and then said it again more insistently. It was on the third go that I cottoned on: I was Uncle George. "It's Mum, for you." I excused myself and put the thing to my ear.

"Hello?"

"George, you should get back here pronto."

"What's up?"

"I have Lucy Booker with me in the office and she wants to talk to you. Also, someone from the nursing home called. A Megan?"

"Everything OK?"

"Yes, it's fine. She said she had some information about the person who visited your dad? I've left her number on my screen."

"Thanks," I said, hanging up before she could ask me more questions.

I lied to the ill-suited man about how we would get back to him about the car hire and we made our way out. As we crossed the road I saw that the Subaru was still there. We'd reached the Golf when I remembered that I'd forgotten to limp. I looked back towards the compound but the guy had disappeared into his Portakabin. In the car I found my notebook and gave it to Jason. I told him to write down the licence plate number of the Subaru as we passed it, just in case.

"Is it following us?" Jason asked. He was looking down at his phone, his thumbs moving quickly over the little keypad.

"I don't think so, but try and concentrate."

"I'm on it, boss. Don't worry." I watched the Subaru, trying to peer through the impenetrable glass, but I saw just the shadows of two men.

I sat opposite Lucy in an otherwise empty Antonio's and we sipped hot cappuccinos from big wide cups. Antonio brought over a small plate of biscotti, delicious morsels made by his wife. I'd brought her over here because Sandra and Jason were in the office, Jason downloading the information from the tracker onto the computer.

Lucy looked even paler than usual with dark rings under her eyes. Eyes which in no way could be confused with her mother's. I couldn't remember which parent eye colour was inherited from or whether it was random, nor could I remember the colour of her father's eyes. She was dressed for Sunday school, a far cry from how she had looked when visiting Quintin Boyd. I'd done the condolences thing, which she barely acknowledged. She could hardly look at me over her wide cup.

"I wanted to thank you for helping me out last Friday," she said, and the memory of it brought some needed colour to her cheeks.

"It was nothing," I said, because it was nothing.

She shook her head and worried at a small cross hanging from her neck.

"No it wasn't nothing. I'm particularly grateful for the fact that you said nothing to Mother about how you… found me." This was all very interesting but not as interesting as the fact that she had come to my office only three days after her father's suicide to tell me this.

"That boy who came back with you to the office. Jason, isn't it?" I nodded. "I've met him before, at the Flying Duck, after rowing." Shit. I'd forgotten about that. "He was there with Rowena and her group of Roughers," she said.

"Roughers?"

"Yes, as in 'roughing it'. They compete to go out with people they deem to be, uh, lower than them in social status." She blushed violently. "I'm sorry, I didn't mean to suggest that Jason was in any way of a lower…"

"Don't sweat it. I'm sure Jason will be quite flattered to be considered a bit of rough."

"Does he work for you?"

"Occasionally," I said.

"Well, he could do better than her."

"I'll tell him." She looked alarmed so I explained that I was joking.

"So tell me, how did you know where to find me?" I asked.

"You told me your name when you drove me home, remember." She smiled. It was a thin, lipless smile. "No, I wasn't that far gone. Besides, it's unusual, so I remembered it when I found your card in Mother's handbag." I didn't ask what she was doing in her mother's handbag, nor did she deem it necessary to explain. I drank my coffee and nibbled a cantuccini, wondering when she was going to mention her dead father.

"What did my mother hire you to do?" She held my gaze but it was an effort for her.

"Who said I was working for her?" She shrugged and examined her nails. If she was looking for one to chew she was out of luck; they were all painfully bitten to the flesh.

"When you rescued me you said you worked for one of her charities." I didn't say anything; it suited me if that's what she thought. Thankfully she was too polite to pursue it. She'd hardly touched her cappuccino. She looked up at me again, her dark eyes brimming. Here it comes, I thought.

"I was hoping you could help me."

"Help you how?"

"Find out why my father killed himself." I looked at her pale face and red nose and teary eyes.

"Have you spoken to your mother about it?"

"Of course. She just says that there were some financial irregularities with the college. I just don't think that's enough, is it, for—" Then she started to cry properly.

I figured it was best to leave her to it and signalled Antonio who nodded and came over with a box of tissues, which he silently put on the table in a practised manner, all the while giving me a disapproving look as if it were my fault. He walked away shaking his head and muttering to himself. While Lucy was busy blowing her nose I wondered whether I should ask her about Quintin Boyd, but that would give away the fact that I knew about him and then she'd know what it was I was doing for her mother.

"I'm sorry," she said, sniffling.

"Nothing to be sorry about. Most natural thing in the world."

"So will you help me?"

"I'm not sure what I can do, to be honest. The police are handling it and no doubt the college will be looking into the financial side of things." I studied her. "Do you have any reason to believe that he had something else on his mind?" She shook her head and absentmindedly moved the cross up and down the chain round her neck.

"No. I just know that a few bad investments is not reason enough for him to… to do what he did."

"Listen, Lucy. You can never really know what is going on inside someone's head. Even someone very close to you," I said. She just stared at her near-full cup of coffee.

"Look, if I find out anything then I'll let you know, but there's no reason to go digging. OK?"

She nodded. Over her shoulder I saw Jason come into the café and wave at me from the door. Lucy looked round and blushed. I signalled to Jason to hang on. Lucy was furiously wiping her cheeks. I couldn't help smiling to myself; even when smothered in grief, life endures.

"You look fine," I said.

* * *

I left Lucy and Jason sitting at stools in the window of the sandwich shop across the way from Antonio's and took my lunch up to the office to see what Jason had downloaded from the tracker. When Jason had come into Antonio's Lucy had gone to the toilet to freshen up, which had given me an opportunity to brief him on the investigator's creed of not divulging client-sensitive information – especially to the client's daughter.

"I know nothing, boss," he reassured me. I wasn't very comfortable with Lucy knowing about me but there wasn't a lot I could do about it and since our attention had now shifted from her to Quintin Boyd I told myself it was not such an issue, even though she was the reason we were interested in him. Still, I didn't want Jason spilling any beans; especially since I'd learnt he was a sucker for plummy-voiced girls.

24

SANDRA HAD ALREADY LEFT FOR THE DAY WHEN I SAT AT MY desk and examined the documents Jason had printed out. There was a map, showing little numbered flags where the Merc had stopped, and a red line marking routes it had travelled. An accompanying sheet matched the flags and detailed when and for how long the car had stopped at each location. It was similar to the one I had given the police that detailed the movements of murdered Trisha Greene. Most of the movements were in Cambridge: the railway station; River Views where Quintin lived when he was in town; then a trip south to the Royston address where the Merc lived when he wasn't. The unknown for me was a trip north out of Cambridge to Waterbeach from River Views last Friday morning. Judging by the time and date it corresponded with when we'd seen the driver pick the black-haired young woman up from Quintin's place. There was an address showing the street he'd taken her to. I'd no way of knowing what was there except by going. I went back to the map, which for some reason looked familiar beyond the fact that it was of Cambridge, but I put it down to the fact that I myself had been to River Views. Something bugged me about it though, a sense of déjà vu if you could have such a thing about a map.

I folded it up and stuck it in my inside jacket pocket where I came across the envelope I'd found in the Bookers' recycling bin, the one with the spiral staircase on it and the PO box on the reverse. I could make a king-sized quilt with the clues I had and yet I had nothing of substance. OK, George, think. Earn your money. I looked at my half-eaten sandwich and made a list – first, find out what the spiral staircase logo was all about; it was on the letter Elliot was holding when arguing with Sylvia and I assumed it was the cause of the argument. Second, track down the woman who'd been dropped off by Quintin Boyd's driver; maybe she could shed light on what these women were doing at Quintin's flat. Third, find out who owned the Subaru that had followed us to Royston. Fourth, find out who visited my father, and why? I switched on Sandra's computer and waited while it took its sweet time to come to life. A yellow Post-it with Megan the care assistant's number on it was stuck to the screen, just as Sandra had promised. I decided to ring her first then go up to the Waterbeach address on the tracker, and see if I could find where that woman lived, then go home and have a bath. However, all I got when I rang was voicemail so I left my home number.

I took a healthy bite from my sandwich while I brought up the Arts Cinema website to see what films were on that night, just to have something to look forward to later. The Italian crime season was over and I had to choose between something starring a permanently pouting Hollywood darling and a French thriller about a man who happens to see his long-dead wife on the Internet. I settled on the thriller and was looking for Kamal's number to see if he wanted to join me in a couple of hours of escapism when the phone rang. I wiped mustard from my chin and picked up.

"Hello, Cambridge Confidential. How can we help?"

"Is that George…" I heard the sound of paper rustling and then slowly, as if being read, "Ko… char… yan?" An Essex voice, raspy with smoking.

"This is he," I said.

"Stay away from Lucy Booker, you and your sidekick," the voice said. "Or else." He was going for menace but coming across like an extra in a bad British gangster film.

"Or else what, you fucker?" I said, opening a drawer in my desk and switching on the tape recorder permanently hooked up to the telephone. "Why don't you come over here and threaten me face to face?"

Again there was the sound of rustling as if the caller were consulting a script from which I'd deviated. Then he spluttered, "I'll show you, you bastard. You'll be sorry." He hung up before I had time to respond. I looked at the telephone display to check the caller ID but it had been blocked.

The call had made what little I had eaten of my pastrami sandwich repeat on me and the rest of it had lost its appeal. I called Jason's mobile, to see if he was still with Lucy. It went straight to voicemail but I left a message for him to call me. I knew he had classes that afternoon that he wouldn't miss, not for all the posh-sounding girls in Cambridge. I supposed the message was from Quintin Boyd or someone working for him.

But it seemed crude for someone of Boyd's type. He was a lawyer after all, and they had perfected the art of threatening people using long words on headed paper. But maybe he wasn't as sophisticated as he liked to portray himself.

There wasn't a lot I could do about the phone call except fret so I thought it more productive to fret while driving to Waterbeach. I took the office mobile with me and once I'd found the street on the map and parked I tried Jason's mobile again: no answer. I contemplated calling Sandra but that would be inviting an avalanche of questions I couldn't answer. Instead I concentrated on my surroundings.

I was on a row of 1980s box houses, half clad in rotting dark timber and topped in mossy concrete tiles. I was outside what I thought was the right house according to the map but GPS is notoriously inaccurate and besides, the driver might have dropped her the opposite side or she might have been asked to be dropped further down from her house. I took a charity ID badge from my glove compartment and a clipboard from the back seat. I got out of the car and tried Jason's phone again. Still no answer. I was deciding which end of the road to start at when a taxi drew up and the woman got out. Same cropped black hair shorter at the back than front, same build, same black shiny coat. At a distance she looked young, but she had a confidence in her manner that made her older. I put the badge and clipboard back in the car and approached her as she was paying the taxi. She looked up and saw me. Close up she was definitely older, tired-looking with a smoker's leathery skin and the jaundiced look of someone on a bad diet. I gave her a smile since she didn't look in the welcoming mood.

"Can I help you, mate?" She took out a coffin nail and lit it, holding her smoking arm at the elbow with her free hand and blowing smoke sideways from the corner of a big mouth.

"I work for Quintin Boyd," I said, in lieu of a plan. She looked wary.

"Oh yeah? I've not seen you before. I usually deal with that Mark bloke."

"You mean his driver?"

"Dogsbody more like. What the fuck does Quintin want so soon?"

"He just wanted me to check that everything was alright after the other night." She took another drag and exhaled sideways, her eyes not leaving mine.

"He's worried about me is he, all of a sudden?" She smiled sarcastically. "I hadn't pegged him as a geezer who gives a fuck as long as he got his take."

"His take?" I asked, stupidly. She looked at me with new interest.

"What exactly do you do for dirty old Quintin then?"

"I watch his back, that's all."

"Well go and fucking watch it then, sunshine. We're done."

"It's been charming," I said.

"Fuck off," she said, and went down a path losing a battle with weeds to a door that had lost its paint to the weather.

* * *

By the time I'd parked in my drive, rain was pounding down on the car roof. I tried Jason again – he should definitely be out of class by now. I wanted to tell him to stay away from Lucy Booker for the time being. It went straight to voicemail again and I left another message asking him to ring me. When I hung up the little screen said I'd missed a call from Kamal. At first I thought perhaps he was ringing about going to the cinema, but then I remembered that I hadn't got round to ringing him in the end. He'd left no message so I rang him back – maybe he'd found a publisher. He picked up on the second ring.

"George, I'm glad I caught you." He sounded anxious, not elated, and I could hear a lot of people noise in the background.

"What is it, Kamal?" I asked, skipping the banter.

"I'm at work, George," he said. "At Addenbrooke's," he added, unnecessarily. He was uncharacteristically hesitant and I could feel my heart pumping.

"Stop dithering, man, and give it to me straight."

"Your boy, Jason? Jason Pike?" He paused again and I shouted into the phone.

"What's happened to him, for fuck's sake?"

"I've just wheeled him up to the ward from A&E. Someone broke his fingers."

25

WHEN I GOT TO ADDENBROOKE'S HOSPITAL I HAD NO recollection of the journey itself except that it was raining hard all the way. I parked somewhere I wasn't allowed to and ran into the main entrance with my raincoat over my head. As promised Kamal was there in his porter's uniform. He filled me in as we walked up to the observation ward where Jason was being kept overnight.

"He had a couple of punches to the head, so it's just a precaution," Kamal explained.

"Is his mother here?" I asked.

"Yes, she got here when he was in A&E, that's how I knew who he was. He looked familiar but I remembered his mother from that barbecue you and erm…"

"You can say her name, Kamal; I've stopped blubbing whenever it's mentioned."

He smiled paternally and patted my shoulder. We stopped outside some double doors.

"He's in here. Oh, and there are a couple of coppers with him, taking a statement."

"Thanks for ringing me, we'll catch up soon," I said. We

embraced, as was his wont, and he went on his way. I took a deep breath before entering the ward.

It was easy to find Jason by the small crowd round his bed – two uniforms, a nurse and his mother. The side curtains were drawn to give an illusion of privacy. When I approached it seemed the police were winding up, one of them folding up his notebook and promising to look into things but there not being much to go on. The other uniform, female, looked at me as if I might be Jason's assailant come to have another go, and Sandra, well, Sandra just ignored me. And I mean she didn't even give me a glance. Jason was propped up against some pillows with his hands resting on his lap, three fingers on the left and two on the right with metal splints on and taped together. I'd pictured his fingers individually plastered up like big sausages, like in a cartoon. The nurse, who'd been waiting for the police to finish, was sticking a thermometer in Jason's mouth and holding his wrist. The police went off and Jason tried hard to give me a smile. A nasty-looking bruise was blooming on his temple, and his right cheek was cut and raised, with strips across the cut. I had an awkward minute as the nurse measured his pulse and Sandra ignored me. Jason rolled bloodshot eyes at her but she just sat there with her hand on his knee. I ignored her right back; she'd talk to me when she was ready to give me an earful. The nurse checked the thermometer and wrote something on the chart.

"I'll be back with painkillers. Are you his father?" she asked, addressing me.

I shook my head.

"Then you've got three minutes." I took her place beside Jason, my mac dripping onto the floor. I pointed to his fingers.

"How long will you be strapped up like that?" I asked.

"I'm not sure, a few weeks," he said.

"He won't be playing the keyboard for a while after that either," Sandra said, her voice dripping like an icicle.

"I'm more worried about other stuff I do with my hands," Jason said.

"George is more worried about who's going to take his beatings for him," she said.

"Mum!"

I turned to her, mustering up what assertiveness I could.

"I know you're itching to have a go at me, Sandra. But why don't you save it for when we're alone, like after I've talked to Jason?" There were a couple of seconds when Sandra glared at me, her eyes bright with anger. I kept eye contact and my nerve. She got up and kissed Jason on his good cheek.

"I'll see you in a few minutes, baby," she said gently, and walked off. I exhaled and turned to Jason.

"OK, now tell me what happened."

Jason and Lucy had finished lunch and then he'd walked with her to Emmanuel College, not ten minutes from the sandwich bar. It seems that they'd hit it off and were continuing their conversation afoot. He'd then walked over Parker's Piece to get to his college on East Road by which time it was getting dark. He was passing the small park on the right going down

East Road, opposite the fire station. After the park there is a church that houses a homeless shelter and a path beside the church leads into the park area, an area often frequented by winos waiting for the shelter to open. Someone called for him just as he was reaching the church. As I recalled the park had mature trees in it.

"At first I thought it was one of the winos wanting some money but a bloke grabbed me and punched me on the cheek. Then he dragged me into a doorway." He lifted a hand and pointed to his cut cheek. The guy must have had a ring on.

"Did you see him?" He shook his head.

"It was dark in there and it happened quickly. He was small and thin but like, impossibly strong. The weird thing was that he was wearing like a suit and tie. That's why I wasn't that worried at first when he called." He paused and smiled. "Never trust a guy in a fucking suit. Anyway, then he had me by the fingers and was pushing them back until I was on my knees with the pain. His other hand was over my mouth to stop me…" He pointed to the water on the cabinet by his bed. I poured some and held it to his mouth. He sipped at it and nodded to indicate he was done and I could remove the glass.

"I wasn't ready for the pain, boss." His eyes teared up and I put a hand on his shoulder. "He told me to stay away from Lucy Booker and let go of my mouth. That's when I told him to fuck off and he did the other hand." He lifted the hand in question in case I was in any doubt.

"Then he said to pass on the message to you and had I got it."

"He mentioned me by name?"

"Yes, but he couldn't pronounce it of course."

"What did he sound like?"

"Essex born and bred. Heavy smoker by the sound and smell of it." My mystery caller from that afternoon. He hadn't lost any time between the threat and carrying it out. Perhaps he hadn't liked my telephone manner. "I didn't tell the police anything, boss, nothing about the case or Lucy Booker." I nodded, although I wasn't bothered whether the police knew. But Sandra and Jason had had their fill of the police from the time when her husband had been a professional criminal. One thing you didn't do if related to a criminal is tell the police anything, whether it benefited you or not. Sandra may have been glad when Jason's father had run off to Spain, but that didn't mean she helped the police get their hands on him and his money once he'd gone.

"I'll take care of it, Jason."

"I thought you might, boss." He relaxed back on his pillows as the nurse arrived with pills. She made him swallow them and drink some water, then he had to lean forward as she plumped his pillows.

"Get some rest now, they'll want your bed tomorrow." She nodded at me. "Your three minutes is up," she said firmly but not unkindly.

"I'm just going."

"Boss." His voice was weak and he was relaxed into the pillows.

"Yes, Jason."

"He got into that Subaru we saw in Royston. It was waiting at the bus stop on Mill Road."

"How the hell did you see him from where you were?"

"I followed him through the park," Jason said. "Before I fainted."

I found Sandra in the day room outside the ward. She was the only one there, standing close to the window and staring at the rain streaking down the glass. Someone had turned the lights off and the room was lit by the yellow street lights outside. I coughed. She didn't look round.

"You told me this job wasn't dangerous, George," she said. "I asked you specifically and you told me it wasn't. And now my baby is…" She gestured towards the ward and then put her hands to her face and bowed her head. I went to her and put my arm round her heaving shoulders. "You bastard," she sobbed. Then she turned and put her head in my shoulder and I held her properly as she cursed me some more, and again wondered if I'd provoked the caller into carrying out his threat.

Some minutes later we were sitting in the day room chairs, Sandra back to her no-nonsense self, me wondering how I could ever make things right.

"I'll find out who did this," I said. "In fact, you can help me find him." I took out my notebook and ripped out the page with the Subaru number plate on it. "See if you can weave your phone magic on this." Before I gave it to her I pulled out the envelope recovered from the Bookers' rubbish and wrote the PO box number underneath the number plate. "And see if you can get me an address for this. I think wherever the envelope comes from was important to Sylvia and Elliot Booker, and what is important to them is important to Quintin Boyd. He's the fucking puppeteer behind all this." She took it from me and nodded.

"I'll do it first thing tomorrow. What are you going to do?"

"I'm going to talk to Sylvia Booker; she's been less than candid with me and I need to know why."

26

I DIDN'T HAVE TO GO TO SYLVIA, BECAUSE SHE TURNED UP AT my house the following morning. But she was not my first female visitor after leaving Jason at the hospital.

My mood that evening was crap, and even the Night Nurse-sized whisky hadn't helped. I'd tried watching a DVD of *The Heroin Busters*, one of my favourites in my collection of *poliziotteschi* films, but it only served to remind me that Jason was lying in a hospital. I turned the film off after a while and paced up and down thinking about how I could tie Quintin Boyd to the thin man who'd broken Jason's fingers. The more I thought about it the better I felt about the police not knowing about the Quintin connection, because I really wanted to meet this thin man myself. An early night would help, and I'd got as far as putting my pyjamas on when the doorbell sounded. It was past midnight. A wet Stubbing was standing the other side of the front door, getting wetter as I watched.

"Going to bed?" she asked.

"Do you know what time it is?"

"Crime never sleeps, Kocky, if anything it wakes up

about now and starts having breakfast." I watched the rain bounce off her unprotected head and waited for her to state her business. "I spoke earlier to the constables who took your boy Jason's statement." Against my better judgement I ushered her in and closed the door, but stayed in the hall so she didn't get any ideas about being welcome. Her being at my house was becoming a bit of a habit.

"So why is CID interested in a few broken fingers?" I asked.

She looked me up and down and I realised that I was in my pyjamas – the second time in her presence. She wiped her face with a wet tissue and I considered offering her a dry towel. *Not* giving her a dry towel sat better with me. "I take an interest in whatever happens to you, George. I wondered if there was anything you wanted to share vis-à-vis the incident reported. The report said he claims he was attacked for no reason. What sort of sicko does that for no reason? It looks like either a punishment beating or a warning to me, Kocky. What do you think?"

"I think that either you fancy me and want to catch me in my pyjamas – which is why you keep turning up at odd hours – or that Brampton sent you here to poke around while she's tucked up with a hot water bottle planning her next career move using you as a stepping stone."

Stubbing reddened like a schoolgirl caught looking at drawings of naked men in an anatomy book.

"What I'd like to know," I continued, "is why she is so interested in Jason's well-being. Or, come to think of it, how she even knows Jason works for me." Stubbing pursed her thin mouth so that it almost disappeared. She pulled her car keys from her wet mac and went to the door.

"By the way, the post-mortem shows that Elliot Booker definitely killed himself, no sign of foul play or even alcohol or drugs. You're off the hook."

"You sound disappointed."

She twisted her mouth in what I took to be a smile. "Let's just say I was looking forward to getting to know you better down at Parkside." With that she gave me a wink and left.

I went to bed, and disturbingly I tossed and turned for a while thinking of Stubbing. Having a woman in the house at night, even if it was only Stubbing giving me abuse, reminded me of how long it had been since I'd been with a woman.

When Sylvia Booker rang the bell I was at my kitchen table enjoying my second piece of heavily buttered white toast which I washed down with sugared coffee. With Olivia gone I could at least enjoy white bread as toast again. She had refused to have it in the house and I had to endure wholemeal toast, which could never be the same. Thankfully I was dressed when I opened the door to Sylvia – I didn't mind Stubbing seeing me in my pyjamas, Sylvia I did. She joined me in the kitchen and sat at the Formica table undoing the large buttons on her black coat while I poured coffee. She looked round the kitchen.

"It's fantastic in here, it's like stepping back into the 1950s."

"I like it," I said. "I don't necessarily think new is better."

"Well I agree with you there, George. Elliot and I are..." She nearly went but maintained her composure. "Were keen collectors of antiques." I thought it impolite to point out that her antiques probably cost a fortune, mine just happened to be part of the house. She coughed and adopted a serious expression, one I imagined she reserved for charity board meetings. "I heard about the boy who works for you, Jason is it?"

I nodded.

"I'm sorry. I just wanted to offer any assistance I could. If he needs to be seen by a surgeon I know the top orthopaedic chap at Addenbrooke's." Of course she did, but why would she care enough about Jason to come out to Chesterton?

"How did you hear about it?"

"Through Lucy; she contacted him last night to tell him about some party, texted him or something. She, ah, told me that she'd been to see you, to ask about Elliot." At this she looked at me with an unarticulated question and I understood her real reason for coming here. I was tempted to let her sweat but she'd already been through enough.

"Don't worry, I didn't tell her anything. I do have a code of conduct when it comes to respecting client confidentiality."

She shrugged as if my reassurance was unnecessary but I could tell she was relieved. She said she'd told Lucy I'd done some work for one of her charities. We synchronised stories then drank more coffee.

"Did Lucy tell you why Jason had been attacked?" I asked.

"No," she said. Trust Jason not to tell Lucy.

"Because we were following her. It was a warning."

She looked shocked, her lovely mouth actually dropped open. I thought it a good time to pounce.

"Why didn't you tell me that you knew Quintin Boyd?"

She did a great deal of foot shuffling and looking at manicured fingers and then something came over her face, perhaps relief at being caught out, or something else I couldn't read. She turned her turquoise eyes on me.

"Yes. I'm really sorry, George. I knew him at university, as did Elliot. I should have told you from the start but I didn't want it to be the issue. The issue for me is his relationship with Lucy." She fiddled with her wedding ring. "Elliot kept in contact with Quintin after university, they did some business. I think he made some investments based on Quintin's advice."

"Are those the ones that went bad?"

"Possibly. I wasn't privy to bursary business. In fact it bored me."

"When's the last time you saw Quintin?" She moved her gaze to the window and then back at me.

"Not since graduation." Not a flicker. I filed that lie for later and tried a new tack.

"Since you knew him why didn't you just ask him about his relationship with Lucy? Or get Elliot to ask him?"

She shook her head quickly.

"I couldn't have asked Elliot to do that. He would have been terribly upset if he knew Quintin was seeing Lucy."

She stood up to go, ignoring the part of my question about why she didn't ask Quintin herself. "Listen, once again I'm really sorry about Jason. If you need anything let me know. I now feel a certain responsibility." She went to the door then stopped. "Do the police know about the connection with Lucy?"

"By the police I assume you mean DCI Judith Brampton?"

She tried to look confused.

"She was at university with you as well, wasn't she?"

She exhaled. "Yes, yes she was."

"In answer to your question, no, she doesn't, as far as I know, although she seemed interested enough to despatch her flying monkey last night to see what information she could get."

"What did you tell them?"

"Like I said, code of conduct, client confidentiality."

"Of course, of course. I'm sorry, George, I'm just..." She curled her fingers as if grasping something that could not be verbalised. I walked her to the door; outside a weak sun was trying hard to dry the street.

As she stepped out I remembered the other thing I wanted to ask.

"Sylvia?" She stopped and turned. It sounded odd, saying her name out loud, like it was the first time I'd done it. "At Morley you all belonged to something called the Cambridge Blue Club. What was it?" She showed nothing on her face but her answer came a little quick.

"It was just a film club, something that Quintin set up. We had weekly screenings. Why do you ask?"

"It was a common factor between you, that's all."

"I don't think it's of relevance. How did you find out about it?"

"It was on the Morley alumni's website. Didn't you provide the details?"

She shook her head. "I don't think so, it wasn't a big part of my life at university. Anyway, I need to get off." She started to walk away again.

"What sort of films did you watch?"

She stopped and turned again. "Pardon me?"

"I asked what sort of films did you watch?"

She looked annoyed and shrugged. "A variety. Fellini, Buñuel, Bergman. The usual film student fare."

"Did that include pornographic films?"

She couldn't help looking around to see if anyone had heard me. "I'm sorry?"

"Well, it's called the Cambridge Blue Club so I just assumed..."

She sighed and her shoulders dropped.

"Well, occasionally Quintin would screen something a little more risqué. We were young, we thought it was, ah, cool."

"Of course," I said. I smiled and nodded to indicate that I didn't care if they watched the odd skin flick. She seemed about to say something else but decided against it and walked off to her Mini. I watched her walk all the way to the car; she looked different now that I knew this about her.

The phone rang as I closed the door and I picked up with a jaunty "hello".

"Oh hi. It's Megan, from the care home? I got your message."

"Ah yes, you had some information for me, Megan."

"Yes, I didn't want to leave a message with the woman at your office, I didn't know who she was." I told her she'd done the right thing. "Anyway, I spoke to Angela, who was on duty that day, and she said that the man didn't give a name and stayed like five minutes. The only thing she remembers is that he wore a suit and was very thin. Also, she told him off for lighting up on the premises. Does that ring a bell?"

"Yes it does," I said, genuinely. It was the man who'd attacked Jason. My guts churned at the thought that he'd been alone with my baby-like father.

"Listen Megan, it would be good to know in future if he calls on my father. Not everyone appreciates his mental state and that he might not recognise them and could be upset. In fact it would be great if I could be told when they are there, not afterwards."

"Of course, of course."

She went on about how she would let Angela know as well and then talked about policies and procedures at the home and I listened dutifully, then thanked her for going to all the effort. This uncorked a gushing stream about how fond she was of my father and nothing was too much trouble, and that I could ring her any time if I was worried or just wanted a chat. I hung up, wondering whether I gave off vibes indicating that I needed a chat.

27

SANDRA WAS ON THE PHONE WHEN I ENTERED MY OFFICE. SHE was saying, in a flirty voice I'd not heard before, "Thank you, Luke, you've been very helpful." She listened to something Luke was saying and made eyes at me. Then, to my amazement, she giggled into the receiver. "You naughty boy, Luke, you've made me blush. Bye now. No, I really need to go." She hung up and wrote on a pad.

"I hope you're not using the office for your other line of work," I said.

She gave me a murderous look and ripped off the sheet from the pad. "That was Luke from the DVLC. He thinks I'm a twenty-something blonde airhead." She handed me the sheet. "This is the owner of the Subaru, one Mark Stillgoe." The note showed an address in Haverhill.

"Quintin's driver is called Mark, I bet even money that this is him."

"You better get on it then."

I looked at her. "How's Jason?"

"He'll be out today but stuck at home for a few weeks. It's going to be difficult to sound sexy on the phone if I know he can hear me." I sat at my desk and wondered if I should tell her that Jason had already heard her. Not really my place, I decided. "Well if you wanted to use the office…"

She smiled. "Thanks, sweetheart, but I've got a dedicated number set up at home and it would be too complicated to get it transferred. Although, imagine how it would go down with the rest of the building."

"They would hold a meeting." I went through my post. There being nothing of interest I put it down.

"I wouldn't have used Jason on the case if I'd suspected it was dangerous. You know that, right?"

"Yes, George," she sighed, "I know that. Let's just nail the bastard that did it."

"Did you have any luck with that PO box I gave you last night?" She rooted round on her desk.

"Yes. I've got an address from the Post Office but no name or anything. It's just a unit number in the Science Park."

"The Science Park? OK, maybe I'll pop there on the way to…" I checked the sheet she'd just given me, "…Haverhill."

I recounted my conversation with the woman who'd been in Quintin's apartment.

"Was she a pro?" Sandra asked, when I told her what she'd said about Quintin getting his take. I recalled the prostitutes I'd come across in the course of my work.

"Could be. She had that hardness about her, you know, but I couldn't really say."

"I could tell you, if I met her."

"You think he's a pimp?"

She shrugged and said, "She was there all night

though, it doesn't really add up."

"Maybe he uses the flat as a brothel. Maybe he likes to watch." She cackled at that and the phone went. It was Addenbrooke's. Jason would be ready to go home in an hour. I suggested we go to the Science Park together and then I would drop her off at Addenbrooke's on my way to Haverhill.

To pass the time driving across town I told her about Sylvia's visit that morning.

"Well, well, who'd have thought little miss Booker had it in her. Do you think they called it the Cambridge Blue Club when they only watched the odd porn film?"

"Not really. Maybe it was the main purpose of the club, maybe the sole purpose."

"Exactly. But why put it on the website? It's not the kind of thing those sort of people want to advertise, is it?"

"I wondered that. She claimed she didn't offer the information."

With Sandra's help I found the right road. I could sense her studying me as we pulled into a car park outside a utilitarian unit.

"You get a kick out of it, don't you? Admit it," she said.

"What are you talking about?"

"I'm talking about the gorgeous Sylvia watching porn films giving you a thrill."

I gave her a smile that I hoped conveyed my contempt as I got out of the car.

* * *

I had only been to the Science Park once before, when I was hired by a management consultancy firm who suspected one of their partners of fiddling his expenses. It turned out he was, using the money to finance a mistress on the side. The guy kept his job and I was made to sign a confidentiality agreement despite declaring my investigator's code of conduct. I studied the buildings before me, one of three on this road, all one storey, a seven-foot layer of brick, then a layer of steel-reinforced window, then corrugated iron topped with a flat roof. More industrial units than offices, each a thousand square metres at most. This was the less glamorous area of the Science Park, not the glass and steel edifice of a management consultancy. No clues as to what went on inside from where I was standing so I looked for the entrance of the right unit. What I was looking for was a sign. And there it was on the first set of frosted glass double doors. One of them had my spiral staircase on it; the other had the words 'Legacy Labs'. I couldn't really reconcile the two things, nor was there any clue as to what Legacy Labs did. I wrote the name down in my notebook.

I asked myself how best to approach things. I could go in and bluff it, or I could go look Legacy Labs up back in the comfort of the office, and at least know what I was dealing with. I tried the door but it was closed, probably for lunch. That deciding things, I rejoined Sandra.

I dropped her off at the hospital, taking some cash out of my wallet.

"This is for a taxi home. I'll charge it to the gorgeous Sylvia."

She took the cash, saying, "Your secret is safe with me, sweetheart."

It was scary how well she could read me, it really was.

I continued out of Cambridge to Haverhill, travelling through the Gogs and past the car park where Trisha Greene had been found topless and dead. I hadn't given her or her husband Al Greene much thought since becoming involved in Sylvia and her world. A world apart, the Bookers and the Greenes. Once I'd left Cambridgeshire for Suffolk I stopped to fill up with petrol and bought an *Argus* and a sandwich.

Parked in a lay-by I looked for an update on the Greene case but found nothing. There was a small item on Elliot Booker, whose funeral was to take place the next afternoon. It said that the college had decided that it would go ahead with the alumni lunch on Sunday because of the number of people who had already made travel arrangements to attend from abroad. Quintin Boyd, as keynote speaker, was quoted as saying he was heartbroken at the news of Elliot's death as he was a 'personal friend', and that he thought the lunch would be a good way to celebrate Elliot's contribution to Morley College. I read all this as I ate my petrol-station sandwich with soggy prawn filling.

I found Mark Stillgoe's address easily enough and cruised past the 1980s semi. I saw no Subaru in the driveway or on the street so I parked pointing the way I'd come. Retrieving my clipboard and fake charity badge from the back seat I went to the front door. It was a PVC door like the windows, which had mock bars in the panes to make them look like they were panelled. I rang the doorbell and Big Ben chimed inside. Someone shuffled up to the door and it opened to reveal a woman in her late fifties. Despite it being the middle of the afternoon she wore a green dressing gown with matching slippers. The whole outfit crackled with static. I was struck by the smell of cigarette smoke, fresh upon stale. A new source of smoke hung from her lip like a protruding tooth on the proverbial witch. She squinted at me through the blue haze, a slack look on a prematurely aged face.

"What is it?" she said, without removing the cigarette. I flashed my fake charity ID at her.

"I'm just doing a survey on behalf of Save Our Trees. Is Mark Stillgoe in?"

"Nah, Mark's at work."

"OK, what time is he likely to be back?"

"It don't matter, since he don't care about saving trees."

"Well maybe you can help me. Can you tell me his occupation?"

"Who is it?" said a male voice from within the house. An Essex voice, a raspy Essex voice. A voice I'd heard on the phone only the previous afternoon, a voice identified by Jason. The woman turned her head to address it.

"It's just someone collecting for charity," she shouted.

"Well fucking get rid of them, you're letting in the cold." She turned back to me and started to close the door, without as much as a goodbye. Some people are so rude. I stuck my foot in the opening. She looked confused.

"What the fuck are you doing?" she asked.

"Coming in," I said. "Saving trees is important." I pushed past her into the narrow hall.

"What the fuck's going on?" That voice, coming from the end of the hall, from what looked like the kitchen. I strode towards the open door where a man appeared, a thin runt of a man. Braces held his trousers up and he too had a lit cigarette dangling from his narrow lips. It was clearly the way to smoke in Haverhill. At least he removed his to speak.

"Who the fuck are you?"

"I want to talk to you about where you were yesterday evening." His eyes narrowed and his right hand went to his trouser pocket. I noticed a big ring on his middle finger, a gold coin mounted in a claw.

"Who the fuck are you again?" he said. He took his hand from his pocket but I couldn't see anything in it.

"You remember breaking someone's fingers yesterday? A young lad, long hair?" His wrist moved and a narrow blade shot from his fist. Then his eyes flicked behind me and I remembered my back was to the woman. I turned just in time to see her with a baseball bat over her head that was about to start its downward swing. I put my palm, fingers spread, into her face, pushing her out of the way. I didn't see the fag in her mouth and her face appeared to emit a shower of sparks, my palm stinging on the lit end. She let out a muffled yelp of surprise. I didn't turn to see what the thin man would do with his blade but I stepped past the woman and headed for the open door. Something caught the back of my jacket but

I didn't stop. It was only when I was on the pavement that I looked behind me and saw the thin man standing in the doorway, his eyes glinting like the blade he was wielding. We stared at each other for a few seconds then he closed the door carefully as if he didn't want to disturb the neighbours. I could feel a wetness at my back but I got in the car and drove straight to Kamal's without daring to check it.

28

KAMAL'S CURRENT FLATMATE, AN IRAQI JUNIOR DOCTOR AT Addenbrooke's, stitched up my shoulder with four of his best while I sat, stripped to the waist, the wrong way round on a chair, resting my forearms on the back. We were in Kamal's room in a small flat over a Chinese supermarket on Mill Road. One of his walls was decorated with floor to ceiling paperbacks, one had a bed against it, the third had hooks in the wall with coat hangers on them and served as storage for his meagre wardrobe. The fourth had a desk and chair under the window and it was here that I sat looking at the ancient laptop that Kamal wrote on and gritting my teeth with every new puncture of flesh – there was no anaesthetic. Kamal supplemented his income by subletting a room in his flat to a succession of Arab medical students.

The thin man had sliced through my raincoat, jacket, shirt, vest and skin, leaving a three-inch-long gash in the lower right shoulder. Kamal was wittering on instead of refilling my glass with Jack Daniels, and he was beginning to get on my nerves. For the son of Palestinian exiles I always expected him to take a dim view of authority, or at least to be wary of it, but he had spent the last couple of hours bemoaning the fact that I hadn't gone to the police. I'd explained that I'd come to him rather than going to Addenbrooke's precisely because I wanted to avoid the police. Doctors were required to report knife crime and I didn't want to risk a protracted explanation to the police of what I was doing in the Haverhill house. The woman had only to say I had forced my way in and punched her in the face. And the thin man had only to say that he was defending her from my vicious attack and for there never to have been a baseball bat. The tables would be turned on me in no time. Despite Kamal's nagging he'd done the right thing and called in his flatmate who told me he perfected his sewing technique by practising at the kitchen table on pork skin.

"I don't eat it myself," he said, tugging at some thread and causing me to wince.

"Religious, eh?"

"No, I just don't like the taste."

He tied off the last stitch and dressed the closed wound. He told me I should get it changed tomorrow and the stitches would need to come out in a week. I thanked him and he said it was nothing. He went off with his medic's bag; he had a night shift to get through.

"Why don't you pour me some more of your whisky?" I said to Kamal.

"Because you've had enough and I have to make it last. What you need is something to eat."

"You can't cook and I'm not going out. How about a takeaway?" We settled on Chinese and I gave him enough of

Sylvia's money to buy food and a bottle of Jack Daniels as well as a bottle of whisky for his flatmate.

"He does drink, doesn't he?" I asked.

"Like Captain Haddock," Kamal said.

While he was out I rang Sandra to check on Jason. She said he was fine if a little bored. I told her that she should get me out of doing the DWP case as things had escalated. She reluctantly agreed, moaning about losing what could be regular income. Then I told her about my trip to Haverhill and subsequent adventures.

"Maybe you should go to the police, George. This bastard sounds a little dangerous."

"Going to the police means involving Stubbing and Brampton, as they seem to have taken an interest in me, and I'm convinced our knife-carrying finger-breaking friend belongs to Quintin, who is a university friend of Brampton's."

"It doesn't mean they are in cahoots."

"I know, but they studied together and watched porn together so I'm guessing she'd not be happy with me linking him with crims just days before he gives the keynote at the alumni lunch."

"Speaking of alumni and porn, I looked up that website again to see if I could find any other ex-members of the Cambridge Blue Club. I thought I might find someone local we could talk to, get a clearer picture of what they got up to."

"Good idea. How did you get on?"

"Well, the thing is, the site was down for maintenance

until about an hour ago and then when I managed to get back on it again all references to the club had gone. It had just disappeared from everyone's entry." I looked at Kamal's books and felt the throbbing in my shoulder. "George, you still there?"

"Yes. I'm guessing it was probably Sylvia got onto whoever runs the site to take it off. Wants to protect her image I guess."

"And Elliot's," Sandra said. I heard Kamal come in and turned to look at him, yelping as I sent a tearing pain through my wound. "You all right, love?" Sandra said in my ear.

"Yes, just moved the wrong way. Say hi to Jason; I'll pop round to see him tomorrow."

"He'll like that. You need anything, you let me know. I can nurse two blokes as easily as one."

I put one of Kamal's blue porter shirts on and we ate in the small kitchen. After swallowing painkillers with my Kung Po chicken the pain began to ease. After dinner I gave Kamal a general overview of the case, without naming names. When he'd heard my summary he thought for a bit, running his finger up and down his impressive nose. Once, having had too much to drink, we'd measured our noses to see whose was bigger. It was mine.

"I have a question," he said.

"What's that?"

"This glamorous woman is overprotective of her daughter, correct?"

I nodded.

"Yet when you tell her who the daughter is seeing she does not reveal that she already knows this man?"

I nodded.

"Why is this, do you think?"

I recalled how Sylvia had recoiled from Quintin at the railway station. I'd seen no love there but it didn't mean it hadn't existed at some point.

"Because she's afraid of what he might want with the daughter, of his motive for seeing her. She tried to see him soon after her husband killed himself, and they didn't get on from what I could see. Let's say they were an item when they were at university. Maybe she jilted him in favour of the guy she married. Maybe she's worried he's getting his revenge on her through her daughter."

"A lot of maybes there, my friend. But there is something missing: what is she so afraid of with this man – what is he again, a lawyer? Why doesn't she just tell the daughter the truth? If she just told her that she used to date this man it would put the girl off, no?"

"That I don't know. Maybe she's worried the daughter would get a kick out of it, use it to get back at her mother."

"Get back at her why?"

"For being her mother."

He chuckled. "Maybe you should be the writer."

"I learnt something else on Tuesday," I said. I told him about the film club and he conceded that a woman as worried about her image as Sylvia would be embarrassed about such a thing.

"I can't help feeling there's something missing though. This guy with the knife seems a bit over the top."

"I agree with you there." He studied me and smiled.

"I can see you've got that glint in your eye – I've seen it before. Your interest is piqued, is it not?"

"Let's say I'm more curious this evening than I was this morning."

We batted it back and forth for a while without much result except finishing the first bottle of Jack Daniels, but it was good to use him as a sounding board. Sometimes he could be a bit earnest, like when he banged on about me not being in touch with my Armenian roots, but he was a good listener. In return I gave him an opportunity to moan about the lack of balls in the publishing industry until it grew late and I grew weary. When I stood up to go to the bathroom I knew I had drunk too much to drive home.

"Best for you to stay here tonight," Kamal said. "I'll set up the sofa bed."

The sofa bed took up all of the living room when laid out, and I'd stayed on it a few times before quite happily, especially in the days after Olivia had left.

I can't say I slept well; it was impossible to lie on my back due to the pain. And I can't sleep on my front even if I haven't been knifed. I must have drifted off to sleep at some point though because I had lurid half-dreams of the woman in the green dressing gown wielding a baseball bat and a thin man with a blade emerging from his fist. They were both smoking cigarettes and laughing as they approached me from front and back.

* * *

I woke on my front and covered in sweat to find Kamal's flatmate in the room with his medic's bag.

"Sorry to wake you. I've come to check your wound. I just got back from my shift and was going to bed but I saw you in here..."

"Of course. Help yourself."

"Please, stay as you are." He pulled up a chair and peeled off the dressing to have a look.

"I'm very grateful for your help," I said.

"It was no problem. Thank you for the whisky, it was very generous."

"Least I could do. Ouch."

"Sorry. I brought you some codeine from the hospital, you might find it helpful at night. Also, a course of antibiotics and some sterile dressings. The wound looks OK but you need to keep it clean and dry. Do you have someone who can change the dressing?"

"Yes," I said, thinking of Sandra. "I have someone."

29

MY CAR HAD A FROSTY TICKET ON IT BECAUSE I'D PARKED IN A residential bay the previous afternoon, not really caring at the time. It took me several minutes to clear the screen of ice using a credit card that had no available credit on it and using the arm connected to my good shoulder. The back of the driver's seat boasted an espresso saucer-sized blood stain, as did my raincoat, jacket, shirt and vest, increasing until it was the size of a side plate on my vest. Kamal had washed, dried and ironed the last two items overnight, which is when he did most of his writing and washing. He'd even, bless him, had a go at cleaning my jacket and raincoat, but it was a dry-cleaning job.

The car didn't have time to heat up in the time it took me to drive to the office – the best place, I thought, to think about what to do next.

Outside my building Stubbing was hunched against the cold, a sensible shoulder bag at her feet. It was too early for anyone to be in yet.

"Are you stalking me?" I asked.

She shook her head.

"What, no comeback?"

She gave me a tired smile.

"Do you want coffee?" I asked.

"That would be a life-saver."

We walked round to Antonio's who told me that it would be a few minutes before he could get his ancient coffee machine (imported from Turin by his father in 1965) up and running. We took our coats off and sat down at the back of the café.

"What happened to your coat?" she asked.

"I caught it on something," I said.

"What, a sword?"

"You wanted to see me?"

"Yes, I went to your house and then came to the office." She tightened her ponytail, something I didn't think possible. My wound was starting to throb.

"Is this about Jason again? Because I've nothing to add to what I said the other night."

She examined her bitten nails then said, "It's about the Trisha Greene case."

"I've nothing more to say about that either," I said. Gurgling and hissing sounds came from Antonio's espresso machine. She clasped her bony fingers together on the table and looked me in the eye.

"You gave us some evidence relating to the murder in the Gogs car park. You know, the tracker details and dogging photos?"

"Yes of course."

"Well, they've gone."

"They've what?"

She looked round to see if Antonio had heard my exclamation, but he was busy grinding coffee.

"How can they have gone?"

"The tracking details and the photos have gone," she repeated, in lieu of an explanation.

I shook my head and laughed. "Brampton must be livid."

Stubbing's face remained impassive and she said nothing.

"They got copied onto a computer or something, didn't they, the photos? I thought it would go to the techies. How do they disappear?"

Antonio came over with some good-smelling coffee. As he placed the cups on the table Stubbing and I eyed them like dogs eyeing bowls full of chopped sirloin being lowered to the floor. We waited for Antonio to head back to the counter.

"Well?" I asked.

She squinted at me through the steam rising from her cup.

"The memory stick was blank apparently, when the technical guys looked at it," she said.

"What? I checked it after I'd put the files on it. Everything was there."

"I'm not saying it wasn't." I looked at her for clues but she remained emotionless. Then I thought about the time frame.

"But I gave it to you over a week ago. Surely it was checked before now?"

"It seems the techies didn't get it the day you came in, and then they had other priorities, like checking hard drives for child porn. Then I got caught up with Elliot Booker's suicide, remember? Look, we're facing cutbacks like every other public body, and we didn't have unlimited people to start with."

I shook my head in disbelief. "But this is a murder case."

"Yes, but we have already charged the husband, remember."

"So what do you want with me?"

"Copies."

"You want copies?"

"Yes please." She sipped coffee and said, her tone level, "Do you have any other photos you took, or notes that you didn't give us to start with?"

I shook my head. "I gave you everything. I'm happy to go through them with you. You can even have the scribbles I made when I followed her around; they're in the file in the office." Something was nagging me about her request. "I don't really understand – why are you bothered about the photos if you've already charged the husband? You have his belt which was round her neck."

"We do," she said, "but the photos would help."

"So you still have a case then?"

She nodded and leaned forward. "Listen to me, George, I need to get hold of any information you have on Trisha Greene, even if you think it's not relevant." It was the first time she'd called me George. My wound had progressed from throbbing to sharp pain; I'd forgotten about it with all my gesticulating. I don't know why I was getting worked up, it wasn't really my problem.

"OK, let's go to the office. Have you got something to copy the files onto?"

She patted her shoulder bag.

"I've brought my own portable drive."

Hills Road was now busy with nine-to-fivers arriving for work, dragging themselves out of bed into the dark and wet morning to face the daily drudge – young men and women in cheap suits. Nina was outside the front door of my building as we got to it. She was in jeans under her mac and I conjured up a brief image of her changing into her white coat upstairs. She regarded Stubbing with open hostility as she put her key in the mortise lock, perhaps wondering why we were arriving together so early in the morning. But then I remembered that they'd met when Stubbing had come looking for me and upset waiting clients.

"Morning, George. A bit early for you isn't it?"

"The early worm gets the bird," I said, and wished I hadn't.

Nina contemplated Stubbing, who gave her the paint-stripping stare. Nina seemed to be struggling with the mortise lock and turned to the door to take out the key. "Whoever was last out of here yesterday didn't double-lock the door."

She put her Yale key in the cylinder lock and the door opened. We trooped inside and I put the door on the latch. Nina grabbed my arm as I ushered Stubbing up the narrow stairs before me.

"We still on for tonight then?" Shit. I'd forgotten all about it.

"Of course we are." She smiled and I wondered if she'd had her teeth whitened. She touched my hand.

"Eight o'clock. Bring one of your films," she said, and the way she said it sent a nice shiver down my spine.

Stubbing was waiting at the top of the stairs. She wasn't smirking, even though she'd witnessed our brief interaction. I led the way to my office and took my keys out.

I didn't need them. The door was open. Crowbarred open by the looks of it. Stubbing stepped in front of me.

"Don't touch anything," she said. She took a biro from her jacket and eased the door open with it then used it to flick on the light.

The place was a shambles. The computer monitor thrown to the floor, the actual computer box opened up, its insides a mess of wires and electronics. The lockable filing cabinet had been forced open too, files scattered everywhere. I could smell stale cigarette smoke. I went to the small safe; it had been bashed but not opened. I started to pick up the files and put them on the desk; then I noticed the opened drawers.

"Is anything missing?" she asked.

I couldn't find the digital cameras – both were gone, including the expensive infrared Fuji I'd used for night-time shots of Trisha Greene.

"It's not the only thing that's gone," she said. She was standing over Sandra's desk looking into the computer's innards. I couldn't see what she was so interested in.

"What is it?"

"Someone has removed the hard drive. Is there a backup?"

"I think so," I said, remembering Jason muttering about

doing one, but a search revealed nothing.

"They probably took that too," Stubbing said.

"I'd better check to see if anyone else has been burgled."

Stubbing was dry-washing her face with her hands.

"No, nobody else will have been burgled," she said. "Do you have a printout of Trisha's car movements from the tracker?"

"Good thinking; they're with the notes I told you about." I looked through the files on the floor and found the Greenes'. I grinned triumphantly and held it up for Stubbing to see. The grin fell from my face when I opened it – it was empty.

30

"AT LEAST I WON'T NEED TO RING THE POLICE, SINCE YOU'RE here," I said to Stubbing after she'd poked around a bit and I'd established that the tracker was also missing.

"I'd rather the police weren't involved," she said, with no suggestion of irony.

"Why not? What about scene of crime techies?"

"I don't think looking for fingerprints is going to yield anything. Besides, it's hardly good publicity for you, is it?"

She had a point. "So what are you going to do?"

"I don't know yet, but I need some time to find out, preferably without the whole of Parkside knowing."

"You think this was someone from Parkside?"

"I didn't say that."

"What's going on, Stubbing?" Her face went blank and she made for the door. I told her I was going to need a crime number for the insurance. She said she'd sort one out.

When she'd gone I started to clear up but my heart wasn't in it and I couldn't really do much because of my shoulder.

The only person who would be interested in the pictures I'd taken of Trisha Greene would be the person who had really killed her. The only people who had seen them were the police, except now they were saying they hadn't seen them. This did not bode well. Too much was happening at once. I decided to head home – I needed a change of underwear and time to think.

On the way home I remembered that Elliot Booker's funeral was taking place that afternoon. In true detective style I thought I would go out there to see who turned up. I particularly wanted a closer look at Quintin Boyd, perhaps even to speak to him and Sylvia together.

At home I had a half-filled bath that I couldn't lie down in. I shaved and tried to look at my wound in the mirror, but was relieved when I couldn't see it. I made a pot of coffee and a pile of toast. Then I switched on my computer and took out my notebook – Legacy Labs was the last entry. I typed it into Google, adding a plus sign and 'Cambridge' to it to narrow it down – something Jason had taught me. I hit the return button and was rewarded with a short list. I chose the one at the top.

One click and there it was, Legacy Labs, based in the Science Park. Specialising in confidential DNA testing by post. You ordered the tests online: paternity, ancestry, relationship and even tests to prove the pedigree of your dog. They sent you a kit, you took some swabs and sent it back. Then they posted you the results. It was that simple. I was an idiot – the logo wasn't a bloody spiral staircase, it was a DNA symbol. I sat back in my chair and barked with pain.

But why had Elliot Booker ordered a DNA test? It seemed unlikely he was trying to trace his ancestry, so it had to be about Lucy. This must be the reason for his and Sylvia's argument that night. Was it because she wasn't his daughter? Why else would one have a test done? I took the envelope from my jacket, in case it offered up more clues. My mind was wild with speculation but I needed facts. There was a phone number on the website but I doubted they would give out any information that way. I could have given it to Sandra, the queen of the phone, but I felt I needed to do this myself. I would have to go back down there when they were open and see what I could find out.

On my way to the Science Park I called in at Sandra's to see how Jason was getting on. But Jason was asleep, doped up on painkillers, so I told Sandra about the break-in at the office.

"So what were they after?" she said. I'd brought a bag of doughnuts with me and some sweets for Ashley, but Sandra had immediately confiscated them as he was about to have what Sandra called dinner, or what Olivia called lunch. He'd only just stopped sniffling and came to settle in her lap. She stroked his hair and he looked at me dreamily. "Just like his father," she said. I wasn't sure whether this was a compliment or not. Ashley's father had disappeared one week into his new child's life. He was another bloke I'd tracked down for Sandra and he now paid child support from his intermittent earnings as a bouncer.

"So tell me, what were they after?"

"Evidence from the Greene case, it looks like. They weren't exactly subtle about it either. The place is a mess." She said she would get it sorted out next morning and we talked about what we could put on the insurance claim.

"Who would be so interested in the Greene case apart from the Greenes?" she asked.

"Whoever killed Trisha Greene," I said. "There must have been something there for them to be worried about." She was going to say something but Ashley demanded that she stroke his head some more. When he'd stopped whining I asked, "Did you do backups, Sandra?"

She frowned in concentration. "It happened automatically I think. Jason set it up. Wasn't there an external drive on the desk by the computer?" I tried to remember if I'd seen it but couldn't – anyway, if it had been there it had gone this morning. "So we've lost everything?" she said.

"All the paper files seem to be there, apart from the Greene stuff obviously."

"There's a lot of other stuff though, on the computer I mean. Accounts and contacts. A lot of personal client details, George. It's a bloody disaster." She was right, but I wasn't sure what we could do about it. I got up to go. "Will you be back later? I'll change your dressing and you can stay for dinner. Jason will be sorry he missed you."

I didn't tell her I was having dinner with Nina. Maybe more than dinner if I was lucky. "Can I come by tomorrow?" I looked down at her stroking Ashley's head.

"Come by when you like, George," she said, without looking up.

* * *

At the Science Park I stood outside Legacy Labs and mulled over how to play it. Now that I was here I wasn't sure about what I was hoping to achieve, except to get some source material rather than relying on what people were telling me. I stepped into reception, praying that they didn't know Elliot was dead.

"Hello, can I help you?" A twenty-something receptionist gave me a smile she'd learnt on a customer care course. She sat behind a glass and steel desk on which rested a screen, a keyboard, an open copy of a celebrity magazine and a pink mobile phone. She had what Sandra called a muffin-top stomach; it bulged between the top of her trousers and the bottom of her shirt. There was a giant version of the DNA logo on the wall behind her and there were pictures of smiling families on the wall. Not just smiling but the unnaturally happy show-your-teeth type of grinning you saw on the back of cereal boxes and vitamin packets – I lived in a world where the nuclear family was considered the standard; anything else was a deviation. The sound of an arriving text message came from the mobile phone on the desk and I swear the receptionist's hands twitched as she gave it a glance then remembered she was supposed to be interfacing with a customer.

"Can I help you?" she repeated, closing the magazine in front of her. I decided a dose of reciprocated insincerity might bear most fruit.

"I'm sure you can; you look like a helpful person. My name is Elliot Booker and I have a bit of a confession to make." I hesitated to see if she had read the Cambridge *Argus* and knew that Elliot was dead, but nothing registered on the foundation-plastered face. "It's a bit embarrassing though."

"That's OK, we get all sorts coming to us," she said, in an attempt to be reassuring; I suppose customer care courses can only go skin deep.

"I knew when I saw you that you were an understanding sort. You see I'm already a customer and you sent me a letter last weekend which I've stupidly lost. I was wondering if you could give me a copy, I need it for a legal document."

"Was it a kit or results?" I made a crazy guess, as she could have, that it was the latter, since it had come in an envelope.

"Results."

"What was your name again?" I gave her Elliot's name and the Morley College address and her glued-on nails clacked on the keyboard. Her mobile phone announced another text.

"There's nothing under that name, I'm afraid. Can you spell it for me." I spelled it for her but she still found nothing. I shifted so I could try and see the screen but she twisted it round on its stand and gave me a look like I'd tried to grope her. She narrowed her over-painted eyes.

"What is it?" I asked. "Have you found my results?"

"No, results don't come up on my screen. Have you got the reference number?"

"I lost the letter," I reminded her, trying to stay on her right side by giving her a nice smile.

"It'll be on the envelope, if you still have it." I took the envelope from my jacket and looked at it. There was no number on it, back or front, so I handed it over.

She studied it. "That's odd."

"What is?"

"Well, there's usually a reference number printed straight under the address so that it can be checked against the number on the results. Wouldn't want the wrong person getting them, would we now?" I chuckled with her at the idea of someone's results going to the wrong person.

"Perhaps there's been some mix-up," I said. She brightened at this obvious possibility.

"Yeah, that's right, a mix-up. I'll ring Mr Bloom, he'll know what to do." Before I could protest about the involvement of Mr Bloom she'd lifted the phone and dialled an internal number. While she waited she rubbed at the label on the envelope. "That's odd," she said. "Mr Bloom? Tania here. I've got a Mr Booker in reception but he's not on the system, even though he got a letter from us. The thing is there's no reference number…" She listened, pulling at the label until it started to come off. There was writing underneath. "Listen, Mr Bloom, there's something… what? Elliot, Elliot Booker, it's right here on the envelope, except I think there's a problem with the address, it's not—" She listened to some more of what Mr Bloom was saying and her eyes moved to me and became saucers. Her mouth dropped open and her voice dropped to a whisper. "But… that's impossible. He's standing right here in front of me… OK, Mr Bloom." She hung up. "Mr Bloom will be right out," she told me. "He'd like you to wait." It was time to leave; Mr Bloom was obviously a reader of the *Argus*.

"I can't wait I'm afraid." I held my hand out for the

envelope. She shook her head and clutched it purposefully to her bulging midriff.

"Mr Bloom said I should hang onto it."

"You do everything Mr Bloom tells you?"

Given there was no time to charm the envelope off her I thought about going round the desk and snatching it from her fingers but it could have turned ugly so I left before having to explain myself to the mysterious Mr Bloom.

As I drove away from Legacy Labs I looked in the mirror and saw an obese man in an ill-fitting lab coat and a comb-over emerge from the unit. He watched me drive up to the end of the road. Unfortunately I had to stop at the junction to give way to traffic which gave him enough time to write down my licence number.

31

ELLIOT'S CREMATION WAS BEING HELD OFF THE HUNTINGDON Road not three miles up from Morley College. I parked in the busy car park about two-thirty and scanned for Sylvia's Mini. I couldn't see it but did see the silver Mercedes with Mark the driver leaning against the door smoking. He was wearing his uniform, and looked round guiltily when he heard me approach on the gravel, like he wasn't supposed to smoke. He relaxed a bit when he saw me and glanced back across the green slope that led to the crematorium. He wasn't as gym-buff as I'd first thought from afar. He used to be but he'd let himself go. When I reached him he stared at me and I wondered if he recognised me from Royston or outside Quintin's apartment. He had the same slackness of expression I'd seen on the woman who'd opened the door to me at his house.

"Is the Elliot Booker funeral still going on? I'm supposed to pick someone up." He flicked his cigarette onto the well-groomed grass bank at the side of the car park and I resisted the urge to go and pick it up and put it out on his shaved head.

"Yeah, they're still at it, be another fifteen minutes I

guess." He had the same nasal voice as the woman at his house. He studied me some more. "Do I know you, mate?"

"Not really, no." I pointed at the Merc. "Nice car. Is it yours?"

"Nah, it's a rental. I just do the driving. What about you?"

"Me? I just run a taxi, mate, nothing flash like this. Don't have to wear a uniform though." He squirmed as if reminded how uncomfortable his outfit was.

"The company insist on it, so do the people renting. Makes them feel big, know what I mean?"

I nodded sympathetically. "What do you drive yourself then, when you're not in this?"

"I've got a Subaru Impreza 2.5 WRX," he said, full of pride. He checked me expectantly for a positive reaction. I obliged by emitting a low whistle.

"Has a spoiler, tinted windows?" I asked. He frowned.

"Yeah, how would you know?"

"Maybe I've seen it around," I said. His face took on the same expression of confusion the woman had when I'd door-stepped her. They must be related. She was old enough to be his mother. Bloody hell – I'd manhandled his mother. He stood up from the car and shuffled on his feet as if preparing to dance.

"I swear I know you from somewhere."

"No, we don't run in the same circle, you and I."

He looked at me with narrowed eyes.

"Where were you Wednesday evening?" I asked.

"What?"

"Wednesday evening, you picked up a guy in a suit from

the bus stop at the Parker's Piece end of Mill Road. Thin guy from Essex, nasty piece of work, smokes for England."

His face was a joy to behold but I wasn't finished.

"He was camped out at your place yesterday, looking after your mum. Delightful lady."

He looked angry enough to punch me but I held up my hand like I was stopping traffic. Unfortunately it pulled at my stitches and I made a face to suppress a cry. The face scared him and he took a step back. I opened the rear door of the Merc and gestured him inside.

"Let's have a chat in here," I said quietly. He studied me but got in. I got in behind him. It smelled of polished leather. The door closed with a satisfying clunk.

"You're the guy that hit my mum," he said.

"She was going to put me to sleep with a baseball bat. Anyway, I didn't hit her, I pushed her out the way. Tell me though, what sort of man keeps a baseball bat next to the front door?"

"It's hers, not mine," he said.

"Does she live with you?"

"Sometimes. She gets lonely, see, since my dad died." Unbelievable: he actually had a soft spot for the bat-wielding old slapper.

"Tell me about the thin bloke."

"What thin bloke?"

"The guy that's shacked up in your house."

"Who the fuck are you? I don't have to talk to you."

"You're right," I said. "Much better we talk to the police about how you aided and abetted an assault and battery and are harbouring a criminal." I opened the door.

"OK, OK, take it easy," he said. I closed the door. He let out a breath. "He's staying with me, is all, while he's in Cambridge."

"A friend of yours, then?" He shook his head. "Your mother's toy boy?" He gave me a look of disgust.

"He's there as a favour to my boss," he said.

"You mean Quintin Boyd, the American guy you drive around?"

He looked over my shoulder and his eyes widened. I turned to see mourners approaching in the distance over the grass bank. He scrambled out of his side of the car and leaned back in.

"Get out," he said desperately. "Please."

"Tell your master I want to speak to him," I said, taking my time getting out.

Once outside the car Mark opened the driver's door and retrieved his cap, using it to quickly buff a bit of the wing mirror before putting it on. I wandered back to my own car and got in, retrieving the small pair of binos from the glove compartment. I trained them on the group approaching the Merc. I only recognised Brampton and Quintin, having an earnest discussion. What I mean is he was doing the talking, she was doing the listening. It was an intense discourse, not about the weather. When they got to the car park they shook hands with the other guests and went to the Merc. Mark opened the rear door and Quintin gestured to Brampton to get in. She shook her head and pointed off somewhere. I followed her finger with the binos and saw her car with Stubbing sitting at the wheel, who waved at me without smiling. I waved back; no doubt she'd seen me talking to Mark. I swivelled the binos back to see Quintin say something to Brampton. She gestured to Stubbing to tell her she was going with Quintin and got into the back of the Merc. Quintin got in behind her and Mark closed the door.

I watched them drive off with Stubbing following and was about to put the binos away and follow when I spotted Sylvia and Lucy coming over the grass. They were having an equally intense discussion, a restrained argument really. At least Sylvia was being restrained, Lucy was animated and angry, not the kind of upset you might expect from someone who'd just been to her father's funeral. When they got to the car park they stood there looking around as if expecting someone to be waiting. I was curious to see how they were getting home since both Quintin's and Brampton's car had now left. Sylvia stood there in head to toe black: hat, designer suit, gloves, stockings (I refused to believe that Sylvia was the sort to wear tights) and heels. She looked back at the approaching mourners. Lucy was also in black, but without the hat and gloves. They must have done the condolences thing back at the service and were expecting to have left before everyone else. Now they would have to stand there while all the mourners went past to their cars – they were approaching over the bank. I turned on the ignition and eased the car out towards them.

They took no notice of me and I realised that my car was not one they associated with anyone they knew. I leant across and wound down the passenger window.

"Sylvia."

"George?"

"Hello." Lucy blushed at seeing me. "Have you lost your ride?" I asked.

"Judith was going—"

"Let's just get in, Mummy, please."

Sylvia glanced at the approaching group who were now in hailing distance and then back at the car. Either way she was going to be embarrassed. Lucy made the decision for her and climbed in the back, moving papers and cans and the bottle that I use to urinate in when on a stake-out. I opened the passenger door and Sylvia got in.

We drove without talking and it wasn't until I was on the Huntingdon Road and heading towards Cambridge that I realised I didn't know where I was taking them.

"Where do you want to go?" I asked.

"Back to the reception at the college, please," Sylvia said. I could feel her eyes on me. "Thank you for coming to the funeral, George."

"He didn't come for the funeral, Mummy, he came to look for suspects, didn't you, George?"

"Don't be silly, darling," Sylvia said.

"I'm not being silly, I'm being sensible. Why would he come to the funeral? He didn't know Daddy. Besides, look at his suit, he's hardly dressed for a funeral." Sylvia didn't say anything and I kept quiet, concentrating hard on the traffic-free road. "He's looking into Daddy's death, aren't you,

George? The detective always attends the victim's funeral because the murderer always does." Sylvia snapped her head round to look at her daughter.

"Shut up, Lucy." But Lucy ignored her; I could see her in the rear-view mirror looking at the back of my head.

"Do you think that American, Mr Boyd, had anything to do with it? I discovered today that he knew Daddy at university. Do you think that's relevant?"

I glanced at Sylvia but she was looking out at the scenery as if seeing it for the first time.

"He knew Mummy as well there, didn't he, Mummy? Perhaps they were lovers or something."

I risked a glance at Sylvia and saw her turquoise eyes were bright with tears. I wondered whether Lucy knew that Sylvia knew she was seeing Quintin. I would have bashed their heads together metaphorically had they not just come from a funeral.

"Your father committed suicide, Lucy," I said. "The police and coroner confirmed it." Lucy slumped back into the seat. Our eyes met in the rear-view mirror and I could see the hurt but also desperation and confusion.

At Morley Lucy opened the car door before I'd even come to a stop and was up the stairs and at the front door by the time I had. She left the back door open for the heat to escape. I leant back and pulled the door closed, which brought me close to Sylvia's neck and perfume. Sylvia showed no inclination to get out.

"She's been through a lot, George, please excuse her," she said.

I nodded. "What about you?" I asked. "How are you holding up?"

"It would have been better for us if Elliot had been murdered. A suicide is just…"

Her mouth trembled and I wished I hadn't asked; it wasn't the time. She recovered and flashed a joyless smile.

"Thanks for the lift; I have no idea what happened to Judith." I didn't tell her she'd driven off with Quintin. She got out and I was left with the ghost of her expensive fragrance.

32

IN MY BEDROOM I LAY ON MY FRONT AND DOZED FOR A BIT, thinking of my dinner with Nina in a couple of hours and the possibilities that might arise after dessert. I felt like a teenager on a promise of getting to remove a bra, it was pathetic. I had another bath to freshen up, being careful to avoid getting my wound wet. I put on clean underwear and struggled into a fresh shirt. Deciding against the expensive men's perfume Olivia had bought me, I opted for a splash of Bay Rum. Then I went through the difficult choice of corduroy versus Hugo Boss again. Corduroy hadn't worked for me last time so I went for the Hugo. Downstairs I remembered Nina's suggestion to bring a DVD, so I picked *The Cynic, the Rat and the Fist* to take with me.

As I was locking my front door, a paler than usual Stubbing stepped out of the cold gloom like a bad ghost.

"Jesus, Stubbing, you could give a guy a heart attack."

She handed me a piece of paper. "Your crime number, for the insurance."

"Thanks. You learn anything you want to share?"

She shook her head. "Brampton knows about the break-in, by the way, and she wants to see you."

"Now?"

"Yes," she said, pointing to the street. "She's in the car."

"I thought you wanted to keep the break-in to yourself."

"I did."

"So how did she find out?"

"There you go, you're beginning to ask intelligent questions."

"Meaning what?"

"I don't know, George, I'm just the flying monkey, remember?"

My God, Stubbing was feeling sorry for herself.

"So are you telling me Brampton knew about the burglary from the person who committed it?"

She folded her arms. "No comment."

"Interesting. Did you know your boss and Quintin Boyd were at university together?"

"Quintin Boyd?"

"The guy whose car she got into yesterday at the funeral. You saw for yourself. He practically ordered her in and she jumped to it like a cat on heat."

She unfolded her arms and tried to muster a look of indifference. "What are you suggesting?"

"Nothing. They're still chummy now, that's all."

"So they're part of an old boy network, so fucking what?"

"I'm seeing too many old boy slash girl connections at the moment and I don't like it."

"But you're not linking this Quintin to the break-in are you? Unless you have some information that you'd like to share?"

I wasn't ready to confide in Stubbing about the thin man, and his connection to Quintin Boyd through Mark, and to be honest I'd not connected him to the break-in before Stubbing brought it up. But I remembered the lingering smell of stale smoke when we'd discovered the ransacked office; not exactly evidence I know, but Brampton somehow knew about it. But then why had Stubbing refused to get the crime scene investigators to the office? Perhaps she was in cahoots with Brampton and Boyd and they were trying to pump me for what I knew, which was zilch.

"I suppose I better see Brampton since she's made the effort," I said.

"I think that would be sensible." We made our way to the street. "By the way, I saw you talking to this Quintin Boyd's driver at the funeral. Did you learn anything useful?"

"So I'm supposed to tell you stuff, but you don't tell me anything, is that how it works?"

"Yes it is. Well done for recognising which of us is a real detective."

"OK then, I'll tell you what I found out. Brace yourself. Quintin's driver drives Quintin around," I said.

She just grinned like a mad thing until we reached Brampton's car, which was idling in the street, emitting carbon from its rear end to keep her warm. I could just make her out sitting in the back, reading a Cambridge *Argus*. Stubbing opened the rear door and nodded for me to get in. I sat down next to Brampton and was greeted by a cloying perfume; not for her the subtlety of Sylvia Booker. Stubbing opened the driver's door to get in.

"Give us a minute, Stubbing, if you don't mind." I tried to throw a smirk Stubbing's way but she avoided looking at me, closing the door with exaggerated care. With the newspaper down I saw that Brampton was dressed in a sequinned evening gown, a black shawl over her shoulders. Something glistened at her throat. Her hair was different, tied up like Lucy had done hers. It was stifling in the car with the blower going and the perfume. I tried to make conversation.

"Going out, Detective Chief Inspector?"

"Yes, as a matter of fact," she said, treating it as a genuine inquiry. "I'm going to dinner at one of the colleges." My father had worked many of those dinners, not coming home until after midnight.

"High Table I suppose?" I said.

She looked unsurprised that I should know what High Table was. "Look, George, I'll keep this brief. As you know there's been a bit of a cockup, a technical failure of the USB stick you gave us."

"It was OK when I handed it over. I checked it."

"And you're sure there's no backup."

"Stubbing's already asked me if I have a backup. I'm not going to tell you anything different."

"Yes I know she's asked you; I just wanted to check that there's nothing you've found since then. Not that the case rests on your evidence, the belt round Trisha Greene's neck was definitely the husband's."

"You have DNA evidence then?"

"We have enough of a case to present to the Crown Prosecution Service. So, you haven't suddenly found a backup at home or anything?" Still banging on about a backup. I was tempted to ask her how she knew about the break-in but it's always good to have something up your sleeve. So I shook my head and watched her face. She gave nothing away. With Stubbing at least I could tell she was trying not to give anything away, Brampton however was masked by a professional veneer that allowed no emotion unless it was calculated. A woman in the police didn't get to Brampton's seniority by being labelled emotional; you had to appear tougher and be smarter than the men. She sat back against the seat and arranged herself in a more informal pose, her eyes masking what was behind them.

"Are you still working for Sylvia Booker?" she asked, checking her watch to show how offhand a question it was. Attack, I decided, was better than defence.

"How well do you know Quintin Boyd?" I asked. She reached for the newspaper, even though she'd just set it down.

"Is that who Sylvia has asked you to check up on?"

"Why would I need to check up on him? She already knows him."

"Knew him, George, at some point. They were here at Cambridge together."

"Yes I know, at Morley. You were all there. You, Quintin, Sylvia and Sylvia's husband. You all belonged to the same club."

Her thick eyebrows flicked and she put the newspaper down again. Her hands found something urgent to do in her clutch bag. I should have left it at that but I couldn't; I'd found a nerve and I wanted to keep pressing. I wanted to puncture that mask.

"I haven't got that wrong have I, you were a member of the Cambridge Blue Club?"

This time I was rewarded with a blotchy reddening of the neck and face.

"I can't remember, I belonged to a lot of clubs."

"You'd remember this one; you watched porn films together."

Her eyes betrayed a quiver of something I couldn't identify then she leant forward and said, in a low voice, "Don't dig too deep, George, or you might fall in the hole you've made." Then she regained her professional façade and sat back and it was as if it hadn't happened.

"Is that a threat?" I asked.

She generated a fake smile. "Thanks for meeting up with me on a Friday evening, I appreciate it. Let me know if you find anything on Trisha Greene. No need to go through DI Stubbing, come straight to me."

I kept quiet and looked out to see Stubbing hugging herself to keep warm; her coat was on the front passenger seat. Brampton coughed gently into a fist – our meeting was over.

I opened the door and stepped onto the pavement, inhaling the perfume-free cold air deep into my lungs. "You can get in now," I told Stubbing.

I put Brampton and Stubbing from my mind and stopped off at the supermarket for a bottle of wine. Feeling in an optimistic mood, or at least wanting to be prepared, I supplemented it with a packet of condoms. At the five-items-or-less till I was faced with the same bloody checkout woman I'd had the other night. I ignored the people behind me who were eye-balling my purchases and held her gaze as she scanned my two items. I pocketed the condoms as soon as they came down the moving belt.

"Have a nice evening," the checkout woman said with a straight face.

"Fingers crossed," I told her.

33

NINA OPENED THE DOOR TO HER FLAT IN A SWISHY SKIRT AND soft wool cardigan. I stepped inside. It was an open plan affair, flat-pack furnished and arranged to look like a page from the catalogue it came from. I saw no hint of Nina's heritage here, except maybe in the faint smell of incense long since burnt. The lighting was soft and the set table was candlelit. Two doorways led from the room, one doorless but with a bead curtain that obviously led into the kitchen. I gave her the bottle of wine I'd bought which I'd chosen based on price since I know nothing about wine. Nina took it to the dining table.

"I just need to check on something in the kitchen. Take your coat off and open the wine for me will you, I always struggle with corks but you shouldn't have a problem." She swished through the beads behind which a nice smell wafted. I hung my coat by the door and did the manly thing with the corkscrew that was on the table, pouring ruby liquid into large glasses. Nina came back out and picked one up, holding it to the candle. Her soft wool top had lots of tiny buttons down the front, except a third of them were unbuttoned and the rest looked ready to pop. I caught a glimpse of promising shadow.

"Perhaps we should start with a drink, George." Shit, maybe she'd caught me looking down her cleavage. I nodded, glad of the low lighting.

"Let's drink to, let's see… anticipation," she said, looking at me over the top of her glass, her dark eyes flashing in the candlelight. Was she teasing me again? I raised my glass.

"Anticipation," I echoed, although I'd had all the anticipation a man could handle. I was ready to sweep the carefully laid crockery onto the floor and ravish her on the table. The only thing that held me back, apart from Nina's probable objection, was a vision of Stubbing's smirking face as she charged me with date rape.

We ate salmon as a starter followed by stir-fried vegetables. It tasted good despite the lack of meat. I asked her how she became a nutritionist.

"I worked as a beautician for a while, but there were only so many bikini waxes I could do. So I trained as a nutritional advisor and then realised you can sell on herbal supplements as part of a franchise, so that fits in nicely with my nutritionist's hat on. There's frozen yoghurt for pudding, just to prove that being healthy doesn't mean you can't be naughty." She flashed a playful smile and went to the kitchen. I studied the room for clues about Nina's interests and passions but couldn't see much; no books, no music, some inoffensive easy-on-the-eye impressionist prints. I wondered what anyone would make of my surroundings at home; I would have to explain that it was my parents' house and that I hadn't changed anything, that it didn't reflect the real me. Or did it? Nina came back with a pot and a couple of bowls.

"So, George, tell me how you got into your line of work."

"I drifted into it, to be honest." I told her how after college I'd got a job as an assistant for a form verifier at an insurance firm and moved on to checking the facts on claimants' forms for myself. Before I knew it I was staking out health insurance claimants to see if they were playing football when they claimed to have whiplash. I'd enjoyed the non-office based work but not the insurance side of it, as all they were looking for was a reason not to pay out. Eventually I'd set up my own business and expanded into other things.

"Although I still do some insurance work for bread and butter," I said. "As well as benefit cheats and serving court papers. Oh, and the odd missing person."

"You must have some stories?"

"Yes, but I'm not telling."

She smiled. "Do you like the marital stuff best?"

"'Like' isn't the right word. It's satisfying, because it's getting at the truth, although often as not it ruins a marriage and I think people are better off not knowing the truth. The trouble is once someone has come to me things are pretty much over."

We ate our puddings for a bit, then, mainly because I couldn't think of anything else, I asked, "So you've never thought about settling down, maybe having kids?"

"Come on, George. Is that the only choice women have, to settle down and have kids?" She scooped more frozen yoghurt into my bowl. "The way I see it, to have kids, or even a man, is to be weighed down with responsibilities, not something I particularly want. Look at your secretary, what's her name?"

"Sandra."

"Yeah, look at Sandra, she's lumbered with two of them by different fathers, neither of them around. She has no life of her own beyond the kids. It's not for me. I like the idea that I can do whatever I like, go wherever I like without worrying about anyone else."

I waited for her to ask me about my life choices – I was ready to give her my sob story about Olivia – but she hadn't finished.

"That's why Sandra doesn't like me, you see."

"I wasn't aware that she didn't like you," I lied.

"Of course she doesn't. I represent everything she's not. I look after myself, she obviously doesn't. She has kids with no man to help out, the worst possible scenario. I'm childless and free." She laughed. "Did you know she goes on a dating website?" I felt my hackles rise.

"She's had a rough time," I said.

"She looks like she has," she said, smirking unpleasantly. "That's part of her problem. If she lost a little weight, wore something less baggy, maybe had a make-over…"

I put down my spoon.

"Are you full, George? You haven't finished." I didn't want to blow my chances at getting laid for the first time in months but I couldn't keep quiet.

"I don't think you can judge people by their appearances, Nina."

"Don't you? I think in today's world presentation is everything. Your outward appearance reflects the image you want to portray. Look at you, you shaved, put on a nice jacket."

"I'm sorry, but that's bollocks."

She looked taken aback – maybe I'd been more abrupt than I needed to be.

"All I mean is that in my job I come across people all the time who are not what they appear. As for this," I pulled at my jacket, "my ex-wife bought it for me and I wore it just to cover up the fact that I'm a middle-aged man trying to impress a thirty-something woman."

"I'm twenty-nine. And I'm sorry, I didn't realise you had feelings for your secretary—"

"She's not my secretary, she's my assistant, and I don't have feelings for her, not in the way that you're implying."

"Well she obviously has feelings for you. When I told her we were going out last time she didn't seem that pleased."

"She looks out for me, that's all," I said. "She's been overprotective since my wife left." This would have been a good point for her to ask me about my wife but she started to stack the bowls. A chirping noise came from my coat.

Nina stood up and took the bowls from the table. I went to my coat – the chirping was probably the packet of condoms calling out, telling me to take them back to the supermarket for a refund.

But it wasn't the condoms; it was the office mobile being rung by a Cambridge number I didn't recognise. I had to dig it out from behind the DVD I'd brought with me. A DVD that would probably remain in my raincoat.

"Hello?" I said.

An incoherent female voice, upset.

"Who is this?" A sniffle, then a familiar man's voice in the background.

"It's Lucy, George…" She sounded drunk, again.

"Are you OK?"

"No…"

"Where are you?"

"I'm sorry, George…"

"For this afternoon? Don't worry about it."

"No… not that." There was that man's voice in the background again.

"Who's there, Lucy?"

"I… I came to confront him but he's not here. Please will you pick me up?" Her voice was slurring now.

Nina came back into the room with a tray of coffee and a bottle of sweet-looking liqueur. At least she was smiling. The light from the kitchen highlighted her figure; the swishy skirt filtered light between her legs. I looked at the carpet and spoke into the phone.

"Now? Can't you get a taxi? Hello?"

"George, son, it's Eric, at River Views. I've got this girl in my office, pissed as a newt, she says she knows you and wants you to pick her up. Says you're the only person she can trust when she's pissed."

"Can't you put her in a taxi? I'll pay you back tomorrow."

"She won't…" he dropped his voice to a whisper, "I wouldn't put my daughter in a taxi if she was this pissed."

I sighed. "OK. I'll pick her up. Keep her in the office and

for God's sake don't let her go upstairs if the guy on the top floor comes home. Understand, Eric?"

"Yes."

"I'm sorry, George," shouted Lucy in the background. Eric hung up.

I put the phone away and looked up to see Nina sitting on the sofa, legs crossed, the skirt open to the thigh.

"Sounds like you're going to bail out on me again, George."

"I'm afraid so."

"And you put that jacket on just to impress me."

I nodded.

She smiled. "How long do you think you'll be?"

"I'm not sure. Why?"

"Why don't you come back later, when you're done?" She leant forward to pick up her small glass of liqueur and the tiny buttons on her cardigan looked very flimsy. "It doesn't matter how late."

34

I DROVE STUPIDLY FAST CONSIDERING I'D DRUNK THREE glasses of wine. But I reckoned I could get Lucy home and be back to Nina's in forty-five minutes tops if I hurried.

I parked in the car park opposite River Views and checked the top floor; it was dark. The street was wet with fresh rain and Eric was waiting outside the gate. He smelled of mints which couldn't hide the smell of whisky.

"She's asleep in the office."

"What happened?"

"She was pressing the buzzer for ages then she started shouting so I went out, didn't I, to see what was going on. Told me she was here to see Mr Boyd. I told her he wasn't in and she started crying, sort of collapsed on the pavement here." He pointed to near where we were standing as if it were important to know the exact place she had collapsed. "So I told her to come into the office, didn't I?"

I told him he'd done the right thing. We went through the gate.

"She said she wanted to call someone so I told her she could use the office phone." He opened the door to his office and I stepped in. Lucy was in a foetal position on the tiny sofa, her open mouth drooling onto the worn plastic. She looked a little clammy but her breathing seemed regular. Her dress was up around her skinny thighs. I pulled it down over her knees and looked at Eric, who looked away. I wanted to believe she had fallen asleep like that.

"She had your business card on her, so we rang you."

"I think the best thing to do is get her mother down here to pick her up." I found Sylvia's card in my wallet and dialled her mobile. Eric was called to the door and went out to deal with someone. I looked round the office as I listened to Sylvia's phone ring. The door on the wall-mounted shallow metal cabinet that I'd seen last time was ajar. I checked the one-way window and saw Eric helping a woman carry groceries from her car. I opened the cabinet door. Bingo – it was full of keys on hooks. A row of hooks for each floor, a hook for each apartment. One hook right at the top, on its own. The penthouse. It was so tempting. Sylvia's voicemail message came on, clipped vowels and businesslike. I hung up and looked through the window; I couldn't see Eric. I took the penthouse keys and stuck them in my coat pocket next to the condoms – was I really choosing between a chance to use one and an opportunity to snoop round Quintin Boyd's apartment? I still had to decide what to do with Lucy; I didn't feel I could leave her in Eric's boozy care.

I rang Sandra from the mobile and asked her to come down in a taxi to pick Lucy up. It was the wrong suggestion.

"Can't you just put her in a taxi home, for fuck's sake? It's Friday night and I've got a toddler and a teenager who can't hold his own cock to piss to look after here."

"I can't get hold of her mother and she's in no state to put herself to bed, Sandra."

"Then why don't you take her to your place?"

I gave her a few seconds to think about what she'd said while I watched Lucy stir and moan. Sandra's voice came back, sounding less shrill. "OK, I tell you what. Bring her here and she can sleep it off tonight. She'll wake up in a bit of Cambridge she's never seen before and I'll give her some toast and put her in a taxi." I didn't want to leave; I'd have to come back and get Eric to open the gates with some excuse. I looked through the window to see him returning to the office.

"I can't leave here, I've got an opportunity to get closer to this American bastard. I'll put her in a taxi to yours." Sandra agreed to keep an eye out for her and I hung up as Eric came in. I told him to call for a taxi. I shook Lucy by the shoulder; she stirred and opened red-rimmed eyes. When she saw me she sat up.

"Woah, not so fast," I said, as she put her hand to her mouth.

"Taxi will be here in five," said Eric.

"Best get a bucket," I told him. When he'd gone I explained to Lucy what was happening. She nodded.

"What are you doing here, Lucy?"

"I came to confront him about my parents; he knew them but didn't tell me. I overdid the Dutch courage though."

Dutch courage in the form of Dutch gin. I wanted to ask her more but Eric came in with a bucket and Lucy bent over it as soon as it hit the floor. I held her hair out of the way while she emptied her stomach.

* * *

When the taxi driver pressed the buzzer I convinced Eric that he should stay in the warmth of his office while I took Lucy out to the taxi. He didn't argue, no doubt desperate to get back to his bottle in the desk.

I steered Lucy through the gate and wedged it open with my packet of condoms – the best use I was going to get out of them at this rate. The taxi driver whined about Lucy possibly throwing up in the back so I bunged him an extra twenty of Sylvia's money which shut him up and told him someone was waiting the other end.

With Lucy gone I walked away in case Eric was watching through his CCTV and then, with my back pressed against the wall to avoid the camera, sidled to the gate. I went through the gate, pocketing my condoms, and squatted to shuffle underneath Eric's window. Ignoring the lift, the noise of which I figured Eric was attuned to, I found the stairwell and climbed to the top floor.

I got into Quintin's apartment easily enough, but once inside it was dark and I didn't want to put on the lights as I knew they were visible from the street. I let my eyes grow accustomed to the dark and then felt my way to one of the vertical blinds and pulled the cord to open them. That let in enough light to reveal an open plan living area furnished with ultra-modern pieces of leather, steel and glass. The end I was standing in was the seating area with a view over the river to the city.

There were two large sofas facing each other separated by a glass coffee table. The other side of the space had a glass and steel dining table surrounded by uncomfortable-looking chairs. A dresser and a drinks cabinet stood either side of an arched doorway through which I could see stainless steel work units and an enormous American-style fridge. No desk, no bookshelves, no pictures anywhere. One of the walls had a giant flat screen hanging on it with a home theatre system underneath and another arched doorway next to it led to blackness.

I made my way through it and peered into the gloom. There were four doors off a hallway, the first of which turned out to be a large bathroom, the floor and wall done in what looked like black marble. The second door revealed a large bedroom with an enormous bed, a walk-in wardrobe with some nice dark suits and pressed shirts hanging in it, a rack of neatly hung ties and another of belts with shiny buckles. There were a couple of drawers with carefully folded designer boxers and balled socks arranged by colour.

I opened the drawer in the bedside table – nothing in it. The room was devoid of interest: no papers, no receipts in the bin, nothing in the en-suite all-white bathroom except expensive toiletries (all of the same brand) and a stack of very soft and very big white towels.

The third door along the hall was locked, so I moved to the fourth, which opened into what looked like an office. Against one wall stood a large glass drawer-less desk with a very big LCD monitor, keyboard and mouse on it. The computer itself was humming away underneath but the monitor was black.

I moved the mouse and a small box came up on the screen asking for a password. A solid wooden cabinet stood against another wall, with two doors and two drawers underneath. I opened one drawer: it was full of neatly arranged computer discs, CDs or DVDs in transparent plastic sleeves, all labelled with a six-digit serial number and nothing else. Maybe, unlike me, he was anal about his backups, although there must have been a hundred or so discs. I chose the one from the front, took it out of its transparent sleeve and put it inside the cover of *The Cynic, the Rat and the Fist* that was in my coat pocket, so that it was underneath the DVD. I stuck the empty sleeve at the back of the drawer so it wouldn't be noticed. The other drawer had VHS tapes in it, again with serial numbers.

Opening the cabinet doors above the drawers I was taken aback; it was the first bit of colour I'd seen in what was a monochrome apartment – the varied colour of a hundred or so DVD case spines. I pulled one out, called *Behind the Green Door*, a topless woman looking out from the cover. Out of habit I checked the credits; it was made in 1972. Another called *Insatiable*, a woman in cut-off jeans and nothing else, her back to the camera and looking over her shoulder, made in 1980. Another, *The Devil in Miss Jones*, circa 1973. Its cover showed a woman holding a snake near her face, sticking her tongue out at it.

"Hello."

My heart jumped into my throat and I spun round, knowing from the accent who it was. Quintin Boyd stood leaning against the door frame, arms crossed, the very picture of calm. He smiled.

35

QUINTIN BOYD LOOKED AT THE DVD IN MY HANDS.

"Ah, I see you've found one of my favourites. By the guy who made *Deep Throat*, but I believe this to be the better film." He walked towards me, completely relaxed, and held out his hand for the DVD case.

I gave it to him and he examined it as if seeing it for the first time. "There were six sequels made, none of them of course matching up to the raw appeal of this one. Excuse me."

I stepped aside and he put the film carefully back in its place, arranging the DVDs so the spines were all flush. I could see that he owned all the sequels of the film.

"They knew how to make adult films then, George – you don't mind if I call you George? There was a story to the action, a reason for the sex. Nowadays you can go on the web and just watch people fucking – it lacks context. Anyone can upload video of themselves having sex, but where's the story?" He closed the cabinet. "Shall we talk in the other room?"

I followed him to the door. "Take Miss Jones for instance. She's depressed at the start of the film, because her life is so boring, and commits suicide. At the pearly gates she meets Saint Peter and discovers that because she's committed suicide, she's going to end up in hell. She asks to be allowed to go back to earth as the embodiment of lust so that she can at least go to hell for good reason, right? And not just because she was bored with life." We came through the archway into the now lit living room. The besuited thin man was standing at the front door, his flick knife in his hand. "I think you've met," Quintin said casually beside me.

The thin man grinned.

"We've not been formally introduced," I said, "but he showed me his knife."

Quintin gestured to the sofa. "Please, sit down."

I played along and sat down as if I'd just arrived for dinner, which is how he seemed to be treating my presence. He sat opposite me and crossed his legs, centring the crease on his trousers with manicured fingers. He was handsome, but carried it as if it wasn't his fault, just something he had to bear. The thin man dragged a dining chair over the hardwood floor to the front door and Quintin winced at the sound.

"So, where were we?"

"You were telling me about Miss Jones," I said.

"Ah yes. Miss Jones is granted a certain period alive to be as depraved as possible, which of course provides for some entertaining scenes." He smiled and those dimples I'd seen in his photo came to life. "Eventually her time on earth comes to an end, but not before she has, of course, become a voracious sex addict. She's now ready to go to hell, happy in the knowledge that she's really earned it. She meets

Saint Peter again and now she's worried, deciding all of a sudden that she doesn't want an eternity of physical pain. He reassures her that there will be nothing of the sort, that physical pain is simply a mistaken impression of hell held by the living. So she goes to hell and finds herself locked in a room with a man. Maybe, she thinks, she can have more sex after all. The problem is the guy spends his time looking for imaginary flies, and is completely disinterested in her." He made more dimples. "So that was her punishment, George, to be stuck in a room with a man who didn't want to fuck her despite her desperate need. That was her hell." He uncrossed his legs and leant forward. "Now you tell me someone would think of making that sort of adult film today. No, sir. It could have been written by Sartre or Beckett." He spread his arms along the back of the sofa. The smile disappeared.

"But, George, you didn't break in to admire my film collection. Tell me why you're here."

"I'm just interested in renting one of these flats out, so I thought I'd take a look."

"Don't fuck with me, George. I'll call your quaint cops and get them to come and pick you up. In fact in the eyes of the law I might be justified in using reasonable force to protect myself and my property."

"Go ahead and call the police," I said, ignoring his threat of violence. I gestured to the man at the door. "Maybe they'd be interested in what your employee was doing Wednesday evening, when my employee had his fingers broken." Quintin smiled. He got up and went to the drinks cabinet near the dining table.

"What's your poison, George?" he asked, his back to me. "I've even got some Armenian brandy, not bad at all." I glanced at the thin man who was sitting in front of the door cleaning his nails with the end of his stiletto. I couldn't risk trying to get past him with that thing.

"Whisky is good," I said, sitting back in the sofa; the wine I'd had earlier had been scared out of me when Quintin had appeared at the door. I felt for my mobile phone, more as a reassurance than anything.

"Bourbon OK?" he asked, his back to me.

"Yes, but no ice."

"Well done, sir." He came over with two amber-filled glasses and handed me one. "This is Eagle Rare Single Barrel, none of that Jack Daniels crap everyone here thinks is bourbon." He sat down. "Let's discuss this sensibly, *mano-a-mano*." He raised his glass and drank. I did the same. I didn't think much of the Eagle Rare. It tasted too salty.

"I knew your father at Morley," he said. "Kockers, we used to call him. He used to clean up after our gatherings." He grinned, waiting for a reaction, but I didn't oblige. "And now here you are, like father like son, cleaning up after other people's messes. Sylvia's on this occasion, right? She always was one to make a mess." He looked down at his drink as if to contemplate its appeal. "You've been poking your nose in my business, George, and I'm entitled to know what it is you want, or what Sylvia wants since she's employed you." Every time he mentioned her name his full mouth twisted briefly into a smile. I swear he didn't know he was doing it.

"Why don't you just ask her?" I said. His lips pursed as

if he was considering the possibility.

I drank some more salty whisky.

"Did she send you up here to look for something?"

I decided to follow some of my own advice to others and directly ask the question I wanted an answer to. "What is it you want with Lucy, Mr Boyd? Surely you can see the anguish you're causing her mother by seeing her."

He looked surprised then laughed. A forced, harsh laugh that made me feel very tired.

"My dear Kockers Junior, you're completely out of your depth, aren't you? You haven't got a fucking clue what's going on. Sylvia hasn't told you anything, you sap." My tongue felt very thick, like my brain. Quintin was difficult to bring into focus.

"Are… you… shleeping… with… Lucy?"

He smiled, and what I thought he said was, "I suppose that could be considered your business, but not Sylvia's." He then said something else but I couldn't make out his words at all.

Fuck and bugger it.

Salty drink, George. What's your poison, George. I put the whisky carefully onto the coffee table and took out my mobile phone. Someone would need to pick me up; I needed to get back to Nina's or go home to bed. But my fingers were unusually large and I couldn't work the buttons. Quintin leant over the coffee table to take the phone gently from my hands.

I desperately needed to lie down, so I did.

* * *

Someone was doing DIY in my head, knocking through from one hemisphere of my brain to the other, trying to make an open-plan brain.

I was lying down at least, on my side. I opened my eyes; I was hemmed in, seemingly by a wall of fabric. It smelled familiar. My feet came up against something when I tried to stretch my legs out and I was hit with a panic of being boxed in or even buried alive. I sat up quickly, only to find myself on the back seat of the Golf. Someone was tapping at the window but I couldn't see them due to condensation. Although my raincoat was over me I was cold. I rubbed the window and saw Eric looking in. I wound it down and let in a blast of cold air.

"You alright, son?" I had no saliva and words came out unformed. The bastard had slipped something into my whisky, probably GHB given the salty taste. Eric opened the door. I sat up and groaned at the pain in my stitched shoulder; I'd been lying on it.

"You must have really overdone it last night, son."

"How long have I been here?"

"It's six-thirty in the morning, I'm just on my way home." Jesus, just how long had I been out here?

"Did you see them bring me out?" I asked.

He glanced back at River Views and then at me. "No," he said, before disappearing from the window. I felt in my raincoat pocket for my car keys, but pulled out my house keys with Boyd's apartment keys tangled up with them. If Quintin and his henchman had searched me they must have thought they were mine.

* * *

I desperately needed a piss. When I put the keys in my raincoat pocket I felt a piece of paper. I pulled it out to find a folded A5 sheet that when opened revealed a photo of myself passed out on Quintin's sofa. On the table before me was a sex toy, standing obscenely upright. Underneath the photo was printed: "Next time we use this on you." I got out and looked up at the penthouse. The lights were on behind the blinds. I thought about going back up there but my head and legs had nothing in them and I couldn't even formulate what I would say, never mind get up there to say it. I relieved myself leaning against the wall behind a white van, my urine splashing onto my shoes and billowing steam in the cold air. Then I ripped up the photo and scattered the tiny pieces around. Afterwards I sat behind the wheel of the Golf and found the car keys were in the ignition. Something dug against my armpit when I moved to start the engine. It was the DVD case I'd taken to my aborted date with Nina. Inside, still underneath my DVD, was the disc I'd swiped from Quintin's office. Just a serial number on it. My shoulder throbbed like an idling motorbike with no exhaust, keeping time with my head. I was worried that the stitches had come undone when I'd been manhandled to the car. I could go to Kamal's, but I couldn't face another badgering about going to the police, and his pork-sewing flatmate might still be at work or might just have gone to bed after a night shift. Sandra might be up; she didn't work Friday nights so she could be on the ball Saturday for Ashley. I put the car gently into gear and moved slowly off.

36

IT WAS SEVEN WHEN SANDRA OPENED THE DOOR IN HER FLUFFY bathrobe. Her hair was still wet and she was makeup free. She looked pissed off for a second before looking me up and down.

"Jesus, you look like shit."

"I look better than I feel."

She helped me take off my raincoat and we went through to the kitchen. I explained briefly where I'd come from and what had happened last night, leaving out my aborted date with Nina.

"What a bastard. But let's sort you out first. What's it to be – coffee, bath, wound or painkillers?"

"I really came round so you could check the stitches. I'm worried they've come undone."

"I'll run you a bath while I look at it – you smell." I acquiesed in the idea of a bath, feeling too weary to trek home.

She put her hands on my shoulders as if to measure me.

"You're the same size as my first. He left a couple of brand-new Armani suits when he scarpered to Spain. I was waiting for Jason to grow into them but it turns out he's not built like his father. Doesn't look like him either, come to think of it." She winked at me and left. I gingerly took off my jacket and shirt while she ran the bath and fetched my overnight bag from the car – I always keep one in the boot. She came back dressed and with a first aid kit. I sat the wrong way round on a kitchen chair and she stood at my back. I could feel the bandage being pulled away.

"Are you going to the police about Quintin?"

"And say what? He'll claim I got pissed and they helped me to the car; it's not like they did anything to me. Anyway, if he gave me what I think he gave me there'll be no trace of it in me anymore."

I felt the bandage come away and fresh air hit the wound.

"Oh my God," she said.

"What is it?" I asked, terrified of the answer.

"Nothing, just kidding. It looks fine to me. I'll clean it with some disinfectant and put a new bandage on."

Later I sat in the bath and lay back on an inflatable cushion between my shoulder blades, to keep the wound off the back of the bath. It felt good, especially when the painkillers I'd washed down with Sandra's instant coffee kicked in. The pills killed the headache as well as the throbbing in my shoulder, and by the time I'd put on some new undies and a charcoal grey Armani suit I felt almost human. I emerged from the bathroom to the smell of cooking bacon and descended to find Sandra and Jason at the kitchen table. The sound of kids' TV came from the living room where I assumed Ashley was plonked in front of the 42-inch plasma fixed to the wall.

"Morning, boss. Looking smarmy in Armani."

Sandra got up and put bacon, tomato and a fried egg together on a plate.

"Have a seat, George. More coffee?" I nodded. Jason was managing to eat on his own, holding a fork in the palm of his hand with his thumb. His food had been cut up.

"Where's Lucy?" I asked.

"Still asleep," Sandra said, placing the loaded plate in front of me. "There's a girl with problems."

"You had a chat then?"

"As much as I could. She was in a state."

"You find out anything?" I winced as she poured hot water into a cup and added instant coffee.

"Mr Boyd was taking photos of her."

"Photos?"

"Yeah, not what you're thinking. Just glamour portraits, that sort of thing. It's a hobby of his, apparently." I remembered the camera in his office, his visit to the camera shop in town when Jason and I had followed him last week. "Anyway, seems he turned her head with the attention. She found it flattering. Told her she was beautiful, the usual shit."

"And she fell for it?" I asked.

"Jesus, boss, she's not that bad," Jason said.

"This from the guy who said 'let's hope she has a big personality' when he saw her photo?"

"Well, it doesn't do her justice," he said, getting up and going into the other room. Sandra rolled her eyes at me.

"You think Quintin was grooming her?" I asked Sandra.

"She seems a little old to be groomed, but then she is childlike in some ways. That's how it starts, isn't it? Befriend children, take innocent photos of them, then gradually convince them to unbutton their shirt, then take it off. Before they know it they're posing naked."

I considered this scenario and sawed at overcooked bacon.

"Good morning," Lucy said from the doorway. She was in a pair of Jason's pyjamas that suited her boyish figure. I wondered if she'd heard our conversation.

Sandra offered her breakfast but she politely declined and settled for coffee.

"I can't find my clothes," she said.

"That's 'cause I put them in the wash, darling, they had sick on them," Sandra said.

Lucy blushed and looked down at her cup. Then she looked at me. "Thanks for coming to get me. Again."

I shrugged.

"He's a sucker for a damsel in distress," Sandra said. She told Lucy to have a shower and that she'd bring her clothes up. Lucy went upstairs, seemingly unfazed about waking up in a council house dressed in men's pyjamas surrounded by people she hardly knew. I looked at my watch.

"Thanks for breakfast, Sandra. I'm going to visit Dad then get some kip."

"Oh my god," she said. "I've just remembered. Jason has something to tell you." She angled her face towards the sitting room doorway and shouted his name. He sauntered in, arms across his chest to protect his hands.

"What?"

"You've got something to tell George here, remember?"

Jason sat down and tried to look like he couldn't remember what it was he had to tell me but he was too pleased with himself and couldn't keep up the pretence.

"Well, you know the backups you weren't doing in the office."

I nodded. "Your mother was doing them and the backup drive was stolen."

Both he and Sandra shook their heads.

"No, boss. Mum wasn't doing the backups. The backups were done automatically online. I set it up like over a week ago, when I was in the office. They were incremental backups so they were done in the background when the computer was on." He sat back, looking smug. I tried to understand what it was he was telling me.

"You mean that everything that was on the hard drive is on the Internet somewhere?"

"Yep, Mum agreed the payment." I looked at Sandra.

"Sorry, I'd forgotten all about it," she said.

"It's a pretty secure website though, no worries there," Jason said.

"Let's have the discussion about me being kept in the loop later. Right now I just want to know if you can download the bloody stuff."

"Of course. I could try and do it onto our computer here, with a bit of tweaking 'cause it's not the source of the original—"

I stood up.

"OK, then download the photos and the tracking info

from the Trisha Greene case. Somebody wanted them badly enough to ransack the office, so I want to look at them again. Email them to me. And for God's sake don't tell anyone you've got them."

"Like who?" Sandra asked, giving me a dangerous look.

"I'm just thinking of Brampton's flying monkey, or Brampton. I wouldn't put it past either of them to come sniffing round," I said.

She walked me to the door and I told her I would pick Lucy up later to take her home.

"Be careful, George," she said.

"You worried about me, Sandra?"

"You're a regular source of income, of course I'm worried."

I drove straight up to Cottenham to visit my father, stopping only for flowers at a petrol station, more for the benefit of Megan the young care assistant than Dad, who I wasn't sure even knew they were there. Megan, who took them off me to put in water, was reading my mind or expression.

"There have been no more visitors, Mr Kevorkian. I've double-checked."

I smiled and wondered how old she was – certainly not much older than Lucy, but younger than Cathy at McDonald's.

"Thanks, and please call me George."

Dad was sitting in his high-backed chair facing the window in his room. I sat on the end of the bed. He looked round and smiled, like you would at a stranger who had just sat next to you in the doctor's waiting room, then returned his gaze to the bird table outside on which three or four small birds pecked at seed before being seen off by a large pigeon. Some sunshine broke through the layer of cloud and reminded me how quickly one became used to drabness.

I wanted to ask him about his days and nights at Morley College, why he had hated it so much. It was my loss that he hadn't been much more talkative before the Pick's disease had taken over, and less so after my mother had died, when I'd mistaken the early symptoms for grief and withdrawal. It is to my shame that at the time he had needed me most, after Mum's death, I had still been obsessed with Olivia, and hadn't spent the time trying to bring him out of the shell he had retreated into. And even though I now knew it was the illness that caused him to withdraw, it did not absolve me.

Now, making sure the door was closed, I told him all about the Bookers, Quintin Boyd and Trisha Greene. I told him about Jason having his fingers broken, me being knifed, the office being broken into. I told him about being drugged by Boyd and my confusion about the case. I also mentioned the Cambridge Blue Club several times to see if I got any reaction. But there was nothing except when he occasionally turned and smiled as if it was the first time he'd set eyes on me. I left when they were about to serve lunch.

In the car I put on the radio and then quickly turned it off when I heard people speaking in the same educated tones Sylvia did. As I pulled out of the car park the hole that had let the sun through was patched up, as if the weather had realised that it had slipped up and quickly corrected itself.

37

WHEN I TOOK MY KEYS OUT TO GET IN THE HOUSE I PULLED Quintin's – or rather Eric's copy of Quintin's – out with them. And once inside I emptied my pockets and found the DVD with the disc I'd half-inched from his apartment and my now battered and unopened packet of condoms. The latter reminded me that I ought to call Nina to try and explain why I hadn't gone back to her place last night, but curiosity about what was on the disc trumped that. I would call her later, or go round with flowers and chocolates.

I made coffee and put on the Goldberg Variations while my computer started up. I put the disc in the drive and it churned for a while but nothing happened. I took it out and dialled up the Internet. My email programme beeped at me to let me know I had mail. Amongst the usual junk was one from Olivia headed "Restoration continues apace!" but my eye was drawn to two emails from Jason. The first just said, "Photos here, boss..." with a web link underneath. The other said, "Tracker details and map..." and had a Word document attachment. He hadn't wasted any time.

I clicked on the link and waited. Images took an age to load with dial-up and I couldn't do anything else on the computer while it happened. The screen slowly filled with postage-stamp-sized thumbnails, which I recognised as my photos of Trisha Greene with various blokes in the Gogs car park and whoever she had met over the few days I'd followed her. I could make out the ones I had picked out for the husband as evidence of her screwing around; I'd chosen the ones that were fairly innocuous. I started to download them all, but it took ages because of my slow connection. Jason was always banging on about me needing to get broadband – maybe he had a point; I tended to dismiss a lot of his recommendations as uncritical championing of technology, a lot of which exists because it can, rather than because it provides function.

There were about fifty photos in all, some in an eerie black and white that was a result of using the infrared Fuji camera, essential for car park shoots in the dark. I had time to make and eat a cheese and pickle sandwich before the downloads were all done.

I scanned through the ones I'd given the husband, to see if I'd missed anything. I hadn't checked on the man's identity – it hadn't been part of the brief – and went through the others. There were several sets of photos I'd taken of her with various men, one set with a guy in a suit Trisha had hooked up with at the car park, who drove a Volvo estate with a kid's seat in the back. Like the others they'd done the deed in her car, even though his was bigger – perhaps he'd felt bad about doing it where he could see his kid's seat. Again, I hadn't checked up on the guy, although his number plate was in one of the photos.

I wasn't sure where I was going with this, because I certainly wasn't planning to investigate each of the men I'd taken pictures of. These were probably just a selection of the people she'd met up with, any one of whom could have been her killer. The point was that whoever killed her was worried about what might be in these photos, and what's more had an insider at Parkside, someone who knew the killer, someone who could make evidence disappear, and could point them in my direction. Brampton was suspect for knowing Quintin, but in her favour I could not tie Quintin to the break-in or to Trisha Greene, so Stubbing was higher on the list. She just happened to be there when I'd discovered the office had been turned over, perhaps to see whether I would find anything that had been missed. She had even convinced me not to report it and all this business about Brampton finding out from someone else about the break-in could be a smoke screen.

I pulled up the last of the photos just because I'd started the process and needed to finish it for the sake of completeness. I'm glad I did.

Now I knew why he'd looked familiar before: because I'd seen him through a long lens. In the photos I was currently looking at he didn't have his chauffeur's cap on although he was wearing his uniform, but his cropped hair, square head and short neck were unmistakable. In the first sequence he was in the passenger seat and was talking to Trisha. In the next she was talking and then they both left the car and disappeared. I remembered that at the time I couldn't see where they'd got to as they'd gone to a neighbouring bit of the car park that was separated by one of the large grassy ridges that divided it up. I had been about to come out of the bush I called home when a couple of men had climbed up nearby and engaged in some mutually pleasurable business. I'd stayed put, ironically worried about being called a voyeur and getting beaten up or being asked to join in. By the time they'd finished Trisha had come back to her car, doing up her jacket.

I hadn't made much of the incident; after all, nothing much had happened in comparison to some of the other encounters I'd photographed. But here I had Quintin Boyd's regular driver on film, consorting with a woman some days before her murder.

This presented my idea of Stubbing as the possible inside person at Parkside in a new light. Maybe it was Brampton who had recognised Quintin Boyd's driver and alerted Boyd, or, more likely, Boyd had warned Brampton that his driver had known the woman, and perhaps fearing bad publicity by association, had asked her to make the photos disappear. To be honest it was difficult to imagine her jeopardising her career and risking prison for the sake of old friends – after all, the photos themselves were fairly innocuous.

I pulled up the second email from Jason with the tracker information attached and downloaded the file to my computer which, after dicking about with the cable, I managed to connect to the printer.

When I eventually got the printer to start doing its thing the phone rang. I went to the hall and picked up.

"Hi, it's me," Sandra said. "Listen, Lucy's telling me that they've got this alumni thing tomorrow at Morley and Quintin is going to be there."

"And?"

"Well, he's the main speaker isn't he and she doesn't want to see him, does she?"

"She was trying to get into his apartment last night, now she doesn't want to see him? Besides she can stay in the house."

She sighed as if dealing with a slow child. "It seems Quintin will be using the house as a base, so he'll be in and out. I've told her she can stay with us until it's all over. I've also told her you'd take her home to get some clothes and stuff." There went my plans for a nap.

"Fine, I'll take her, I want to have a word with her mother anyway. I'll be there in twenty minutes." I picked up my car keys then went back into the living room. The printer was still working its magic so I pocketed the disc I'd got from Quintin's – maybe Jason could work out what was on it.

38

IT WAS NEARLY THREE WHEN I GOT BACK TO SANDRA'S. LUCY, Ashley and Jason were laughing as they watched a DVD. None of them looked up when I put my head round the door. Lucy did not look ready to go; her bare feet were tucked under her skinny legs on the sofa between the boys and she was cradling a mug of tea from which she gave Jason a sip.

Sandra and I sat in the kitchen drinking tea and waiting for the film to end.

I told her about what I'd found on the photos.

"Are you going to tell Brampton you've got them?"

"I'm not sure yet. What if it's Brampton who wanted them disappeared? I thought maybe it was Stubbing before but it's Brampton who has a history with Boyd, not Stubbing. And now he's connected to the dead woman through his driver."

"Did we check Stubbing on the alumni website?"

"She's too young to have been there when he was. Besides, Stubbing didn't go to university."

"How'd you know?"

"I just know."

"OK, but it's a big thing to do, make evidence disappear."

"You're right, it's career-buggeringly big. Stubbing said something about the USB stick not getting straight to the techies. If Brampton got to it before it was handed in then it would be difficult to prove that there was anything on it in the first place. She could have just zapped it."

"There must be more to it. I mean maybe the driver, what's his name, Mark, was just one of her regular dogging buddies, if they have regulars. From what you describe the photos aren't exactly incriminating, are they?"

I shook my head; I hadn't even seen Mark having sex with Trisha.

"So there must be something more than what is in the photos."

I'd thought all this on my way over, of course, and she was right.

"There's certainly something else going on." I thought of how Brampton had got into Quintin's car like a trained dog. "Let's suppose you are right, and Mark likes a bit of outdoor sex. That still doesn't explain why Brampton would take a risk covering for him."

Sandra shook her head and looked at me with her big brown eyes.

"What are you thinking?" she asked.

I was thinking that she was nice and easy to talk to. "I'm thinking that maybe Boyd has something on Brampton which makes her compliant."

Before I had time to talk that through Lucy appeared in the kitchen and Sandra gave her a cloud-busting smile.

"Have you come to take me home?" Lucy asked.

"Yes, are you ready?"

She nodded. She started to thank Sandra for offering her a haven and while they hugged I went to find Jason. I handed him the disc.

"Can you see what's on this for me, I can't seem to read it on my computer."

He took it between his thumb and little finger. "Yes, boss."

"Be discreet, I don't think it's family viewing. Call me on the office mobile when you know." I went back into the kitchen and Lucy went to say goodbye to the boys. Ashley ran in from the living room.

"Mummy, Mummy, Jason and Lucy are kissing!"

"Only on the cheek," Lucy protested from the other room but her giggle was plain to hear.

"It's good to hear that girl laugh," Sandra said.

In the car I asked Lucy whether her mother knew where she'd been.

"No. I'm afraid I was a bit of a coward and I got Sandra to ring her last night to say I was safe, and to tell her that she was a friend of yours, but I told her not to tell her where I was. I haven't spoken to her today and she doesn't know I'm coming home to get some overnight things. It was great of Sandra to offer."

"You don't want your mother to know where you are?"

She shrugged. "It feels good to be somewhere she doesn't know about, with people she doesn't know." She looked at me. "Do you understand?"

I nodded. It was probably why she spent secret time with Quintin Boyd, because she thought he was someone her mother hadn't known about. I drove for a while, feeling sorry for Lucy, and turned onto the Huntingdon Road.

"I'm beginning to grow fond of this car," Lucy said.

"It grows on you."

She released a long breath as we pulled into Morley College, and I noticed that her hands were placed carefully on her thighs, as if consciously trying to relax.

I parked behind the Mini. Elliot's Saab had gone. Lucy seemed reluctant to get out.

"You haven't admired my Armani suit," I said.

She smiled. "A bit short in the leg when you're sitting down but otherwise absolutely fab, darling."

The office mobile rang as soon as we got out.

"Can you talk, boss?"

"You go up. I'll follow," I said to Lucy. She hesitated and I gave her a firm wave. When she was up the stairs at the front door I put the phone back to my ear.

"What is it?"

"It's the disc you gave me. It's a DVD, that's why your old computer drive couldn't read it." He paused.

"Come on, boy, spit it out."

"It's porn."

"Well that's no surprise. He's got a collection of the stuff. It's probably ripped."

"This isn't ripped. It's home-made stuff and it's got that

woman in it. You know, the one we saw coming out of River Views." The foul-mouthed woman I'd confronted outside her house in Waterbeach. She'd said something about Quintin getting his take, now I knew what she meant.

"It's also got the driver in it, and the thin guy who broke my fingers. She gets quite pally with them. She's done this before, I'd say, definitely."

I looked up to the porch and saw that Sylvia had opened the door. I waved and she gave me a polite smile. Lucy went in and they immediately started arguing in the hall.

"Are you still there, boss?"

"What about Quintin, is he in it?"

"No, he doesn't appear in the action, but he's sometimes in shot. This stuff is all filmed from a fixed point of view, in HD. You can hear him giving instructions. But also, he occasionally appears in shot with the small camera I saw him buy in the shop, doing like close-ups? It's all unedited, this stuff, so I'd say it's possible the camera was recording straight onto DVD." Quintin, it seemed, was an amateur pornographer.

"You've done well, Jason. Your mum didn't know you were watching it, did she?"

"Don't worry, boss, there are some things I can do in private."

Sylvia was standing expectantly at the open door. I hung up and took the worn steps up towards her.

39

SYLVIA STOOD ASIDE AND I PASSED HER INTO A HALL LARGE enough for ballroom dancing. The ceiling went all the way to the top of the house, with a spiral staircase winding round the fuck-off chandelier I'd spotted before. Lucy had disappeared. According to the grandfather clock under the stairs it was just after four.

"I have to thank you, George, for rescuing Lucy yet again. It's above and beyond the call of duty." She moved from one small bare foot to the other. Despite the time of day she had on some sort of silk pyjama outfit with matching robe – perfectly respectable, but clingy at the same time. "We must seem dysfunctional to you, as a family." I could smell gin on her breath and her jewelled eyes glistened like the crystals in the chandelier. This was not the Sylvia I had come to know.

"I've no yardstick by which to measure it. Besides, you've been through a lot," I said.

She closed the front door.

"Come in and have a drink. I could make some tea," she said, not disguising her ambivalence towards the idea.

"I'll have whatever you're having." I followed her through

one of the many doors off the hall into a large sitting room. The room looked over the back garden that I had trespassed in; we must have been on the other side of the house where I'd found Elliot. There were numerous sofas and armchairs and pools of light were provided by black-shaded lamps. Sylvia closed the heavy door and moved to a large drinks cabinet, which held pretty much every drink I knew of except Quintin Boyd's special bourbon.

"I'm drinking gin and tonic," she said.

"Then perhaps a whisky."

"I didn't think you were a G and T man. Single malt OK?"

"That would be acceptable." I felt self-conscious here, in Sylvia's space, like the gardener who's been asked into the house after only seeing it from the outside for years. She brought me a drink and appraised my Armani suit, although she had the grace not to comment.

"Let's sit, George." I followed her to a couple of large high-backed floral-patterned Chesterfields that faced each other across an antique coffee table. Her movements were looser, more relaxed than I'd been aware of before. Maybe it was the gin; maybe it was the fact that I was alone with her in silk pyjamas and subdued lighting and drinks in our hands. Maybe I was still recovering from a GHB-induced stupor. I reminded myself that she was a six-day-old widow on the verge of a possible breakdown. I sat opposite her and noticed that her hair hadn't been styled, probably contributing to her more relaxed look. That and the gin; the gin had definitely softened her face. She put her feet under her thighs, just as her daughter had done at Sandra's. I sipped my drink and tried to pull my trouser legs down over my socks then looked out at the dark garden. I could feel those eyes on me. I turned my gaze on her, studying her face.

"I met with Quintin Boyd last night," I said.

She sipped her drink and blinked.

"Lucy went to see him, to confront him about something, probably about him knowing you and not telling her, but he wasn't there." She said nothing so I upped the stakes. "She says he's been taking photos of her."

It was as if I'd slapped her. She put her drink down on a coaster on the coffee table.

"What sort of photos?"

"Portraits, that sort of thing. Nothing untoward as far as I can gather."

She shook her head and then put her hands to her face.

"He wouldn't. Even *he* wouldn't."

"Wouldn't what?"

She looked up, as if surprised I was there. She shook her head again.

"What wouldn't he do?" I pushed. "He wouldn't take pornographic pictures of her?"

"Why would he do that?" she said quickly.

"Because it's what he does. He's moved on since the Cambridge Blue Club. He makes pornographic films now, not just watches them, although he still does that as well."

"You're just trying to shock me," she said.

"Yes I am," I said harshly. "You haven't told me the whole truth about Quintin, first pretending you didn't know him, then when I caught you out about that, pretending you hadn't seen him since university. You may have your reasons, I don't know, but I don't really know what you want from me any more. I know that Quintin is a nasty piece of work and that he has some hold on you. Perhaps you're afraid of him." I stood up. "I can't help you any more, Sylvia. I can't work for someone who constantly lies and withholds important information. Jason's fingers were broken by Quintin's sidekick because I took your case, and I've been stabbed and threatened."

I was about to add 'Good day' and walk out when she covered her face with her hands and muttered something.

"Sorry, I didn't catch that," I said.

She shook her head, taking her hands from her face. Her cheeks were wet and she wouldn't look at me. I looked round for tissues and found some on a dresser. They were disguised with a silver box with a slit in the top. I put it on the sofa beside her. She took one out and I took our glasses to the corner drinks cabinet to refresh them. There was a lot of nose blowing and pulling of tissues and by the time I got back with new drinks she'd regained some composure, but sat slumped and red-eyed on the sofa, barely acknowledging the drink that she took from me.

She took a deep breath and exhaled through dried lips.

"He hasn't moved on," she said, her voice dropping to a husky whisper.

"What do you mean?"

"He's filmed before, when we were here as students."

"You mean you weren't watching films?"

"No, we watched the films, quite a big group of us did, but Quintin really wanted to make one."

"So he did?"

She nodded, looking down, twirling the rings on her finger like they would make her disappear. I didn't know how to ask the next question but I was guessing that she wanted me to ask it.

"And did you…?"

She nodded without looking up then hid her face with her hands.

"It was just the once, after one of his screenings," she said from behind her fingers. I had to lean forward to hear her. "A few of us stayed behind. Things got out of hand, we'd had a lot to drink. I don't even remember a lot of it, it was like a dream."

I thought I was beginning to understand what was going on.

"He still has the recording, doesn't he?" I asked, thinking of the VHS tapes I'd seen in his collection. She removed her hands from her face and looked at me.

"It's like a sword hanging over me. It was a terrible mistake, and something he's used against us for eighteen years."

"Us?"

"Elliot and me."

"And Brampton?"

She hesitated then, almost imperceptibly, nodded. I put my drink down on a coaster. It had the Morley crest on it with the motto underneath, *Aut viam inveniam aut faciam*. I had no idea what it meant. What she had told me explained the hold Quintin had over her, the investments Elliot had made with him, the fact that Brampton was in his pocket. Something else occurred to me.

"Why did Elliot go to Legacy Labs?"

Her head shot up and she frowned. Strands of hair stuck to her wet cheeks.

"How did you… No he didn't…"

"Was it Lucy? Did he suspect Lucy wasn't his?"

"No, no he didn't suspect…"

"Well what is it then?" I said, raising my voice. Then I remembered that Elliot's name wasn't on the system at Legacy Labs.

"Was it you? It was you, wasn't it, who requested the test."

"No, no, no. You've got it all wrong."

"How have I got it bloody wrong?" I shouted.

"Shush," she said, looking at the door. "It was Quintin."

"What? Quintin? You mean…"

"He got the test done." She lowered her voice, glancing again at the closed door. "He must have suspected Lucy wasn't Elliot's. Elliot didn't know, it didn't even cross his mind that Lucy wasn't his. So Quintin ordered the test and got the results sent to Elliot." She looked out of the French windows into the dark. "It pushed Elliot over the edge, what with the bad investments Quintin had made him put college money into. The timing couldn't have been worse."

Or better, I thought, if that had been Quintin Boyd's intention.

"So Quintin is Lucy's father?" I said more quietly.

She dried her face and took a long drink, avoiding my gaze. If she nodded it was slight.

I was about to push her again but the door opened and she managed a fixed smile to greet her daughter. Lucy asked her mother about some missing item of clothing and Sylvia got up unsteadily and left the room.

I felt weary and my shoulder began to throb. I had the painkillers with me but I wasn't sure they mixed well with single malt. The truth is I liked the throbbing, it kept me awake. Awake enough to do some maths. Sylvia must still have been at college when Lucy was conceived. Perhaps Elliot had done the right thing by her after she'd found out she was pregnant; perhaps she'd got pregnant at this session they'd filmed. However, I didn't really trust Sylvia to be completely honest, despite her sudden revelations. She came back into the room.

"Lucy's nearly ready. It's probably for the best that she goes with you; there's the alumni gathering all day here tomorrow. Quintin is giving the keynote and I'd like to avoid a confrontation between them. Obviously I would expect you to charge me for looking after her."

"I won't charge you for babysitting. It was Sandra's idea, anyway."

"Ah yes, the woman who phoned me last night."

I stood up, draining my glass. "Will you be alright here on your own tonight?"

"I won't be on my own; there's a formal dinner I have to attend here."

"They expect you to attend?"

"I usually accompanied Elliot to High Table; it was thought it would send the right message if I took his place."

I shook my head; these people were crazy. To put her up there for all the students to gawk at. "You're going on your own?"

"Quintin will be there," she said, lowering her eyes.

No doubt sitting in Elliot's chair, I thought.

She stepped forward and placed her hand on my arm.

"Would you get the tape for me, George? I'll pay you well, whatever you want." I could see the desperation in her strange-coloured eyes, smell it in the gin, feel it in her grasp. That American brute had kept her guessing for over eighteen years and it was becoming too much for her to bear.

"I'll see what I can do," I said. "What time is he here tonight?"

"Seven. He'll be here for a couple of hours at least."

"You have my mobile number. Ring me if he leaves early for whatever reason."

Nodding, she mouthed, "Thank you." But no sound came out.

"I can't promise anything," I said.

She was trembling. I instinctively opened my arms and she came to me gratefully, her head against my chest. I wrapped my arms around her, her body soft and warm under the silk gown. Lucy came to the door, bag in hand. She looked at me in disgust and withdrew to the hall. A second later the front door slammed and Sylvia was jolted out of my embrace.

40

IN THE CAR LEAVING MORLEY LUCY LOOKED OUT OF HER window, saying nothing. I'd come out of the house and found her sitting in the passenger seat studiously looking ahead as I descended the steps. On the Huntingdon Road I spotted the McDonald's I'd stopped at the night I'd found Elliot. I turned off into the car park.

"Hungry?" I asked.

"Are you sleeping with my mother?" She was still looking out of the window.

"No I'm not. She's going through a rough time, that's all. What do you take me for?"

"A man."

I parked, silenced the engine and looked at Lucy.

She looked down at her feet, rubbing a pair of worn silver ballet pumps together. Not what I would call sensible autumn wear.

"The food here is made for people who are hung over," I said.

* * *

I sipped coffee while Lucy devoured a cheeseburger, checking her face for any resemblance to Quintin. I couldn't see it, myself, but then these things sometimes skip a generation. Cathy, the woman who I'd talked to the night I'd found Elliot Booker dead at Morley, came over carrying a glass pot of coffee.

"Can't keep away eh?" she said, giving me that smile I remembered. Maybe I was too much of a sucker for women's smiles.

"How'd your essay go? What was it? Don't tell me... erm... hybrid polymers."

"Yeah, well done, you get a free coffee refill."

Lucy got up and excused herself.

"Is she a relative?" Cathy asked when Lucy had gone towards the toilets. Her smile had transformed into what I took to be a smirk – had she said 'relative' with virtual quotation marks round it?

I shook my head, annoyed at the second implication in the same hour that I was some sort of lech taking advantage of the recently widowed and their impressionable daughters. The annoyance must have shown in my face.

"I didn't mean anything by it," she said. "It's just that—"

"Forget it, I'm tired," I said.

She poured some coffee, saying, "Yeah, you look knackered."

"Thanks."

She smiled – her teeth weren't as straight as Nina's, but that gave her smile authenticity. "By the way," she said. "A rude detective stopped by my house a few days ago, wanted me to give you an alibi for Sunday night. What happened?"

"I was in the wrong place at the wrong time. Sorry you got dragged into it."

She shrugged. "It's no biggie. In fact it's the most excitement I've had all week."

"Really? I thought student life was a continuous round of binge drinking, May Balls and punting."

"Yeah, right. Some of us have to work evenings to make ends meet so drinking is out. May Ball is a hundred quid at least and I've never been in a punt."

I nodded understandingly and sipped coffee, the sole virtue of which was its heat.

"Well," she said, "if you need another alibi you know where to find me. I'm usually here Sundays, Mondays, and Tuesdays, six 'til closing. I'm just filling in for the other work-shy manager today. Just ask for me." She pointed at her name badge and walked off as Lucy came back to the table.

I watched Cathy walk away. Lucy sat down and let out a long belch.

"My goodness, excuse me. I've not eaten one of those before," she said, looking at the mess of greasy paper in front of her. She nodded in Cathy's direction. "She's pretty. Is she the reason we came in here?"

"No."

She put on a contrite expression. "Look, I'm sorry I accused you of sleeping with my mother."

"Don't worry about it, it made sense for you to ask. Let me ask you something."

"What about?"

"About Quintin Boyd."

She frowned and pursed her lips. "What about him?"

"Well, where did you meet him?"

She started to fold up the paper wrapper from her meal. "This is going to sound weird, but I met him after my first bridge club, through a girl in the photography club. I didn't know her particularly well but she told me he was a semi-pro photographer who had seen me and wanted to take my picture. He said I had an interesting face, which I thought at least was honest. I know I must sound naive, but he was very respectable and treated me with courtesy. He's the first real man to pay me any attention, not counting the drunk boys at college."

"Do you think that's all he wanted from you, to take photos?"

She blushed and cocked her head. "What makes you think I didn't want something from him?"

I sat back, thrown by her answer. She folded the wrapper into smaller and smaller halves.

"He made me feel special, like I was the only person that mattered. He's very charismatic and has always been a perfect gentleman, at least the first few times."

"What happened?"

"Well, he'd been taking photos, just portraits, you know. Like I said, I wasn't being naive, I knew, at least I thought I did, what he really wanted. And to be honest," and here she reddened again, "I would have gone further – I gave him enough hints, tarted myself up..." She studied the table. "Then I realised that he wasn't interested in me in that way. I mean why would he be, I'm not beautiful or anything."

I considered telling her that she was beautiful or that beauty was in the eye of the beholder but I didn't think she was fishing for compliments or would put up with being patronised.

"Then something changed," she continued. "He changed, became more pushy. He asked me if I would take my top off, maybe pose for some more risqué photos. Artistic of course, nothing sordid." She blushed again, perhaps realising how silly it sounded out loud.

"When was this?"

"The last couple of times I saw him. Anyway, after wanting him all along to suggest it I got cold feet when he did. Besides, I never had much time before getting back for the end of bridge club."

The timing of this change of attitude didn't make sense to me. Presumably that was when he'd done the DNA test and discovered that she was his daughter. What sort of sick fuck was he?

"What does your mother say about him?"

"She refuses to talk about him. When I discovered, at Daddy's funeral, that he knew my parents, it came as a bit of a shock. All she told me was that they were at Morley together. And the fact that he never said that he knew them…" She shook her head and looked at me. "Do you think he and my mother were… you know?"

I kept my face noncommittal, draining my coffee, and looked towards the counter where I caught Cathy looking at me. I wondered whether I should leave her my card on the way out.

"Let me get you back to Sandra's."

I stood up and so did Lucy.

"What do you think Quintin wanted with me? Why didn't he tell me that he knew my parents?"

"I really don't know, Lucy. All I know is that despite his appearances and charm, he's a bit of a shit and you're better off avoiding him." Even if he is your father, I thought.

I didn't leave Cathy my card, because of how it would look to Lucy.

41

AFTER DROPPING LUCY OFF I CONSIDERED STOPPING OFF AT Nina's to apologise for last night but I felt shattered. The whisky I'd had at Sylvia's hadn't helped and I could only think of getting home to have proper coffee followed by a microwaved pizza from the freezer, maybe washed down with a beer. Then bed. I decided, as I pulled into my drive, that I would ring Nina between the coffee and the pizza. I didn't see Stubbing until I put the key in my front door.

"Jesus Christ. Do you live in the fucking hedge or something?" I said.

"Can I come in?"

I went inside leaving the door open and put lights on. The door closed as I went to the kitchen and filled the kettle. Stubbing came into the kitchen. She was dressed in jeans and a woolly jumper under an unzipped puffer jacket. The jeans made her look more stick-like than her work suit. The suit hid the fact that you could pass a paperback between her thighs when her feet were together.

"What are you doing here on a Saturday night?" I asked. "Is there nothing on TV?"

"Nice suit," she said. "Although it's a bit upmarket for you, isn't it?"

"It was a gift."

"I meant style-wise, not money-wise."

"Nice. It's a wonder you're still single, it really is. Seriously, why are you here?"

She stood against the wall next to the fridge as I put ground coffee into the pot.

"What did the boss say to you in the car?" she asked. I poured hot water onto the coffee grains and watched them swell and rise to the surface before pushing down the plunger.

"Let's go somewhere more comfortable."

As I led Stubbing past the dining room I saw the computer was still on as I'd left it, although the screen had gone to sleep. The sheets in the printer tray reminded me that the computer had been in the middle of printing the GPS information from Trisha Greene before I'd gone out. I ushered her into the living room and as she passed me I caught a whiff of her stale sweat. I put some lamps on and we sat down.

"Your boss wanted to know whether I had copies of the missing photos, but you knew that already. What gets me is why she would be so interested in something that made no difference to the case. Since the husband confessed and you've got his belt, why the interest in the photos?"

She just looked at me and took off her puffer jacket.

"Did she have access to the USB stick before you did? Before the techies did?"

"No comment."

"She's also a little touchy about her past," I continued. "She belonged to some club at university started by Quintin Boyd. They used to watch porn films together."

Stubbing made a noise like a dog with something stuck in its throat. "I can't see Brampton watching porn, can you?" she said.

"There may be more," I said.

She leaned forward.

"They may have made films together, not just watched them."

Stubbing whistled, low and long. "That would explain a lot," she said.

"Like why Brampton sits up and begs when Quintin says so?"

She nodded, and I could see her working things out, piecing it together.

I sat back in my chair, pressing painfully against my wound. "I think she's worried about the photos turning up, is what I think, not the fact that they're lost."

Stubbing leant forward and stared at me. "You've got copies, haven't you?"

"What would you do with them if I had? Give them to Brampton?" I was going to add 'like a good little dog' but I was hoping our relationship might move somewhere more mutually beneficial.

She went pale and her lips disappeared. "I've been taken off the Greene case," she said, her voice hard.

"Why's that?"

"Officially it's because there are more important things

to be working on but basically 'cause I don't think Al Greene killed his wife. I know his belt was round her neck but I've interviewed him three times and he's not the killer."

"But you got a confession."

"Brampton got a confession. I wanted to talk to some of the pig men his slut of a wife used to meet up with. But then the photos disappeared and I came to see you." She leant forward. "So, George, do you have anything you want to share?"

"Just with you, not for Brampton?"

"Look, I'm just as anxious to get to the bottom of this as you are. Brampton isn't the only one with a career. If she goes down for something she may have done I go down, unless I can come up with something."

I studied her for a few seconds and stood up. "You know what, Stubbing, you're in for a special treat."

She stood up and pushed her rucked jeans down her skinny legs. "Maybe you should start calling me Vicky."

"I'm not quite there yet," I said, and she grinned.

In the dining room Stubbing looked at the chessboard laid out on the other end of the table.

"Who do you play chess with?"

I moved the mouse and the computer came to life. "I don't. It's a chess problem."

"You mean you play on your own?"

"Yes. Come and look." The photos of Trisha Greene appeared, little thumbnails that filled the screen, and she joined me. We hunched over, our heads together, and I caught that sour smell again.

"It's a seedy job you've got, Kocky," she said, as I scrolled through the pictures.

I shrugged, bringing up the pictures of Quintin's driver and Trisha Greene, walking off together, then her coming back alone. "You know who that is, right?"

She nodded. "Mark Stillgoe, Quintin's occasional driver." She stood up and folded her arms, staring down at the screen. I picked up the sheets from the printer, one listing the postcodes Trisha had been to in her car, the other a map showing the same. I stared at the map. Had Jason sent me the wrong one? This looked like Quintin Boyd's map: his road was flagged on it, but Trisha's name was clearly marked at the top. I checked the list; again, Trisha Greene's name was at the top. From the map I looked at the River Views postcode and scanned the list of postcodes on the other sheet for it. It appeared. She had been there a week before she died.

Stubbing was going through the rest of the photos, pulling them up one by one and moaning about my slow computer. I shoved the printout under her nose.

42

OVER PEPPERONI PIZZA AND BEER AT THE KITCHEN TABLE Stubbing and I talked. If I'd been worried that she'd rush off to Brampton with the news that the murdered woman had known her university buddy – or at the very least parked on his street – I had no need. It was becoming apparent to me that Stubbing, or Vicky as she wanted me to call her, was no fool. I brought her completely up to date, telling her about my run-in with Quintin's knife man, my discovery of his DVDs and my confrontation with the man himself last night, ending with the fact that he was making his own movies. I didn't tell her about the nature of the warning he'd made against me or that he was probably Lucy Booker's father or that there existed a sex tape of Sylvia in Quintin's apartment; that was between me and Sylvia.

"Sounds like he used a date-rape drug on you. You sure he didn't put you in one of his films?"

"My arse isn't sore, if that's what you mean. But maybe he uses it on the women who come to his place, I mean the ones he doesn't pay or who aren't willing."

"Some people take it recreationally in smaller doses.

Maybe that's how they get in the mood to be filmed. Maybe he even filmed Trisha Greene, in which case that's something to take to Brampton that she can't ignore."

"Or make disappear," I said. I leaned back and pulled out another couple of beers from the fridge.

"The thing is that even if I was in a position to try and get a warrant to enter his place, I've got very little to go on. That's why it would be good to get hold of actual footage. Your photos tie the driver to Trisha and the GPS data shows she parked on Quintin's street for a couple of hours a week before she was killed. It's not enough. If we could show she was there on the night, for instance."

"Unfortunately I took the tracker off before then."

I got up and went into the hall, rummaged in my coat pocket and pulled out the crushed box of condoms, the DVD that I'd picked up from Jason when I dropped Lucy off and the keys to Quintin's penthouse. I put the condoms and DVD on the hall table next to the phone. In the kitchen I tossed the keys onto the table in front of Stubbing. She picked them up.

"What are these?"

"The keys to Quintin Boyd's apartment. And," I added, before she could ask where I got them, "I happen to know that he'll be out tonight." I looked at the clock on the wall. "In about an hour in fact."

She sat back in her chair and shook her head. "Do you know what you're asking?"

"I'm asking you to accompany me when I go to someone's house to pick up a DVD he was going to lend me. That's all. I'm not going to break in; I have the keys." I didn't mention that I also wanted to pick up the tape of Sylvia.

She looked at the keys, unconvinced.

"You wouldn't want me to get drugged again, would you? It could be worse this time if I'm caught," I said, thinking of the photo I'd woken up with.

"If I was caught in his flat my so-called career would be buggered, never mind you. I'm already off Brampton's copper-of-the-month shortlist."

"Does Quintin know what you look like?"

"I don't think so, but—"

"So even if he were to turn up—"

"Save your breath, George. Listen, most I'll do is wait outside the residence while you pick up the aforementioned DVD from the apartment whose owner gave you his keys with the express intent that you could enter his premises."

I sat down. It was the most I was going to get out of her, but it would be good to know that she would be watching my backside while I was inside.

"OK, we've got an hour to kill. Do you want another beer?"

She shook her head and leant forward, giving me a blast of pizza and beer. "Why don't we watch that DVD you got hold of from his apartment?"

I shrugged. I'd planned to watch it but it wasn't an experience I wanted to share with Stubbing of all people.

"It's just professional, Kocky, to see if there's anything on it we can use against Quintin Boyd."

* * *

For all his pontificating about the artistic merit of 1970s porn, Boyd's own efforts were laughable. Jason was right; it obviously wasn't a finished piece, more a series of scenes taken from one camera. The woman who'd been dropped off by Quintin Boyd's driver and who I'd spoken to outside her house was the star of the show. I was embarrassed to be watching this sat next to Stubbing, professional or not, and my embarrassment grew when a man's arm came into shot and started to pull her dress up. She protested but her heart wasn't in it. I glanced at Stubbing beside me who was leaning forward, intent on the small screen. I tried to study the setting where it was happening.

"Is that in his apartment?" I wondered aloud, my voice at odds with the over-the-top moaning coming from the screen. It was in a room I didn't recognise. In the middle was a small bed, more like a massage table, on which the now naked woman lay back, and I had to endure her use of a variety of weird-looking sex toys, culminating in the use of two at once. All the while she was pretending she didn't want to do it, looking behind the camera and pleading with whoever was there to stop filming, but Quintin's voice was heard telling her to do what she was told. None of it was going to win any Oscars, not even those obscure ones nobody cares about except the recipient.

"She's definitely a pro – over the hill mind – but a pro," Stubbing said, and I gave her a questioning look.

"I've had to watch lots of this stuff."

"How about a cup of tea," I said, getting up and moving to the door – I just wanted to be out of the room.

"*He's* definitely not a pro," I heard her shout as I filled the kettle. "He must have lighting set up in the room, and he's using a high definition camera."

I put on the kettle but Stubbing kept up her loud commentary.

"She's good, it takes practice to do that without gagging. But the two blokes are amateurs."

In the kitchen, I tried to drown out the sounds of the film by washing two mugs up. By the time I'd poured hot water over teabags it had gone quiet.

"Too hardcore for you was it?" Stubbing said from the kitchen door. "Believe me, that was pretty tame." I turned to see her leaning against the frame, arms folded, grinning.

"Well? Did you learn anything?" I asked.

She shrugged. "She wasn't drugged, she seemed willing enough; there was no coercion, not on film anyway, even though she's pretending she's being forced into it. There's nothing disturbing or unusual about it, it's not like it's kiddie porn. The only thing that's odd is who's made it. You don't generally find someone of Quintin Boyd's type making porn – it's not like he needs the money and it's pretty lame stuff compared to what's out there. Also, it's unedited. It's all one take. He's even in shot using a small camcorder for close-ups."

"I'm told the big camera records straight to DVD, so it's just the raw footage."

"That makes sense, he probably edits it together with the stuff from the small camera on a computer."

I glanced at the clock. "We've still forty-five minutes to

kill. Do you want some tea?" I held up a steaming mug.

"No thanks." Her expression changed into something I'd not seen before and she said, matter-of-factly, "Do you want to have sex?" She held eye contact, and I looked in vain for signs of sneering or mocking.

"OK." I put the mugs in the sink.

"You've got a condom, I assume?" she asked.

"Yes, as a matter of fact, I have."

43

STUBBING AND I SAT IN MY GOLF IN THE CAR PARK OPPOSITE River Views. A fine drizzle meant that I had to occasionally flick on the wipers to look up at the penthouse apartment and see if the lights had gone out. Stubbing was drumming her fingers on the dash – she had no fingernails to speak of.

"I see your windows don't steam up. The old taxi driver's washing-up liquid trick?" she asked.

"You pick these things up if you've sat in a car long enough," I said.

She nodded. "I tell you something. Pissing in a car is easier for men." She took out a small pot of Vaseline and applied some to her thin lips using her little finger. Part of me was now regretting that we'd had sex. Part of me was extremely glad we had. However, if I'd expected cuddles and pillow talk afterwards I was a bigger fool than I already knew I was.

"That was a one-off, Kocky, it doesn't mean I'm giving you my phone number or that we're going to the cinema together," she'd said, pulling on her once-white underwear and faded jeans over her stubbly long-distance-runner's legs

– we hadn't made the time to get her jumper off, never mind her bra, and she hadn't even made eye contact during the short time she'd frantically ground her hips against mine, testing the condom to near destruction. Seconds after, we were finished, and I was lying on the bed, my trousers and pants round my ankles, making sure the condom had held up to the rigours of Stubbing's furious fornication. Indeed I half wondered whether I should provide a testimonial to the manufacturer.

"I know it was a bit, erm, hasty, but in my defence it has been six months," I said. "Maybe next time we can—"

"I've just told you there won't be a next time. It was a one-off thing that we both needed. Now let's go to Quintin's."

Stubbing hadn't bothered to wash after sex and in the enclosed stuffiness of the Golf her stale sweat and the smell of sex combined in a heady mix that made me wish that I could crack open the window. But I didn't want to be obvious and besides, it was cold outside and had started to rain.

"How will you know which DVD to pick up? You can't bring the whole lot out," she asked.

"I've thought about that," I said, taking the DVD we'd watched from my pocket. "There's a serial number on this – there's one on all of them – so there must be a book or something that references them. If I can find that then maybe it will point me in the right direction."

She turned to look at me for the first time since we'd got in the car and I had trouble believing that just thirty minutes ago she'd been riding me with wild abandon.

"Your plan is flawed," she said. "One, if there is such a

list it will most likely be computerised. Two…" She stopped and stared at the DVD in my hand. "Hang on a minute," she said, looking back at me, "you know from your GPS tracker the date Trisha was parked here, right?"

I nodded.

"Then all you need to do is pull out the DVD with that date on it." She grinned in what I took to be a patronising manner since I hadn't a clue what she was on about.

"What?"

"That's not a serial number, George, it's a date."

I looked at the number. True, it was six digits, the last two ending in what could be a year, but the middle two numbers were twenty-three, and the first two eleven. Just how stupid was she?

I gently pointed this out.

"You're being thick, Kocky. He's an American, you fool."

"So?"

She stared at me until a light bulb went on in my head.

"Of course, they swap the day and month."

"There you go."

I looked at the date on the DVD. It corresponded with the date I'd seen the woman in the film leave his place.

"Now, do you remember the date Trisha was here?" Stubbing asked.

"Mmm, let's see, I could work it out…"

She rolled her eyes. "It's a good job I can remember it, isn't it?"

I was spared the need to answer by the silver Merc pulling up outside River Views. I flicked the wipers on and off. Mark the driver spoke into his earpiece as the car idled and proceeded to check himself in the rear-view mirror.

"There's our man," said Stubbing. She wrote down the date I was looking for and wished me luck.

"Have you got a mobile on you?" I asked.

She looked at me suspiciously.

"Jesus, woman, it's just so you can ring me in case they come back."

"OK. Give me your number."

"I don't know the number," I said. And when she gave me another look I told her it was the office mobile and I never rang it.

"Give it to me," she said. I handed her the phone and she fiddled with it then keyed a number into her phone – one that looked more ancient than mine.

The lights went off in the penthouse and a few minutes later Quintin emerged from the gate of the apartments. Mark sprang out of the car and opened the rear door of the Merc. I spotted a bow tie under Quintin's coat. Mark did a three-pointer, pulling briefly into the car park entrance requiring us to duck our heads to escape the headlights. Our heads touched beneath the dash and oddly enough it was a more intimate moment than the one we'd had on my bed earlier. When the lights had gone we sat back up, but not before I'd noticed the build-up of wax in Stubbing's ear. A pizza delivery scooter pulled up outside the gates. I saw my chance; it would save me pressing all the buzzers on the off-chance someone would let me in with the old 'it's me' trick.

"OK then, I'm going," I said. "I shouldn't be more than twenty minutes."

She nodded. I got out into the rain and walked over to the gates as the helmeted teenager pressed a bell on the panel. I hoped Eric the concierge (if he was on duty) didn't come out of his room. I put my mac over my head to protect myself from the rain and the CCTV camera. The gate buzzed as I reached it and I went through behind the pizza boy, following the lovely smell. A smell that promised more than it delivered – like Chanel No. 5 on a woman who turns out to be wearing polyester underwear, or indeed a man in an Armani suit who buys his underwear in packs of five from the supermarket. At least when it came to Stubbing, what you saw is what you got.

44

IT WAS DARK INSIDE QUINTIN'S APARTMENT BUT THIS TIME I knew my way around. After dropping my wet raincoat over the back of a dining chair I went straight through the archway and down the hall to the office at the end, passing the bedroom and the door that was locked last time. The office was lit only by the computer screen. The computer, which was humming, hadn't yet put the screen to sleep; presumably because Quintin had been using it just before he left. I approached the desk and studied the screen more closely than I had last time. The computer was an Apple Mac, so I understood even less what I was looking at than usual. Some programme was running, a completion bar was nearly complete. I gave up, deciding I would look more closely when I had got what I came for, and went to the oak cabinet.

I opened the right-hand drawer and located the empty sleeve I'd left behind, slipping the DVD I'd borrowed back in the correct place. I flicked through the rest; it seemed they were arranged by date going back several years, the most frequent one being last week. This wasn't a recently acquired hobby, it was something he'd been developing for some time.

I moved forward through the discs until I found the only one with a date that coincided with Trisha Greene's visit.

Then I had a brainwave, the sort that hits you every now and then and makes you feel more intelligent than you really are. I looked for DVDs with the date of the night of Trisha's death. Yes, there was one. I put both DVDs in my jacket pocket.

I closed the drawer and was about to open the left-hand drawer with the VHS tapes in when the room went dark – the screen on the desk, which had been providing all the light in the room, had gone black. I went to the desk and jogged the mouse and got the dialogue box asking for a password. Now I felt stupid for not having a closer look when I'd had the chance. Then I heard a key in the front door and froze. I heard the front door close. Why hadn't Stubbing rung me?

It was quiet and no lights came on. What was he doing? Perhaps he'd forgotten something and gone to the bathroom. Shit: I'd left my raincoat over the back of a dining chair. I didn't understand why it was so quiet; the whole place was wood-floored so you would hear someone walking down the hall. I decided he must have gone to the loo so it was a good time to sneak out – in which case I'd have to forget about Sylvia's tape – or I could wait it out and hope he left without noticing my coat. I looked out into the dark hall and the last thing I saw before understanding why Stubbing hadn't called was a gold coin mounted in a claw heading for my eyes.

Surprised rather than stunned, the back of my head hit the door frame and I found myself on my arse looking at a pair of stockinged feet. No wonder I hadn't heard the fucker coming. A hole in the left sock allowed a long toe with a yellowing and cracked nail to protrude. Blood trickled down my nose and I tried to get up but cold sharp steel pressed against the side of my neck and stale cigarette breath came down at me.

"Don't fucking move."

I considered sweeping his legs from under him but my left arm was jarred from taking the brunt of my fall and my right hand was better occupied carefully feeling the damaged flesh between my eyes. My legs were splayed; the right inside the office, which meant the left was my only properly useful limb. But the thin man, as if anticipating my thoughts, moved to the side of me – any heroics would have to wait.

"OK, get on your front. Slowly." The cold of the knife contrasted with the warmth of the underfloor-heated hardwood against my cheek as I lay down.

"Now put your wrists together behind you."

I did as he said – I needed to find the right moment to strike the bastard and lying on the floor with a sharp point in my neck wasn't it. I heard rustling and looked up to see him undoing his tie with one hand. If he was planning to tie my hands he would need both of his – this could be my chance. But he had simply loosened his tie and slipped the noose over both my wrists with one hand and then pulled it tight. Still, I thought, a Windsor knot would be easy enough to loosen. But then the knife left my neck and was replaced by his foot and he swiftly bent down and secured the tie ends properly. It all took a couple of seconds and the knife was back on my skin. Then his hand gripped a handful of hair at the back of my neck and pulled.

"On your fucking knees, arsehole."

It's not easy getting on your knees from a prostrate position with your hands tied behind your back. And they were tightly tied, so tight that my fingers were beginning to lose feeling. I struggled to my knees and felt the point of the knife move to the back of my neck. He pulled my hair back which made it stick painfully into my skin.

"Easy," I said evenly.

"Shut up and start walking on your knees."

"Where to?"

"The next room."

I shuffled forward until we reached the door which he opened with his free hand. A light came on and revealed the massage table in the middle of the room – the table I'd seen in the film earlier. A large, professional-looking camcorder sat on a heavy duty tripod at the foot of the table. Another handheld camera was on some units along the right-hand side wall. A light with a large diffuser was mounted on another stand near the table.

"What now," I said.

"Just get on the fucking table, face down."

I stood up gingerly, my knees cracking. All this with him remaining behind me. There was a hole in the head of the table in which he told me to stick my ugly mug. He took his hand from my hair and leaned over me. I thought he was going to whisper in my ear but something came over my middle and arms and was tightened hard. Then another strap, the sort you use to tie luggage to a car, appeared in my vision and I could feel it being tightened hard over the back of my neck. Another strap was tightened over my ankles. I heard the door close and after a few seconds realised I'd been left alone. All I could think of was the message written on the back of the photo I'd woken up to last time I was here: next time we use this on you.

I tried to move but the most I could manage was to swivel my eyes. My hands were becoming increasingly numb, and no amount of movement would loosen the tie. Even if I could get my hands free, I was still strapped like a rolled-up carpet to a roof-rack. I relaxed, tired from thrashing about, and tried to make sense of my surroundings, the bits I could see anyway.

I was lying head towards the door. To the right of me I could make out the bottom of a leather sofa against the wall. To the left I could see vinyl cupboard doors, like in a budget kitchen. I knew, from when I'd come in the room, that they sat under a counter with a sink in it and a paper towel dispenser and a first aid kit above. The first aid kit worried me. I heard a voice from the other room, just the one. Sounded like the thin man was on the phone to his American master. Stubbing probably hadn't phoned because she didn't know this guy from Adam.

It went quiet and he came into the room, stepped up to the table and I felt him go roughly through my pockets.

"You don't have to do this," I said. He pulled out my mobile phone, then the two DVDs I'd taken from the office.

"Yes I do." He rapped me three times on the back of the head with the phone and left the room, closing the door behind him again. My head stung and I could hear his one-sided conversation again; or rather I could hear him talking without making out the words. I struggled at my ties and discovered that if I rocked left to right I could make the table move. How this was going to help I didn't know but I did it anyway, since action seemed preferable to none. Then the door opened again and the thin man's legs came up to the table and disappeared to my left. He dragged the table back to the middle of the room – he was strong for such a slight man, I'll give him that. Then he pulled my jacket over my shoulders, then my shirt, forcing it over my back until the top buttons popped and the cloth scraped my shoulder wound and was bunched down at the strap that was over my waist and arms.

"What the hell are you doing?" I asked, trying to go for dignified outrage rather than helpless terror – at least he hadn't pulled my trousers down, yet. "That's an Armani suit you're ruining." I could hear him panting with his efforts. I wondered how long it would be before Stubbing started to fucking worry and come up to check on me.

My dream of being rescued was painfully interrupted by him ripping the bandage from my shoulder.

"Listen to me," I said to the floor. "There's a copper waiting for me downstairs, a very mean detective."

"Of course there is. And Kim Kardashian is waiting for me in the bedroom with her legs spread." He laughed and it turned into a giggle that he cut short, perhaps aware that it didn't sound too manly. I heard him light up and caught the fresh smell of cigarette smoke.

"Only five stitches, eh? You'll be needing more than that when I finish with you."

"What would the point of that be?" I said, adopting the firm voice I'd heard Sandra use with Ashley when he demanded sweets before dinner.

"The point, you cunt, would be to teach you to stop messing in Mr Boyd's personal business." I felt the cold steel of his knife running between my shoulder blades and tensed.

"So you're just doing what you're told, right?" I said. Then I remembered something. "Why did you visit my father in the nursing home?" The knife stopped.

"Your father?"

"Yes. What the hell were you doing there?"

"Stop fucking talking," he screamed, but only after a very slight pause. I'd hit a nerve, not a good thing.

I felt the knife move to the wound and immediately began to sweat from places I don't usually put deodorant. I couldn't make out what his game was here. Worse case was he just liked hurting people, but he was still an employee, and that meant he was ultimately beholden to the boss.

"Mr Boyd won't want you committing a crime in his flat. This is already kidnapping, don't make it worse."

He giggled and I knew I was lost. Boyd had probably sanctioned this.

"What is it that you want?" I asked.

"I want you to tell me where Lucy is," he said. "But first I want you to scream." I felt the knife point in my wound. He flicked it upwards, cutting the first stitch and then pulling the semi-healed flesh apart.

And scream I did.

45

I MUST HAVE FAINTED AT SOME POINT BECAUSE I OPENED MY eyes and saw the thin man on the floor, his hands handcuffed behind him in the same position he'd had me. Someone loosened the strap around my head followed by the ones over my middle and ankles. I caught a whiff of Stubbing and relief washed over me, but it was immediately substituted by the pain of trying to move.

"Easy, George," I heard Stubbing say. "You've been operated on by our amateur surgeon here."

"How bad is it?" I asked.

"I've seen worse. It's not bleeding too badly but you'll need to get it seen to. I'll patch it up for now."

I cautiously sat up on the table – difficult with the shirt and jacket round my arms – while Stubbing got the first aid kit from the wall. I was covered in a cold layer of sweat. I looked down at my torturer and wondered if I could get away with stomping on his head. Stubbing, though, was attuned to my mood.

"Don't worry about him," she said. "Did you get what you came for?"

"He took it off me."

It was all he got off me though. In between removing my stitches he'd kept asking me about Lucy and where I'd hidden her. I hadn't told him anything, not because I was a hero, but because I'd been in too much pain to talk.

"Keep still," Stubbing said. She ripped open a sterile dressing and placed it over the reopened wound then taped it down. She pulled my buttonless shirt and jacket gently back over my shoulders.

I got off the table and went to the sink. As I splashed cold water on my face and used the mirror to examine the damage between my eyes, Stubbing had a look round the room.

"So this is where all the action happens." She moved to a narrow wall cupboard to my left and I heard her open the doors and whistle. I looked round. A variety of sex toys, a couple of which I recognised from the film, and one I'd posed with in the photo, were aligned neatly on a shelf in an upright position. Different colours, sizes and textures, they stood like a mismatched platoon of proud soldiers waiting to be given the order to stand easy. There were enough of them to play chess with. I'd once opened Olivia's bedside cabinet to look for something and I'd found one of these things stuffed at the back of the drawer. It seemed odd that a lesbian would need one, but then maybe it wasn't so odd, maybe it made perfect sense: all the benefits of a man without all the hang-ups.

"This would make your eyes water," Stubbing said, pulling down a large pink specimen with nobbles along its length. She twisted the bottom and it started to judder obscenely. "He must spend a fortune on batteries." She put it back carefully where she'd found it.

A noise made me turn to see the thin man getting awkwardly to his feet from his knees.

"Hey," I shouted.

Stubbing was faster than me and in two strides had reached him and kicked him under the kneecap. I winced as he screamed and dropped back to the floor. He lay on his side making strange noises through his open mouth. I had to sit down again as a tsunami of pain spread over my shoulder. Stubbing was manipulating the limping prisoner out into the hall. I followed them to the living room. She plonked him on a leather sofa. I searched his pockets, pulling out my mobile phone, his mobile phone, some loose change, the wrapper from a Mars bar, his flick knife and a wallet containing several store cards (the man's name was Kevin Chapman) and a wrinkled ten-pound note. There were no DVDs.

"I don't know what he's done with the DVDs," I told Stubbing.

"DVDs, plural?"

I nodded. She bent down and stuck her face in Kevin's. He sat back to create distance between them but she just followed, putting her hands either side of his head on the back of the sofa. If it weren't for the narrowing of her eyes and lips and the throbbing veins in her neck you'd think she was about to tongue him.

"Where're the DVDs, arsehole?"

"What DVDs?" He couldn't control the small smile that flashed across his anaemic face. Stubbing stood up and kicked him under the knee that hadn't been kicked. He yelled and bent over in pain.

"For fuck's sake," he cried, tears running down his cheeks. She pulled his head up by his hair and stuck her face back in his.

"Where're the DVDs?"

"You're hurting me."

"Maybe you should break his fingers," I said. "You know, like he did Jason's."

Stubbing looked at me.

"This was the guy?"

I nodded.

"Well why didn't you say so? I wouldn't have been so easy on the fucker."

"You can't do this," Kevin whined. "You're police aren't you?"

"I'm off duty," said Stubbing. "This is how I like to relax." I was beginning to believe her as she yanked Kevin off the sofa and made him kneel on his damaged knees. She stood in front of him and leaned forward to pull up his handcuffed hands until his head was forced against her midriff. She grabbed hold of a little finger and held his arms up by it. He started to whimper. I didn't like the look on Stubbing's face, regardless of my disgust for Kevin, but then I remembered that he'd been alone with my father.

"Maybe he just put them back," I said.

"Did you put them back?" she shouted, yanking his arms up.

He shook his head, tears streaming down his face.

"Just tell us where the DVDs are and this will stop," I said, looking at Stubbing since he couldn't see me.

Stubbing gave me a look to tell me what a wimp I was. "I flushed them," Kevin said.

"You what now?" she said.

"I broke them up and flushed them."

"Did Quintin tell you to do that?"

"Who?" Stubbing pulled his finger back and he yelped.

"Mr Boyd. Did Mr Boyd tell you to?" I asked.

"Why didn't you say 'Mr Boyd'? Yes, yes. He told me to. Please stop."

"I interrupted him in the loo when I was let in by the caretaker," Stubbing said. "He was standing over it flushing. I just thought he was trying to get rid of a floater."

I went to the all-white bathroom and looked into the toilet bowl – nothing. Then I caught a glint of something on the floor behind the basin. There was one of them. He must have stashed it there when he'd been interrupted by Stubbing. I picked it up and went back into the living room. Stubbing was holding Kevin's head to her midriff and stroking his hair like a mother who has reprimanded a child too severely and needs to comfort it. It was creepy but at least she'd let go of his fingers. I waved the DVD at her, then thought to check the date on it. It was the one from the day Trisha had died.

"You should have microwaved them, you moron," she said to Kevin, cuffing him aside the head. Then, to me, she said, "I'm going to take little Kevin down to Parkside and book him."

"OK, but can we talk in the other room?"

She moved Kevin over to the radiator, uncuffed his hands then recuffed one of them to the pipework. She patted him on the head and said, "Don't go anywhere." He scowled but it was half-hearted; he was a broken man.

We moved to the studio where Stubbing retightened her hair which had come loose in her manhandling of Kevin.

"He destroyed one DVD but didn't have time to destroy this one." She looked at it and I turned it so she could see the date.

"Bloody hell, George, you're not as stupid as you look."

"Well, it could contain something unrelated of course."

"Yeah, but it's more than a stab in the dark."

"Are you going to Brampton with him?" I asked.

She shook her head.

"With what? I'll book him for assaulting your boy, say I picked him up in a pub with that knife he's carrying. He'll play along 'cause otherwise it would be kidnapping and assault, but I'm assuming you don't want to press charges?" I shook my head. "Good, my being in here would be a bugger to explain." She rubbed her face. "I need more before I can go to Brampton. It needs to be watertight and undeniable otherwise she'll fuck me with something bigger than all the toys in that cupboard put together. What I'm going to do is get this turd to give me something on Quintin, which might give me enough to come back here and seize his computer, which might give me enough for Brampton. In fact I'll take the DVD from you; if there's anything on it I'll claim I found it on him."

I reluctantly handed it over.

"Right now we need to leave before Boyd gets back."

I hesitated. I hadn't got Sylvia's tape, but with Stubbing

here it was impossible. And any chance to ask Kevin what he was doing in the nursing home with my father would have to wait.

Being Stubbing she sensed my hesitation. "After you, Kocky."

Kamal's flatmate was mortified when he saw my wound because at first he thought his stitching wasn't up to much and it had somehow unravelled. It took as long as it did for him to restitch me for me to reassure him that it wasn't his fault. But there was no way I was going to go to Addenbrooke's and explain a knife wound that had become unstitched.

Kamal was not impressed with my story, telling me that I'd 'gone rogue' and needed to bring things back to the right channels. I let his voice wash over me, I was dog tired and spaced out on a cocktail of painkillers and whisky. My thoughts though were on the fact that I'd failed to recover the tape for Sylvia. Quintin would most likely be back home right now and removing everything to somewhere more secure, although Sylvia hadn't rung me to say he was leaving. Worse still is that Stubbing was planning on going back there if she got a warrant, and the police would end up with the tape, and this time Brampton wouldn't be able to dispose of it.

The office mobile phone went in my jacket. It was Sylvia – it was also approaching midnight.

"Hello?"

"George?" Sylvia's voice, urgent and low.

"Yes, is everything alright?"

"I have to be quick, he's just gone to the toilet before he leaves," she whispered. "Did you find the, erm, tape?"

"No I didn't; I was waylaid by his sidekick."

Kamal glared at me disapprovingly.

"But you have to get it, George, you must, you don't know what it's been like…" Her voice wobbled.

I wanted to tell her what I had been through already that night, that I needed to go home to bed and forget her sordid sex tape. But I recalled her face when I was round there earlier, recalled her smell when I'd given her a hug.

"Can you keep him there? I can go back but I need more time."

Kamal threw up his hands and shook his head in despair.

"I don't know, it's difficult. He'd like nothing more than to stay but I can't do it… not anymore…" She broke off.

"I need an hour," I said. "I won't get another chance, Sylvia."

"You don't know what you're asking me to do."

And you've no idea what you've asked me to do, I thought. "It's now or never," I said. "Once he gets home he'll remove the tape and store it somewhere else. He already knows I was there this evening, his sidekick called him."

She went silent and I thought she'd hung up.

"Hello?" I asked.

"He's coming back," she whispered. "Just get the tape. I'll keep him here, whatever it takes." She hung up.

"You're going back?" Kamal asked, wide-eyed in disbelief.

"Yes, I have to. Will you drive me?"

"No, I most definitely will not."

46

THIS TIME I DIDN'T BOTHER WITH TRYING TO SNEAK INTO RIVER Views. Fifteen minutes after hanging up on Sylvia I pressed the caretaker's buzzer, and Eric, who was on duty, shuffled out of his small office, popping a mint into his mouth. As anticipated, he didn't look pleased to see me. From my coat I pulled a quarter bottle of whisky I'd taken from Kamal's kitchen. He shook his head but opened the gate, slipping the flat bottle into his jacket pocket.

"I suppose you want me to let you into the penthouse, like I did that bloody policewoman?"

"No," I said. "I've still got the keys."

His mouth fell open. "I got into trouble for losing those keys. I knew you must have taken them."

"Borrowed them, Eric, borrowed them."

I made to step past him and he said, "I had to pay for new copies to be made from my own pocket."

We stood there for a second then I pulled out my wallet and handed him a tenner. He didn't take it, saying, "Those keys aren't like your normal keys you can get cut in a shoe repair shop, you have to send away for them to be done."

I attached another tenner to the first which he took and folded into three then slipped into his back pocket. Then he shuffled back into his cubby hole without as much as a nod.

In the lift to the penthouse I became aware of my shoulder. It had felt like a frozen leg of lamb; now it was beginning to thaw, letting the pain back in.

Quintin's apartment was becoming a home from home. I moved quickly to the office at the end of the hall, putting the lights on and going straight to the cupboard which contained the films. The computer was still humming, making the occasional grinding noise as the hard disk worked away at whatever it was doing. I opened the left drawer which held the video cassettes and looked at them more closely than I had before. There weren't as many as the DVDs but they also had American dates on them, printed onto labels on the spines, and were organised chronologically like the DVDs. The earliest was the year he'd graduated. It was the only one for that year. I pulled it out. Then I checked in the DVD drawer to make sure that there were none dated the same year.

I was in spitting distance of the front door when it opened. I stepped back involuntarily. Quintin came in and closed the door behind him. He stood against it, his raincoat dripping onto the hardwood floor, glancing at the cassette in my hand and grinning unpleasantly.

"Do you take me for a fool, George?"

I shook my head in genuine denial.

"Did you think I wouldn't be suspicious that Sylvia

unexpectedly turns on the sex appeal and wants me to stay with her? I knew she'd been on the phone when I was in the john. And who else would she call but her Armenian knight in shining armour. She never wants me to stay, never wants to fool around. Not willingly anyway." His full lips twitched momentarily into a brief smile as he took off his raincoat, carefully hanging it in a narrow cupboard next to the door. He was in his tuxedo, black tie undone at his throat, looking like he'd come straight from the set of a James Bond film. Then he moved to the drinks cabinet. "I'd offer you a drink but I suspect you'd decline."

I glanced at the front door.

"Go ahead. Run to the lovely Sylvia with her sex tape. Everyone wants to do her bidding. Everyone falls in love with those eyes."

I turned to look at him, pouring his poncy bourbon into a heavy glass. "You know it's not going to help her – having the tape – it won't free her from her past," he said. He went over to the leather sofa and sat down, legs apart, leaning forward with elbows on thighs, glass cradled in both hands. He contemplated the golden liquid inside and took a pull. It looked good, the drink, so I went over to the cabinet and poured an inch of what he had poured – if he was drinking it, it couldn't be spiked.

I sat down opposite him and wetted my lips. Nice, no salty aftertaste this time.

"So why won't her having the tape help her?" I asked. "It will finally get you off her back, won't it?"

His lips twitched again. It was an involuntary expression of pleasure, is what it was. One that he wasn't aware he was making.

"Because, Kockers, technology has moved on from VHS. How do you think people watch porn nowadays? How do you watch it?"

"On the Internet."

"Indeed."

I waved the VHS tape. "You mean, this…"

"Yes, Kockers, you've got it." He gestured towards the office. "It's sitting on a server in there, available to a few select members of my virtual film club along with some other special clips." He looked pleased with himself, like a conceited chess player declaring that he would win in three moves before you'd had a chance to work it out yourself.

"Film club? You mean like the Cambridge Blue Club?"

"Yes, very good, Kockers, it's developed a bit since its early days. Just a small group of broad-minded people who share the same interests."

"Like films of women who've been drugged?"

He deliberately adopted a very relaxed pose, leaning back and crossing his legs. He smiled his dimpled smile.

"I don't know what you mean."

My phone rang out but I didn't answer it – I wasn't about to have a conversation in front of Quintin.

"That's probably Sylvia asking you to hurry to her with the tape. She might be very grateful if you're lucky, although I'm not sure you're her type."

His smugness was beginning to get on my nerves. I wanted to tell him that his flick-knife friend hadn't managed to destroy both DVDs but I didn't want to land Stubbing in hot water just yet, and it was always good to keep something up your sleeve. Instead I hit him with information that I had found out myself. "You obviously know that I was following Trisha Greene, 'cause I assume it was you who arranged for my photos to disappear, and for my office to be knocked over."

His face was fixed in an expressionless smile.

"The thing is there was a backup after all…"

That caused a break in his expression and he struggled to recover the smile.

"…and the police now know that she was probably in your apartment a week before she was murdered."

"A nice if stupid bluff, Kockers. The police know nothing of the sort. Assuming that's based on your silly tracker all they know is that she was parked outside here a week before her murder."

"But coupled with the fact that your driver was seen with her at the Gogs, I'd say there was strong circumstantial evidence that you knew her."

He shrugged and removed his black tie.

"You're not worried? I suppose because of what you have on Brampton?" I held up the tape. "Is she on here too?"

"She and Sylvia together," he said, smacking his lips. "It's worth watching just to see a DCI go down on a socialite. Of course they were just girls then."

"Brampton can't stop this now, it's too big. Trisha Greene was strangled remember."

"Trisha was trash, if you'll forgive the alliteration. She went too far with her sexual cravings. I applaud her for not being hung up like most English women but she became a slave to her own desires and there was a tragic inevitability about how she died."

"So you did know her then?"

"Yes, I'll even admit she was here, but nothing was done to her that she didn't want doing."

"What people think they want and what they might need are two different things. You took advantage of her addiction, just like you take advantage of Sylvia's indiscretion."

He laughed. "George, you delight me with your insight, even if it is disappointingly prosaic. Let me give you a real insight. Sylvia is not a hostage to her past, to one night's indiscretion, as you put it, recorded on tape. She's a hostage to her middle-class English need to keep up appearances. She's so consumed with what people will think of her that she will do almost anything to prevent the truth coming out. Yes, I've benefited from that, just as I benefited from Trisha's needs. In fact I was desperate for them to meet. But alas, I could only push Sylvia so far; asking her to do something more extreme than what I already had her on film doing didn't work. That's why I never filmed her again, alas." He swallowed more bourbon – he clearly enjoyed gloating about how many lives he'd fucked with.

"What about Elliot?" I asked.

"Ah yes, Elliot." He nodded and wagged a finger at me. "Elliot, may he rest in peace, was trapped by the same fears. So much so that he preferred to kill himself rather than face loss of respectability."

I raised both the tape and my eyebrows in a question.

"Yes, he's on there. But his main concern was protecting

Sylvia from exposure. The poor sap adored her."

"So you used that to get him to make dodgy investments, which became another secret that needed hiding when they went tits up."

"Well, let's say I convinced him to invest in some highly speculative unregulated hedge funds. Then I lent him the money to cover his ass. The funny thing is that Morley are working their balls off to stop his financial indiscretions coming out." He chuckled. "It's deliciously ironic that they've asked for my help; they're terrified of how it might reflect on the college."

"But what really tipped him over the edge was when you told him Lucy was yours, or at least got him DNA tested without his knowledge. That's what did it for him wasn't it, learning that Lucy was yours."

The beginnings of a frown then a satisfied smile. "Actually, George, you're off track there: I told him that Lucy wasn't *his*, not that she's *mine*." Before I had time to digest what he was saying he stood up. "Where is Lucy by the way?" he asked. "Are you hiding her somewhere?"

I put my glass down and stood up too.

"Does Sylvia know you've made the tape available on the Internet?"

"Sylvia understands even less about technology than you do. It's the tape she wants. It would never occur to her that it could be copied to a different media. Now leave. Take her the tape and tell her what you like."

I stepped outside and he said, "Give me the keys will you, I'm sick of you turning up here." I handed them over and walked to the lift. Then his voice at my back: "Oh, and make sure you watch the tape, before you give it to her." I turned to check his expression but he had closed the door.

47

I WONDERED, IN THE DESCENDING LIFT OF RIVER VIEWS, whether to go home and, as Quintin suggested, watch the video I was carrying. Although I was curious about it on a purely carnal level that curiosity didn't overcome my discomfort about who was on it. If I'd not known Sylvia, not known the anguish the tape's existence was causing her, I would of course have watched it, which I know makes me a hypocrite. I did feel a sort of loyalty to her (she was a client after all), and I just wouldn't have been able to face her if I had watched it. Besides, having Quintin tell me to watch it made me determined not to become part of his machinations.

After a long minute waiting outside the bursar's lodge at Morley the porch light came on and Sylvia opened the door slightly, popping her head round it to peer at me. She was makeup free with red-rimmed eyes, pale lips and rumpled hair. Her face was colourless and pasty.

"Thank God it's you, I thought it was..."

"Quintin?"

“Do you know what time it is?”

I looked at my watch – it had gone one. “I’m sorry, I wasn’t thinking. I thought you’d want to…”

“It’s cold, you better come in.” She opened the door just enough for me to squeeze through and shut it behind me. She was in an ankle-length dressing gown which she clutched to her throat against the cold. She peered at me and pointed.

“What happened to your forehead?”

I felt the wound between my eyes. “Nothing. I thought you’d want to have this as soon as possible,” I said, fishing the tape out of my pocket in what I judged to be an understated but dramatic gesture.

She didn’t jump up and down, or clasp me to her bosom in joy, or kiss me passionately on the lips in gratitude. If anything she looked insulted by my bringing something that unsavoury into her house.

“He didn’t find you in his apartment then?”

“Yes he did, as a matter of fact.”

“I’m sorry, I did try and ring you.”

“It really doesn’t matter. It’s done,” I said, although if it was her that had rung when I was talking to Quintin then she’d left it a bit late.

“What did he say?”

“He wanted me to watch the tape before I brought it over,” I said.

We stood there for a few seconds, me holding the tape, she looking at it.

“And have you watched it?” she whispered.

“No, of course not, why would I?”

She put her hands to her cheeks, as if her head had become too heavy, glanced at me then looked away. "Watch the tape, George, then we'll talk."

"What?"

Her eyes locked on mine. "Please, just watch it. All the way through."

She moved to the door and opened it.

"I don't understand, why would you want me to watch it?"

"You'll understand when you see it. But watch it to the end, not when you think it's finished."

Studying her I thought it best not to argue. I stepped outside and she closed the door behind me. I felt like the cat who's brought a dead bird into the house for its owner and has been hurt to learn that they don't like dead birds. I sighed and looked down the stone steps at my car. Then the porch light went out, leaving me in darkness.

Arriving home I half expected Stubbing to jump out at me from the undergrowth but all I found was a note trapped in my letterbox. I put lights on in all the downstairs rooms. It was cold, an established cold you get after hours of no central heating. The note was from Stubbing: 'TRIED TO RING YOU. DVD IS DYNAMITE. RING ME.' She hadn't left a number. I checked the mobile and saw the call I'd missed at Quintin's but the number had been withheld and there was no message. It wasn't Sylvia that had rung me then. Maybe she'd wanted Quintin to catch up with me. I yawned and stretched which made my freshly stitched wound pull and the pain was enough to incapacitate me for a few minutes. Once it had faded I checked landline messages. There were two, one from Sandra left a couple of hours ago telling me that all was well at her house but where was I so late at night, and please would I check in. The other message was from Stubbing who reiterated her wish that I call her, however late, and this time she'd left a number.

I rang it from the office mobile, and by the time she answered I had the gas fire on in the front room.

"Hey," I said.

"Hey, Georgie Porgie. I've watched that DVD. Your hunch was right. That was a good call, picking it up."

"That means a lot coming from you," I said, only half joking.

"Fuck you." I heard her take a drink, ice on glass.

"So what was on it?"

"Trisha Greene was on it. In a big way, yes she was. So was our little torturing friend, so was the driver, so was Mr US of A."

"Sounds like some orgy."

"Bloody right it's an orgy, Kocky. Makes the film we saw earlier look like the *Teletubbies*."

"The what?"

"It's a kids' programme, for fuck's sake."

"Please tell me you don't have children, Stubbing."

She mumbled something and I heard liquid being poured. I wondered how much she'd had to drink. "So did you learn anything new?" I asked, fingering the forming scab between my eyes.

"Yes, your hunch paid off alright. It shows Quintin filming Trisha on his sofa while Mark pleasures her with those toys we saw and, get this, Kevin strangles her."

"Bloody hell. Quintin recorded her murder?"

"No, nothing so convenient. It was just a bit of erotic asphyxiation, all part of the show he was filming."

No wonder the thin man (or Kevin as I could never call him) was keen to get rid of the DVD, but what the fuck was erotic asphyxiation? I was being immersed in a world I didn't want to be part of. I felt very tired. Plus the cold wasn't helping my shoulder. Stubbing's voice grated in my ear.

"At the end of the footage she's fine, laughing and getting dressed and she even suggests doing some more filming outdoors. Guess where?"

"The Gogs?"

"Spot on. Can you believe it?"

"But wouldn't the post-mortem have shown finger marks? I thought she was killed with the belt."

"He was using the belt," she said, her voice rising an octave in excitement. "The very one she was found with round her neck at the Gogs."

I wasn't in much of a state to process what she was telling me. "Her husband's belt? I don't understand."

Stubbing chuckled at my incomprehension and I wandered into the kitchen to put the kettle on. "Trisha was wearing the belt at the beginning of the film, like an accessory around her dress."

"She was wearing the belt the night she was murdered?"

"Will you stop repeating everything I say for fuck's sake."

I poured hot water onto a teabag and waited for Stubbing to take a gulp of whatever she was numbing herself with.

"There's no real way to prove the date and time the film was recorded but it was already dark when the footage was taken."

"Which means after four. Of course she could have gone home afterwards and been confronted by hubby – remember that's the day he learnt about her – then driven him to the Gogs to show him what it was all about and then he lost it."

"Maybe, but he would have needed another car to get back to Haverhill, unless he walked the thirteen odd miles."

"How does he explain it, then, since he confessed?"

"He doesn't. He's saying nothing, just that he killed her. There's nothing to pin on him except the belt."

"So the husband's off the hook?"

"Not necessarily – it explains why his belt was round her neck, but the main thing is that it provides a credible alternative to his story."

"So what now?" I asked, taking my tea to the glow of the gas fire.

"I don't know. Technically I'm not on the case and I'd have to run all this by Brampton, so I still don't have enough really."

"You're telling me that you've got footage of Boyd's henchman strangling Trisha on the night of her murder in some sex game and that's not enough? And didn't you say she suggested going up to the Gogs afterwards?"

"Think about it: we can't yet prove it was actually filmed on the night, just because Quintin wrote a date on it. There's no time and date code on the actual video. And even if there were and we could get at the camera, it would mean that the camera would have to have the correct date and time set on it. As it is we have fuck all."

I was pretty sure that if Quintin was anal enough to date his films then he was anal enough to get it right, but I could see Stubbing's point. I was still confused though.

"I don't know much about it but it seems to me that you've got enough at least to get a warrant, I mean they're using the same belt on her for fuck's sake. I'll bet you anything he has a copy on his hard drive and your techies will be able to establish when it was put there which will narrow it down."

It went quiet and I could hear only the sound of ice.

"Hello?"

"You're right," she said, then belched. "You don't know much about it. I'd have to go to Brampton, right, who would warn Quintin and he'd get rid of anything more he might have on his computer. Or, I'd have to bypass her and explain to someone why I was doing it. Do you know what that means, going above your boss's head? No, of course not, you're a free agent, you don't have a career to worry about, feeding at the bottom of the swamp as you do." If I'd hoped Stubbing would be a pleasant drunk then I was wrong.

"OK. I'm going to hang up now."

"George..." she said, her voice softer. Then another belch. I hung up in case she offered to come round and tuck me in.

I hooked up the video player to the TV in place of the DVD player and popped the VHS cassette in. I settled down to watch Sylvia Booker have sex.

48

THE GRAINY FILM STARTED WITHOUT PREAMBLE, THE CAMERA wobbling everywhere. Then it settled on an empty room, high-ceilinged with a chandelier, sofas and armchairs, an upright piano in the corner. A large fireplace formed the centrepiece, logs burning in its grate. Above it an oversized mirror with peeling silver backing that revealed in its reflection floor to ceiling heavy curtains that kept the outside from view. Before the mirror were candles that were the only lighting in the room apart from the fire. I assumed it to be a common room at Morley; it had that sort of shabby opulence that lacked any personal touch, photographs or knick-knacks. The camera defocused then focused until finally fixing on a large sofa in front of the fire. The scene shook briefly and a blurry form came into view very close, then disappeared off camera. It was very unclear on my small black and white screen and for the first time I wished I had a bigger, colour TV. I leaned forward and turned the sound up but there was no sound.

Some minutes went by with nothing happening and I noticed a carriage clock on the mantelpiece that said it was five minutes to twelve. Then three people entered the frame from the right, a woman between two men. Even in the gloom the woman was obviously a younger, incredible-looking Sylvia. Dressed only in a flimsy-looking white cotton shift that reached mid-thigh she was being helped along by the two men. It was difficult to see who they were as they had eye masks on; the elaborate sort you see in costume dramas when they have fancy balls. And that's all they had on. I wondered if it was Quintin and Elliot. One of them was taller and thin, not so confident in his nudity, whereas the other seemed assured in his bearing, his measured steps marking this as a sense of occasion.

Sylvia looked drunk, having to be helped to the middle of the room, her head lolling occasionally. Another woman came into frame from the right, naked, solidly built, but youthfully firm-bodied. She wore a mask like the men that revealed only her mouth. From her build I took her to be Brampton but it was too grainy to be sure. Whoever it was stepped forward and stood before Sylvia. She took hold of her flimsy dress at the neck and ripped it open from top to bottom. Sylvia didn't seem to react at all; her head flopped back and jerked forward again. The woman in the mask knelt down and kissed Sylvia's breasts and stomach. Then Sylvia was lain on the sofa, one foot on the floor, the other on the arm of the sofa, the leg bent at the knee.

I fast-forwarded the film at this point. Suffice to say that Sylvia was the object of intense sexual activity, and Quintin was right about the future DCI going down on the socialite. It seemed easier to watch sped up, making it seem less like what it really was. The two men took turns, the taller one first then the other, who had to be Quintin. I stopped and rewound the tape to where he got up from between Sylvia's thighs. He leant over and grabbed Sylvia's head with his hands, lifting her head from the sofa and spitting a word at her, then he stormed off. She was on her own and I played the video at normal speed. The picture was like this for thirty seconds, then a minute, and I began to think it had frozen except the fire was still burning. Then she pulled her legs together and turned onto her side facing the room. She drew her knees up and tried to cover herself with the torn fabric of her shift. Another minute and nothing much happened except one of the candles went out and the fire died a little. The clock now read twelve-thirty. I was about to turn it off when I remembered Sylvia's insistence that I watch it to the very end.

Another long minute later a figure, fully clothed in black, came into frame from somewhere behind and to the left of the camera. He looked back from where he'd come, his face away from the lens, seeming to listen to someone, nodded, then he approached the sofa warily, as if afraid to wake Sylvia. The way he walked and stood looked familiar. He sat straight-backed on the edge of the sofa and started to stroke her hair. She turned her head and it looked as if she was smiling. I couldn't see the man's face but could see his hand move over the curve of her body. Then he stood up, his back to the camera, and removed his jacket. I thought he was going to cover her with it but then he draped it over the back of an armchair. He removed his trousers and placed them neatly on the same chair. This act seemed so familiar and domesticated that the next thing he did, even though it was expected, seemed all the more shocking. He gently rolled Sylvia onto her back and got between her legs, pulled his underwear down and lowered himself. I grabbed the remote and fast-forwarded; I just couldn't watch any more. The speedy jerking up and down made comical what was obscene. I pressed play when he had finished and watched him get dressed just as carefully as he'd got undressed. Then he went to the mirror over the fireplace and adjusted his tie in it. His face became visible close to the candles and fire.

I stood up, appalled. No wonder the clothes-folding had seemed so familiar. I had seen it before. Just as I had seen the face in the mirror every day of my childhood. I stood mesmerised as he turned, picked up the coverlet on the back of the sofa and pulled it over Sylvia, who had resumed a foetal position on the sofa. He then walked off screen the way he had come.

49

I DIDN'T SLEEP THE REST OF THE NIGHT. I FELT SIMULTANEOUSLY sick and wired, not helped by the mixture of coffee and whisky I absorbed in a bid to clear my head and cope with what I had seen. My own father – a… I couldn't quite say it. Was it rape? Perhaps it had been consensual. I was kidding myself, of course. Clearly it was why Sylvia had wanted me to watch the tape, but what was she expecting from me? An apology, or just to get back at him through me? I needed to speak to her: I think at the very least that's what she was expecting me to do.

At five-thirty I threw up and felt better. I took painkillers with a pint of water, washed my face and armpits, brushed my teeth and gargled, then put on a clean shirt.

At six-thirty I sat in the Golf in the dark outside the bursar's residence at Morley for a few minutes, glancing up at the dark house, mulling over what I was going to say, just as I had all the way here. I mean, what the fuck *could* I say? The light in the porch lit up as the front door opened and Sylvia looked down at me then disappeared, leaving the door ajar. Picking up the tape from the seat beside me I dragged myself up the steps into the house.

We sat in the same seats we had the day before. I put the tape beside me on the sofa. Sylvia brought in a tray of coffee with proper cups and saucers and matching milk jug and sugar bowl, which was filled with crystals of brown sugar. She was dressed in a dark suit with a faint stripe and wide lapels over which white shirt lapels neatly sat. Her hair was tied up at the back and she looked professional and unrecognisable from the woman who had needed comforting the night before and who had begged me to help her. She sat with her back straight, knees hard together, and poured coffee.

"Milk or sugar?"

"Neither, thanks."

She passed me the fragile cup and saucer which I held precariously on my lap.

"I'm assuming you've watched it, George?" she said, nodding at the tape. Her voice was cool and businesslike, her eyes remained steady – it was as if she was interviewing me for a job, not asking me if I'd watched a film of her being drug-raped nearly twenty years ago.

"Yes I have."

"Did you watch it right to the end, and not when it seemed to have finished?"

"Yes."

"And what were your impressions?"

"My impressions?"

"Yes. What was your feeling when you saw it?"

"I felt sick," I said.

She nodded, as if I'd told her the coffee tasted nice. "My part in it wasn't as voluntary as it might have appeared."

"I didn't think it was. Did you know you'd been drugged?" I said.

"No. We'd taken it once before, but I didn't like it. Quintin put it in my wine. I believe it's now known as a date-rape drug, but at the time it was more of a relaxant."

"So you knew what was going on?"

"Yes I did, but it was like being in a dream you can't escape. What I didn't know was that Quintin was filming it. He showed it to me straight after Elliot and I got married."

"And took great pleasure in doing so I imagine."

She nodded and sipped at her coffee.

"And he used it to blackmail you?"

"Yes. Among other… things, he wanted me to convince Elliot to listen to his investment advice. I thought he just wanted to make some money out of the college but really he wanted to destroy Elliot's reputation."

"I think he wanted to destroy Elliot full stop, not just his reputation. Hence the paternity test showing Elliot that Lucy wasn't his."

She sighed. "You're not curious as to why he wanted to do all this?"

I shrugged. "Perhaps he was envious of what you and Elliot had, including Lucy. Maybe he wanted Lucy for himself." Then I remembered Lucy telling me that he'd changed a gear up with her around the time he'd learnt Lucy was his, although he'd told me I was on the wrong track when I'd confronted him with that. "Perhaps he's just psycho."

"Well actually he does satisfy most of the criteria that define a psychopath."

"So do most of our captains of industry and politicians. It's more common than we think."

She nodded distractedly and studied her cup.

I put my cup down on the Latin-engraved coaster and sat forward.

"I'm not sure how to say this..."

She sat back and watched me. "Just say it, George."

"I feel I need to apologise, really, for what happened. At the end of the film, I mean." Jesus, I sounded like I was clarifying a misunderstanding over the splitting of a bill.

"You mean when your father raped me?"

It came out loud and sharp and I sat back, unable to even acknowledge what she'd said with a nod.

"Sorry," she said, blushing, "that was a little harsh of me."

"But the truth, nevertheless," I said.

She glanced down at the china on the table, then out of the French windows at the light now appearing, then returned her gaze to me and exhaled through parted lips. "Look, I'm under no illusion that Quintin put him, your father, up to it, even convinced him I was OK with the idea. He'd seen what sort of parties we had, the screenings of Quintin's films. He cleaned up after them so it wouldn't have been that unreasonable for him to assume I was a willing participant. I wouldn't judge him too harshly."

"It's not you who should be making me feel better about it."

"It was a long time ago."

"Do you think it's why he retired early?"

"I'm not sure what happened. As far as I know nothing came out. The only person who knew apart from me, and of course your father, was Quintin, and I certainly didn't mention it to anyone."

"But I thought Elliot saw the film."

"Not the end of it, he didn't. Quintin kept that up his sleeve. He kept threatening to show it to Elliot if I didn't..." She faltered in her self-composure for a second but I looked outside as if I hadn't noticed – I had a pretty good idea by now of the nature of Quintin's abuse. When I looked back she'd recovered. The issue of whether my father's retirement was caused by what he'd done was going to be something I would have to take up with Quintin.

"There is something else," Sylvia was saying.

"What's that?" I put my cup on the tray. She did the same and placed her palms on her thighs, looking down and taking a breath. The doorbell chimed. She sighed and looked at her tiny gold watch. The doorbell was pressed again. She stood up, smoothed her skirt and excused herself. I stood up as she left the room and went to the French windows.

Then I heard his voice, the American twang, brash and confident in the hall.

"Is he here?"

A mumble from Sylvia.

"And have you clued him up?"

More mumbling.

"You stupid bitch. I'll do it myself."

"No, Quintin, please." They were in the room. I turned

and saw her composure shattered, her face pleading, pulling at his sleeve as he strode towards me. It made me wince, to see her like that.

"Ah, here's the poor Armenian sap, blinded by the femme fatale. Have you fucked her yet, Junior, like your dad?"

"Why don't you shut the fuck up," I said. He stopped an arm's length away and undid his jacket so he could ease his hands into the pockets of his Savile Row trousers.

"Ah, isn't this sweet, standing up for the lady while she's here. Don't tell me you've actually fallen in love with her?" Beneath the bluster he looked tired.

"You're still drugging women to make films then?"

"Some women like to loosen their inhibitions, so fucking what? It's a very English thing to have to do."

"So you don't spike people's drinks?"

He smiled. "Only yours." I tried a different tack, hoping I wasn't overplaying my hand.

"What about Trisha Greene? Did you drug and film her?"

Sylvia, standing behind Quintin, gave me a puzzled look. Quintin studied me carefully.

"Trisha? Maybe I did film her, but Trisha wasn't one to need her inhibitions loosening. In fact she left the night she was in my apartment on her own two feet, saying she was going to look for more of the same. It seemed the fun I provided just got her warmed up, but she was a slut like that." He moved over to the sofa. "Anyway, Junior, this is all an irrelevancy. Isn't it, Sylvia?"

He sat down where I had been sitting, next to the VHS tape, and felt the coffee pot.

"Fetch me a cup, there's a good girl," he said, without looking at Sylvia. She just stood there twisting the wedding ring on her finger like it could set Quintin on fire if she did it fast enough.

"Don't," she said.

But he glanced her way coldly and said, "A cup."

She turned to leave the room. He smiled at me. "Sit down, Junior, and I'll tell you what Sylvia didn't have the balls to."

I stayed standing, fists hard behind my back, my shoulder throbbing like buggery. I had a bad feeling rising in my gut.

"Suit yourself," he said. He relaxed into the sofa, stretching his arms out along the back, taking his time to tell me whatever it was he was going to tell me.

"It's about Lucy," he said, glancing at the tape then fixing his eyes on me.

I was aware of Sylvia coming into the room, the rattling of cup on saucer, but I continued to stare at Quintin, whose full lips were twitching in anticipation.

"To be more accurate, it's about your father. You see," Quintin said, "Lucy's your sister."

The cup rattling stopped. Quintin's grinning face, in fact the whole room, disappeared behind a white mist. What did he mean? I knew what he meant. How? Pull yourself together. He's lying; it's what he does.

"You look discombobulated, old chap."

I shook my head. I needed to sit down but I wouldn't give him the satisfaction.

"OK, George, you got me," he said, putting his palm to

his chest. "So I exaggerate, she's your half sister. It's quite simple. George Senior was the last person that night to deposit the good stuff in our English rose here. I've had him DNA tested and there's no doubt about it. Sylvia is, in effect, your stepmom."

"You had him tested?" I asked.

"Yes, I sent someone to swab him at the home Morley is generously paying for." Yes, that explained the runt visiting him. I felt sick.

Sylvia came into my field of view behind the sofa on which Quintin was sprawled – I could discern the cup and saucer in my peripheral vision, but I couldn't bring myself to look at her. I kept my gaze on the smirking Quintin. I was fighting to remain standing when Sylvia extended the cup and saucer with her left hand over the back of the sofa into Quintin's line of vision. He half-turned to take it and her right hand appeared from behind the sofa and rose above his head. She was clutching a small kitchen knife.

I cried out.

Quintin jerked his head round to see the knife descending and tried to get up but he met the blade as it arced down. It sliced through his left ear and sank into his shoulder. He let out a horrible squeal and released the cup to clutch his bloody ear. My immediate thought was whether the broken cup on the carpet was replaceable.

50

BLEEDING FROM THE EAR IS ALWAYS PROFUSE, AND QUINTIN was no different from human beings in this regard. Sylvia stood frozen, clutching the knife. Quintin staggered around moaning then sat on the other sofa. Sylvia came round and picked up the pieces of cup and put them on the table.

"He needs an ambulance," I said.

"No he doesn't. He needs to have his testicles removed," she said calmly but confidently. "I've had enough of his… his endless chatter. Talking, he's always talking. What have you got to say for yourself now, Quintin?"

He glared at her.

"Don't drip on the carpet, please," she said. Quintin, as if in obeisance, pulled a handkerchief from somewhere and pressed it to his ear. It immediately turned red.

"Sylvia, we need a first aid kit," I said, taking her wrist in case she decided to emasculate him herself. She was in shock, as probably was I.

"In the scullery," she said, staring at Quintin.

"Show me," I said, not wanting to leave her alone with him, and not quite sure what a scullery was. She let me take the knife from her hand and we found our way to the kitchen. It was a massive rectangular room with a farmhouse-style table down the middle with twelve chairs round it. A huge Aga-type stove took up one side and wooden cabinets lined the other. Opposite was an arch into another area with sinks and work areas, where Sylvia led me. This was where the actual food preparation was done. A magnetic knife holder on the wall had ten knives ordered by size stuck to it. The smallest was missing: it was in my hand. I washed it thoroughly and put it back on the rack using a tea-towel. Sylvia handed me the first aid bag and back in the kitchen area I sat at the end of the large table to gather my thoughts – let Quintin fucking bleed.

Lucy was my half-sister. Was Quintin lying? Sylvia stood at the opposite end of the table and put her palms on the wooden surface.

"I'm sorry you had to hear it from him. I was about to tell you myself."

"So it's true?"

"Yes, I've seen the DNA results myself, assuming of course that the sample was from your father, but I've no real doubts." She walked round and sat next to me. I noticed a tiny drop of blood on the collar of her white shirt, but it wasn't the time to point it out. "It is obvious if you look at the two of you together." I remembered Cathy at McDonald's thinking Lucy and I were related. Lucy's nose, a nose I was cursed with myself.

"Why didn't I see it?" I said, shaking my head.

"Why would you? You weren't looking for similarities. Anyway, I'm glad it's out now. I needed you to know."

"When did you know?" I asked, not quite being able to look her in the eye.

"I suspected some years ago. I wasn't lying when I said Elliot thought she was his, it's incredible how self-delusional men can be. But Quintin, being who he is, had his suspicions. And when Elliot couldn't get me pregnant I was pretty certain. You see, his sperm count was low. I think that's when he began to have doubts about Lucy. He never articulated them of course but I saw the way he looked at her. His unspoken fear was that Quintin was her father."

"But why isn't Quintin a candidate?"

She shook her head. "He can't do it. Erectile dysfunction. He can't get it up, not when there's a woman present, anyway."

"No, of course he can't – all those… things in his apartment."

"Yes. That's what he's reduced to. Won't even try anything that could fix it. He thinks it's our fault."

"Ours?"

"Women."

"But hang on, in the video with you—"

"He's faking, or trying and failing. You can only tell if you look carefully but take my word for it, it's one of the few things that evening that I can recall clearly. It made him livid." It wasn't clear on my tiny black and white TV, except his angry reaction when he'd stood up from between her legs. And then of course my father…

Quintin's bellowing came through from the other room, even though it was half a mile away.

"This is too much to take in," I said, standing up. "I'm

not sure what I'm supposed to do with the information."

"Do? It just is, George. It's just something that you need to accept."

Quintin had found the tissues in their disguised box and had a wad of them pressed to his ear. They were rapidly going crimson. He'd managed to get his jacket off and it was thrown over the back of the sofa.

"Where the fuck have you been?"

I stood behind the sofa and opened the first aid case, picking out a dressing, tape and a pair of scissors. His shirt had a five-inch long rip, through which I could see split flesh. Bleeding, but not as bad as his ear.

"Let me have a look at your ear," I said. I told him to release the wad of tissue. An inch-long gash in the ear caused a corner to flop over like banana peel. Blood seeped out in a steady stream. I pressed the dressing to his ear and told him to hold it. Then I taped it to his head. With the scissors I cut his expensive shirt from the collar to the wound, then down and under the armpit back to the lapel. With his hand temporarily removed from his ear I pulled the sleeve from his arm. I felt his house keys in one of his jacket pockets as I leant over the sofa. I unwrapped another dressing and with my right hand pressed it onto the cut on his shoulder. He groaned and I let my left hand wander into the pocket with his keys. I pressed a little harder on his wound and closed my fingers tightly over the keys so they wouldn't jingle, pulling them out.

"That crazy fucking bitch. I need to call the police."

"You'll need to get that ear and shoulder stitched up," I said, leaving the first aid kit by him on the sofa after taping the dressing to his shoulder. I walked to the door, his voice shrill behind me.

"Where are you going, you Armenian bastard? Call my driver, he's outside."

I turned away from his ashen face, then remembered the video tape. No point leaving it with him. I slipped it into my raincoat pocket with his house keys, left the room and closed the heavy door behind me. Sylvia was coming across the hall from the kitchen.

"Are you leaving?"

I nodded, managing to look her properly in the eye for the first time since Quintin had told me about Lucy.

"You'll probably see Lucy before me," she said. "But I'm sure you understand that I'd rather tell her myself."

I looked back at the living room door where I could hear Quintin's muffled voice cursing and groaning. I took a step closer to Sylvia, getting in her personal space.

"Was Elliot a good father to Lucy?" I asked.

Her brow furrowed. "What do you mean?"

"I mean did he raise her properly, read to her, look after her when she was ill, go to her school plays, help her with her homework?"

"Yes, of course, he was an excellent father. He loved her."

"Then for God's sake what would be the point of telling her?"

"Because it's the truth," she said.

"Don't, I'm begging you. Think of what you would be telling her. That her real father is a college butler, not the bursar? That the person she thought of as her father killed himself when he learnt the truth? That she was conceived during some sex party that was filmed and by the way, would she like to see it? That her real father is now a mute simpleton abandoned in a nursing home with Pick's disease – he doesn't even recognise me for fuck's sake. Do you really want to dump all that on her?"

"You're hurting me, George." I was grabbing her wrists. I let go and she rubbed them. I took some deep breaths.

"The truth isn't all it's cracked up to be," I said, more gently. "It has consequences, and they're not always good. At least think it through."

"I've spent the whole of my life living a lie, putting on a façade, paying for my fear of the truth coming out. And I'm glad you now know, I'm relieved. I needed to be free of it," she said.

This is why she'd come to see me in the first place. This was the reason she'd chosen me, a two-bit operator over a big London-based firm run by ex-coppers. So I could reach this point and lance her festering boil for her.

"Just think about what it would do to her," I said. "You're riding the crest of a wave at the moment but like all waves it has to crash somewhere."

She nodded. "Maybe I haven't thought it through, but it's a secret I need to be free of."

I opened the front door then stopped, pointing to the living room door. "Can you deal with him?"

"He doesn't scare me anymore." I believed her.

"You won't stab him again?" I asked.

"Do you care?"

"Not about him, no."

She smiled humourlessly.

"What if Quintin decides to tell her?" she whispered, the old fear returning momentarily to her face.

"Quintin has other things to worry about, and besides, he doesn't know where she is. Neither do you, for that matter."

She looked relieved and nodded. At that moment Quintin came crashing out of the living room, trailing bloody bandage clutched to his ear, and made for the front door, glaring at us as he pushed past.

I stepped out behind him and followed him down the steps to his Merc which was parked behind my Golf. Mark was asleep in the driver's seat. Quintin rapped loudly on the window and startled him. Mark wound down the window, his mouth agape at the sight of his boss.

"Get me to hospital, you cock-sucker. And you might want to open the fucking door."

The Merc sped out of the drive in reverse, showering the back of the Golf in gravel.

I looked up to the front door but it was closed. I had one last thing to do to finish this.

51

THE SUNDAY MORNING CAMBRIDGE I DROVE THROUGH WAS dark, damp and empty. I wondered whether Quintin would press charges against Sylvia for cutting him, and whether he would make the alumni lunch – if he did he would be heavily bandaged. I calculated that I had an hour before he got to Addenbrooke's, was stitched up and made it back home to change, since Sunday morning would be quiet in A&E. Plenty of time for me to do what I needed to do. The last thing I wanted was Stubbing getting hold of Quintin's hard disk copy of the film showing Sylvia and my father. I wasn't sure whether I was doing this for Sylvia or him, or maybe even myself, since Dad would be none the wiser even if he watched it.

I parked in the car park opposite River Views and put on some silk skin-tight gloves, the sort bikers wear under their leather gloves, and with Quintin's keys let myself into the front gate. I doubted Eric would be on duty – his night shift would be over – but I didn't care if he was. There was little he could do except ring Quintin or perhaps Mark, and Mark was a pussycat compared to Quintin's knife-wielding minion who was in Stubbing's custody.

* * *

As I emerged from the lift on the top floor a young woman with a mascara-streaked face rushed by me into the lift, pressing furiously at the lobby button and ignoring my stare. She didn't look much older than Lucy. I let myself into the penthouse. A half-empty bottle of wine and two glasses sat on the coffee table – the girl (she was really no more than a girl) who'd passed me must have arrived last night after I'd left. I went to the hall leading to the bedrooms and office.

Quintin's bedroom door was open. The bed was unmade and two sex toys from his vast selection sat on the bedside table. At the foot his semi-pro camera was fixed to the tripod and aimed at the now empty bed, no doubt recently occupied by the same girl – another unwilling recipient of the Quintin magic. It's probable that she'd arrived voluntarily but what had happened in here was not done by consent. Quintin did not have relationships with women who wanted to. His *modus operandi* was to pay, drug and blackmail them into it, excepting perhaps Trisha. I found a DVD in the camera – he'd obviously not had time to catalogue it – so I took it out. At the oak cabinet in his office I ignored the cupboard full of bought porn and opened the drawers below. I took out all the carefully dated DVDs from their sleeves, and the VHS tapes from their cases, and carried them all into the kitchen. I put the DVDs into the microwave and set it to high, for three minutes. They sparkled and popped alarmingly as I filled the oven with the tapes – including Sylvia's in my pocket; I ripped the tape out of it for extra measure – and set the dial to high. Then it was back to his office.

I found that the actual computer, under the desk, was a silver metal tower with a mesh-like back and handles at the top. The front of it was facing to the left, the long side towards me, a large Apple logo on it. Kneeling down, I eventually found the switch on the back and turned it off. The low hum subsided. I couldn't work out how to open the thing to get the cover off though, there didn't seem to be any screws. I thought of smashing it but it was made of aluminium and I might not be able to destroy the hard drive inside, and even if I thought I had, the police could recover things from the flimsiest of evidence. I remembered the computer in my office: someone had removed the hard drive from it – it was the only way to be sure that nothing was left behind. I took out the mobile and dialled Jason's number. He answered on the third ring, groggy with sleep.

"Morning, son. You up for providing computer support?"

"Do you know what time it is?"

"I'm kneeling in front of an Apple Mac with the prospect of the Mac's owner appearing any minute. You told me you use Macs at college, didn't you?"

"What do you need to know?"

I explained my desire to extract the hard drive from the machine. He asked me the model which I got from the back.

"You're in luck then; it's a doddle on that machine, you won't even need any tools." He guided me to the lever embedded in the back, which I pulled, enabling the panel with the logo on it to come clean off.

He talked me through removing the drive, which, as he'd

promised, was straightforward. Then he told me how to put the panel back.

"Is there a backup machine attached to the computer?" he asked.

"How do I know?" I asked. "There doesn't seem to be anything connected to it apart from a camcorder."

"Well, if you don't find it, and he's bound to have one, what you've just done is next to useless."

"There's nothing coming out of the computer," I said.

"Then you better hope there is a wireless backup somewhere in the house and that he wasn't doing it over the Internet like we were. Although that's unlikely given his material."

"Shit. What am I looking for?"

"A box somewhere. It might be in another room or in a cupboard or something, probably next to the router."

"That's helpful. Perhaps you could tell me what the router looks like?"

I trawled the house and came across a cupboard next to the front door in which sat a variety of equipment that left me bewildered. It was like a mini disco going on what with all the lights flashing in there. With Jason's help I identified the culprit backup drive from which I unplugged a power cable and a network cable connected to the router, which was distinguished by its antenna. It was bigger than the drive I'd taken from the computer in the office and wouldn't fit in my pocket.

* * *

Fiddling around under the desk and in the cupboard hadn't helped my shoulder and I tried not to think of what it had done to my fresh stitches. Checking my watch told me I must have been at it for forty-five minutes or so. The smell of burning plastic from the kitchen reminded me that I should check my cooking.

I turned off the oven and opened the door, releasing acrid black smoke. Once I'd cleared the smoke inside I established that the tapes were a molten mess. I nearly had a heart attack when the smoke alarm went off over my head and I had to get on a chair and smash it with the heel of my shoe, spluttering in the smoke. I switched on the extractor fan over the hob before putting Quintin's keys on the dining table – he might think he'd left them there himself, until, of course, the smell hit him and he went into the kitchen.

As I was about to leave something nagged at me, so I decided a last sweep of the place would be prudent; it's not unknown for things to drop out of pockets or a mobile phone to be left behind. I looked in the bedroom, studied the large camera aimed at the bed. I remembered what Stubbing had said when she'd rung me early this morning, about tying the Trisha strangling footage she'd described to the camera now before me. Could she use it if I took it to her? My scant knowledge of the law was that here, unlike in the US, evidence could be admissible however it was obtained. But it was a large piece of equipment usually used on a tripod or carried on the shoulder, which presumably is why he had the other, smaller handheld camcorder. Besides, I wasn't about to do Stubbing's dirty work for her, just because she was worried about her career.

The nagging feeling amplified. What was it? Something about the cameras. There were two. It was the smaller handheld, that's what it was. The one Quintin used in addition to the fixed camera I was staring at. The small one. The one, had he taken Trisha up to the Gogs that night, he would have used, not the big one. Where was the raw footage from it? All on the hard drive, I supposed, so anything incriminating would be on there. But what was it recorded onto in the first place? Not a DVD, it was too small, but a memory card. Memory cards that we'd seen him buy that morning in Cambridge. I went to the office, where the camcorder was connected to the computer. Cameras and camcorders I could understand, and it wasn't long before I saw that it contained one of the largest capacity cards you could buy. The adrenalin made my hands tremble as I flipped open the screen and navigated the menu system to play back what was on it.

52

MY ORIGINAL IDEA WAS TO GET JASON TO DELETE THE offending footage of Sylvia and my father from the drives and to help me look for further evidence of Quintin and friends' involvement in Trisha's sad end. But there was no need for that now, not after what I'd seen on the camcorder, which left nothing to the imagination. I put the camcorder in a Waitrose carrier bag I found in the kitchen and left. In the car I made a phone call to Kamal, who listened and said he would get back to me. Then I drove home.

Through the brambles at the bottom of my garden is the small shed where my father kept his tools. I went there with the hard drive and backup drive and a small blowtorch Olivia had used once to sear the top of some crème brûlées for a dinner party. Inside the shed, tendrils of bramble had snuck through the large gaps in the rotting slats and were thriving despite the gloom. I fought them and large cobwebs to reach a dust-covered worktop to which a rusty vice was fixed. I jammed the drive in it, turning the handle and increasing pressure until it cracked and bits pinged off. Jason had said that I needed to get at the circular wafers inside. Once I had done the same to the backup drive I was left with a collection of thin brown magnetic discs to which I applied a blowtorch causing them to melt and contract into dark brown balls of plastic.

As promised Kamal called me back, and after talking to him I rang Stubbing, having to leave a message on her voicemail – no doubt she was sleeping off last night's self-pitying binge. I drove to Addenbrooke's.

Quintin had bagged himself a private room. According to Kamal's nursing contact he was waiting for a neurosurgical consultation, due to possible nerve damage in the shoulder. He was sitting up in bed, his ear bandaged to his head like an extra in a Second World War film. His left arm was in a sling and judging by his vague expression he was on strong painkillers.

"Ah, Kockers Junior, at last, I've been ringing for ages. I need you to hold my pecker so I can have a whizz."

I put the Waitrose bag at the foot of the bed.

"Did you bring champagne?"

"Why did my father retire early?"

He smiled, as if realising why I was here, and shifted his buttocks on the bed.

"Because, you Armenian retard, I showed him the film.

I gave him a choice. I'd show the film to his employers, the relevant bit anyway, and he would be sacked with no pension and charged – although to be honest the spineless wonders at the college would do anything to avoid a bad name – or, he could retire early voluntarily. It was a no-brainer. As it was he lost five years of his pension."

"But why?" I said, more curious than angry. "What had he ever done to you?"

He shrugged and grimaced, as if remembering something unpleasant. "Nothing. He was always around, always there, waiting for us to finish so he could clean up. He watched the films, knew what was going on. He was almost part of the club." He picked up a glass of water. "But I did it mainly because I could."

So that was Quintin's reason? Not because of what my father had done to Sylvia, no, but simply because he could. He didn't give a shit about Sylvia. Quite the opposite.

"You set him up with Sylvia, didn't you?"

"Yes, I thought it would be good to mix things up. There should be more intermingling of the classes, I feel."

"And your interest in Lucy? What was that about?"

He sipped at his water and smacked his lips.

"Just more sport. I thought it would be fun to do the daughter of the mother, catch my drift?" He smiled that sensuous smile. "Especially when I'd had a hand in creating her." Here he guffawed and if he'd been hooked up to a life support system I'd have happily unplugged him and locked the door to prevent his resuscitation.

"Except you can't, can you?" The laughter stopped.

"Can't what?"

"Do her, of course. You can't get it up, can you? It's all trouser with you and no cock. You can't stand up for women, if you catch my drift." He tried to get comfortable in the bed, his gaze unfocused and wary, his smile fixed. He opened his mouth to speak but I cut him off. "I don't know what happened to you, or what caused it, and I don't really give a shit. But you probably thought, in that mess of a mind of yours, that you could compensate with your artificial substitutes and coerced victims, and that putting it on film for your sad little friends gave you some sort of masturbatory satisfaction."

"It gave us plenty of satisfaction as a matter of fact. And I gave pleasure to plenty of women." I ignored going down that twisted route and carried on.

"Not Trisha, though. Trisha was different, wasn't she?"

At that point Stubbing came into the room, looking like she'd just got out of bed having slept in her clothes.

"Who's this?" Quintin demanded.

"Detective Inspector Stubbing," said Stubbing, in a hoarse voice.

"What's she doing here? I called Brampton." I exchanged a look with Stubbing.

"It'll become clear why she's here," I said. That's when Brampton came in, looked surprised to see me and Stubbing, and went straight to Quintin's side, glaring at us with all the distaste of someone who's found a pubic hair in a sandwich they've already bitten into. All I needed now was Sylvia to arrive and I could do a Poirot and dazzle the gathering with my deductive powers.

"Ah, Judith, better late than never," drawled Quintin. "I want you to arrest Sylvia Booker for assault. This gumshoe here is a witness to her unprovoked knife attack."

"Shut up," I said. "She's had years of provocation from you."

"What are you doing here?" Brampton spat at Stubbing.

"I was just about to explain about Trisha Greene," I said before Stubbing could answer. It was Brampton's turn to look confused.

"What's going on?" she demanded of Stubbing.

"Just listen, ma'am," Stubbing said. I went to the door and closed it. Quintin was protesting to Brampton.

"I was wondering," I said, cutting him off midstream, "why Quintin here would want to do what he did to Trisha. Strangle her all the way, I mean, not just a little bit for perverted kicks." A gratifying hush filled the room. "A psychiatrist could get a fat research grant to look into this but my take, for what it's worth, is that it's because she was the only one of Quintin's conquests, if I can call them that, who actually wanted sex on his terms."

Quintin laughed again and shook his bandaged head, almost in sorrow. "I already told you she was a slut. But I didn't kill her. You've completely lost the plot. Why would I kill her if she was giving me what I wanted, you idiot? Besides, I only did to her what she wanted done."

"Exactly. You gave her what she wanted, but that's not how you roll, is it? She irritated you because you didn't need to coerce it out of her, that's the thing. No blackmail, no date-rape drug. And you didn't like that, did you? Trisha made you angry, didn't she, because she actually took everything you threw at her and enjoyed it?"

"What the hell is going on here, George?" Brampton said, her brow furrowed with worry. Quintin was reaching for the buzzer that summoned a nurse. He'd be lucky if he got a response on a Sunday with all the staff cuts. I looked at Brampton.

"I bet you a high-table college dinner that if you checked the back seat of Trisha's convertible you might find a hair or even some fibres that match our American friend's tailor-made trousers."

"Why on earth would she want to do that?" Quintin shouted.

I shouted back: "You're forgetting, Boyd, your compulsion to film every fucking thing you do."

There was a silence like the sort experienced in the seconds after an explosion. Brampton was staring at Quintin with disbelief.

"I gave her what she wanted, that's all. It was the natural conclusion," he said, as if explaining why he'd given someone too much cake and they'd been sick.

"You filmed it," Brampton said to herself. "You bloody filmed it."

"Where is it?" Stubbing asked. I picked up the carrier bag with the camcorder inside it and handed it to her.

"Everything is on there, the critical bits are filmed by his sidekick Kevin. Try to make sure this one doesn't get damaged or wiped."

She opened the bag and smiled, then showed it to Brampton,

who made to take it from her. Stubbing pulled it back and looked askance at Brampton, who nodded in resignation.

I left as Stubbing was formally detaining Quintin Boyd as a suspect in the murder of Trisha Greene.

53

STUBBING ARRIVED THE NEXT MORNING, EARLY, HER HAIR bound tighter than ever. She followed me – without mentioning my pyjamas – into the kitchen where I sat at the table. I poured her some coffee, yawning.

It was only after she'd added two sugars to her mug and stirred it to buggery that she spoke. She was still standing.

"I suppose I should thank you," she said.

"Consider us even."

She smiled. "Do you want to press charges against little Kevin?"

"I don't think so. Besides, he's got enough heat without me wasting my time on him."

She nodded. "That's true enough, plus he's got form. He's been singing like a canary since I showed him the video." She sniggered. "He was just following orders, apparently."

I sipped my coffee. "Have you seen footage like that before?"

She sat down opposite and looked at her mug. "I've seen some pretty sick stuff, mainly with kiddies, but this is disturbing in a different way. It's like he lost it at the end and wanted to see how far he could go."

I didn't agree with Stubbing's evaluation of the video. All I'd seen was the concentrated hate and effort on Quintin's face while he was doing it, then the relief and pleasure when he'd finished. He'd collapsed in the back seat, panting, and I wouldn't have been surprised if he'd smoked a cigarette then had a nap, except that the runt, realising what he'd just filmed, had called out to his boss, "Mr Boyd, what the fuck have you done? Mr Boyd? Fuck." He'd put the camera down on the bonnet of the car without switching it off, and it had desperately tried to autofocus on the windscreen and Trisha's just-dead face at the same time. The face that had kept me awake all night. Then you could hear the runt dragging Quintin from the back seat, trying to pull him from his trancelike state, all the while grunting and swearing with the effort. Then he'd picked up the camera and it had gone dead.

We sat for a bit, drinking our coffee, then Stubbing got to why she was here.

"So, George, anything to say about all the DVDs and tapes cooked in the arsehole's flat, not to mention some missing hard drives?" She was oddly calm, perhaps realising the futility of her task.

"Not really," I said, sipping my drink. "He must have done it himself when he knew you were onto him."

"Don't try and give me a warm feeling by pissing down my leg, George. You're not going to hand over the hard disks you took from there?"

"What hard disks?" She put her mug on the table.

"So if I get the ferrets in here to rip the place apart they're not going to find anything?"

"Not a sausage." She raised her thin eyebrows.

"Was it something to do with Sylvia?"

I weighed up the option of stonewalling against telling the truth and hoping I touched some human streak of decency in Stubbing.

"He did have something that belonged to Sylvia. It has nothing to do with Trisha."

"And because you have a hankering for posh quim you removed any possible copy of it on Quintin's hard drive, thinking she might be grateful enough to throw a desperate dog a bone."

I looked impassively at her over my cup.

"Women like that don't put out for blokes like you," she said.

"I'm sure you're right."

"And Brampton, how was she involved?"

"Like I told you, they were all at university together, watched a bit of porn, that's all." Stubbing sneered as only she can and made a noise like an asthmatic pug.

"She seemed bloody relieved that Quintin's computer had no data on it." That didn't surprise me. She must be as relieved as Sylvia, especially since disembowelling his computer, which was running as a server, meant there'd be nothing available online anymore, something Sylvia seemed blissfully unaware of. But I wasn't expecting a thank you card from Brampton.

"What's going to happen to her?"

"What do you mean?"

"I mean about her wiping the memory stick. She did do it, didn't she?"

"Well, all I know for certain is that she was the first person to get her hands on it. Waylaid young Turner as he was taking it down to the tech unit, saying she would take it down herself. It didn't get there until last thing Friday and she told them it wasn't a priority." She shrugged. "But I can't prove anything. I mean maybe the techies could show that the files were deleted, but to be honest she probably just gave them an identical brand-new one." Her jaw tensed and her eyes went hard like marbles. "And of course anything he might have had on her has conveniently been destroyed." She mimicked something disappearing with her hands and shook her head in disgust, not looking at me. I said nothing, waiting for her to calm down.

"Maybe she'll move on," I said. She looked up.

"She'll probably be promoted out the way," she said. "That's what usually happens."

"Will you apply for her job if she does?"

She made another pug-like noise and took a deep drink of coffee. She studied my face and I raised my eyebrows – I'd seen that look before; it resulted in putting on a condom. But to my relief she must have thought better of it because she sighed and slowly got up. She put out her hand and I took it.

"It's been a pleasure working with you, Vicky."

"Likewise, George."

* * *

Midmorning Monday Sylvia came into the office. After writing a cheque she sat back in her chair.

"To be honest I didn't think he was capable of murder," Sylvia said. "Manipulation and abuse, yes, but this?" She was a lot more relaxed than when she was last here. No unnecessary sunglasses, no twiddling of rings. She wore a black trouser suit that had been tailored with great care and sat up straight with her hands flat on a black leather portfolio resting on her thighs. "Judith says the whole thing was filmed?"

"Old habits die hard, I guess."

"At one point I wondered what had made him the person he is."

"Probably something to do with his mother," I said, then wished I hadn't because something flickered across her face.

"Mothers are blamed for most things," she said.

"I'm sorry, I didn't mean…"

She waved my apology away. "He wasn't all bad, you know, he used to contribute generously to charity."

I declined to comment and she had the grace to look embarrassed. "I must say you don't seem surprised by any of this."

"Nothing surprises me," I said.

"Really? Even Lucy?"

"Well, maybe that," I granted. I gazed into her turquoise eyes but they looked less alluring to me than two weeks ago. And I no longer fantasised about her whispering into my ear.

"I want to thank you, George, for what you've done."

I shrugged in an it's-all-in-a-day's-work manner.

"No, Judith told me that… his hard drives had

disappeared and someone had destroyed all the recordings?"

I nodded.

"Oh, I nearly forgot," she said, in a way that suggested she hadn't forgotten at all. She unzipped the portfolio and took out two white envelopes. She handed me one with my name on it.

"What's this?"

"It's the DNA results that Quintin had sent to Elliot. I thought you might want to see them." I put it unopened in my jacket pocket; I didn't want Sandra opening it. I hadn't told her about Lucy and didn't really want to. She'd been trying to pump me on the phone the night before, but I'd put her off, accepting an invitation to eat with her and the boys that night when I promised to reveal all.

"When do you plan to tell Lucy?"

"I don't know. She's taking some time out so we're going away. I might tell her then." She half-smiled and her fingers moved to her rings – she was getting cold feet about telling Lucy the truth. I myself had given it more thought since yesterday morning and changed my mind, if for no other reason than Lucy could still hear it from Quintin from behind bars. If of course they kept him there – he would no doubt have a team of lawyers who would prove it was Trisha's fault she had died – a woman can't enjoy sex for its own sake without being judged.

"Do you still think I shouldn't tell her?" Sylvia was asking.

"It doesn't really matter what I think," I said.

"Yesterday you made a passionate plea for me to tell

her nothing." She raised her eyebrows questioningly. They looked unnatural in their arched perfection.

"I don't know. What you said made sense, about the burden of carrying around secrets. I don't mean about the video, or how she was conceived – in a way that's your business. But the question of who fathered her is her business. What I'm trying to say, not very well, is that if you're carrying a secret about someone else, someone you love, then I think they have a right to know. Otherwise your relationship is built on a pretence." I was spouting stuff I wasn't sure I believed but I was worried she had lanced one boil only to cover another in makeup.

"I still need to think about it."

"Where are you going?"

"Pardon?"

"Next week, where are you going?"

"Somewhere we've never been before."

"An excellent choice, if I may say so." We both smiled and I gazed meaningfully at the other envelope in her hand.

She cottoned on and handed it over. It had Jason's name on it.

"I know I've paid you but this is specifically for Jason. Erm, cash, compensation for his injuries."

"That's really not necessary," I said, taking it from her.

"No, but it would make me feel better." I shrugged and we stood up. I walked her to the door.

"He and Lucy have grown quite fond of each other," I said. She stopped and turned to me, putting her hand on the door to stop me opening it.

"In light of his relationship to you, and yours to me, I'm not sure it's healthy for him and Lucy to, erm, maintain contact, do you?"

I thought it extremely healthy but I knew what she was really saying. She'd made it clear when she'd given me money for Jason: her daughter was not going to date someone she had employed.

"They are adults," I said, out of pigheadedness. She nodded, but we were no longer having a discussion.

"We'll be moving away from Cambridge when we come back; obviously we can't continue to live at the college and I think a fresh start would be good for both of us. I'll be discussing it with Lucy when we're away, but I've already made enquiries this morning about getting her transferred out of Emma." It sounded like they'd be having a fun mother and daughter trip, and I felt sorry for Lucy; in one respect nothing had changed for her, except she had lost her real father because of her biological one.

After Sylvia was gone Sandra rang and I reassured her I hadn't forgotten about dinner. I left the office, passing Nina in the hall, who blanked me. Fuck her, or not, as the case now seemed to be. I drove home and mooched about. I tried to set up a new puzzle on the chessboard but the heavy pieces just reminded me of my father, and his reverence of the Armenian chess grandmaster Tigran Petrosian. I packed the chess pieces into their felt-lined box with the sliding lid and took them and the board to the car, which I pointed towards

Cottenham. I'd have to face him at some point.

He wasn't in his room. I followed the sound of the decrepit piano to the day room – he was there with the other residents. Someone was playing Gershwin songs quite badly, but still a pleasant contrast to the TV being on full blast. I saw Megan, the care assistant, standing behind my seated father, her hands on his shoulders. Unseen, I went back to his room where I put the chessboard on the small table used for flowers. I set up the pieces and left before the piano playing stopped.

Back home I remembered my invitation to dinner at Sandra's. But I didn't feel I could face her, especially not to go over everything again. I rang to tell her I was knackered and needed some rest. I could hear the disappointment in her voice as she told me to take it easy. I could have rung Kamal and asked him to come round but hesitated; the truth was that I wasn't ready to talk to anyone just yet. I would have to at some point, if only to stop it eating away at me, like it had eaten away at Sylvia.

I fiddled around on the computer but decided it wasn't what I needed. I didn't know what I needed, just what I *didn't* need. I knew I was hungry, but a search of the kitchen revealed nothing. I decided I needed to go out, out of my father's house.

* * *

I drove round Cambridge for a bit, finding myself on the road to Morley College. I stopped at the McDonald's.

Sundays, Mondays, and Tuesdays Cathy worked there, and it was a Monday. I was hungry, after all.

EPILOGUE

THE COUNTY COUNCIL PUT GATES ACROSS THE ENTRANCE TO the Magog Down car park a few weeks later, so no one could have sex in cars there, not after hours anyway. I guess they just found somewhere else.

As if to give the finger to my cynicism Quintin Boyd was sentenced to life imprisonment for murder, although his team of lawyers are planning an appeal. His stiletto-wielding sidekick Kevin was convicted as an accessory. Mark the driver was acquitted, since he wasn't present when it happened.

I've not heard from Sylvia, or Lucy for that matter. I looked Sylvia up once, to see that she was a trustee on the board of a high profile national charity based in Oxford. I have stopped looking at other women online, as it doesn't really do anything for me anymore, that sort of thing. I'll always associate it with Sylvia's tape, and the sort of people who watched it. Although to be honest, it's easy for me to take this moral stance since I'm having regular sex. When that stops my standards will no doubt slip. As for the dating website, I let my account gather cobwebs, much like my father's shed, and eventually Sandra gave up bothering me about it.

I still haven't come clean to Sandra about Lucy, but I did get it off my chest. I ended up telling Cathy about it one Sunday morning, as she lay next to me in my parents' bed. She laughed hysterically, which is exactly the response I was looking for.

GEORGE KOCHARYAN WILL RETURN IN

THE RUNAWAY MAID

MARCH 2017

ACKNOWLEDGEMENTS

I'M GRATEFUL TO ANGUS, PAM, JONATHAN, JOHN AND MARY, all of whom helped by being generous with their professional know-how.

ABOUT THE AUTHOR

E.G. RODFORD IS THE CRIME-WRITING PSEUDONYM OF AN award-winning author living in Cambridge, England. Rodford writes about the seedier side of the city where PI George Kocharyan is usually to be found.

Twitter: @eg_rodford

ALSO AVAILABLE FROM TITAN BOOKS

HACK

AN F.X. SHEPHERD NOVEL

KIERAN CROWLEY

It's a dog-eat-dog world at the infamous tabloid *The New York Mail*, where brand new pet columnist F.X. Shepherd accidentally finds himself on the trail of The Hacker, a serial killer targeting unpleasant celebrities in inventive—and sometimes decorative—ways. Luckily Shepherd has hidden talents, not to mention a hidden agenda. But as bodies and suspects accumulate, he finds himself running afoul of cutthroat office politics, the NYPD, and an attractive but ruthless reporter for a competing newspaper. And when Shepherd is contacted by The Hacker, he realizes he may be next on the killer's list...

"A witty and incisive mystery set in the raucous world of tabloid journalism. Laugh out loud funny and suspenseful."
Rebecca Cantrell, bestselling author of *The Blood Gospel*

"A rollicking, sharp-witted crime novel." *Kirkus Reviews*

"It's a joy to read and captures the imagination from the start."
Long Island Press

ALSO AVAILABLE FROM TITAN BOOKS

DUST AND DESIRE

A JOEL SORRELL NOVEL

CONRAD WILLIAMS

Joel Sorrell, a bruised, bad-mouthed PI, is a sucker for missing person cases. And not just because he's searching for his daughter, who vanished five years after his wife was murdered. Joel feels a kinship with the desperate and the damned. He feels, somehow, responsible. So when the mysterious Kara Geenan begs him to find her missing brother, Joel agrees. Then an attempt is made on his life, and Kara vanishes... A vicious serial killer is on the hunt, and as those close to Joel are sucked into his nightmare, he suspects that answers may lie in his own hellish past.

"An exciting new voice in crime fiction" MARK BILLINGHAM, No. 1 bestselling author of *Rush of Blood*

"Top quality crime writing from one of the best" PAUL FINCH, No. 1 bestselling author of *Stalkers*

"Take the walk with PI Joel Sorrell" JAMES SALLIS, bestselling author of *Drive*

TITANBOOKS.COM

ALSO AVAILABLE FROM TITAN BOOKS

THE BLOOD STRAND

A FAROES NOVEL

CHRIS OULD

Having left the Faroes as a child, Jan Reyna is now a British police detective, and the islands are foreign to him. But he is drawn back when his estranged father is found unconscious with a shotgun by his side and someone else's blood at the scene. Then a man's body is washed up on an isolated beach. Is Reyna's father responsible? Looking for answers, Reyna falls in with Detective Hjalti Hentze, but as the stakes get higher and Reyna learns more about his family and the truth behind his mother's flight from the Faroes, he must decide whether to stay, or to forsake the strange, windswept islands for good.

PRAISE FOR THE AUTHOR

"Unmissable and thrilling fiction… a tough-talking, brutally honest lesson in the harsh realities of youth crime."
Lancashire Evening Post

"This is bound to be a highly successful series." *Hearthfire*